# The Wrong Idiot

## Tim Reardon

ALL THINGS
THAT MATTER
PRESS

*For all the characters from The Sunset*

# Acknowledgments

Thanks to early reader and "title guru" J. Danford Harlan. Much appreciation to Kathleen Reardon for her honest editing. Special thanks to Laura Ferry Kelly for her always meticulous editing and spot on character recommendations. And finally, a shout out to Phil & Deb from ATTM Press. Thanks for your loyalty!

# Part One

## *Eddie Bilker*

A double bind is far worse than a straightforward damned-if-you-do, damned-if-you-don't dilemma. It requires you to obey two mutually exclusive commands: Anything you do to fulfill one violates the other.

—Deborah Tannen

To Eddie Bilker, foggy days in the city always seemed to be full of ghosts, drifting through the neighborhoods, looking for trouble, and eventually loitering over the Sunset District, where Eddie's little office was located—stuck between Seal Rock Cleaners and Ace Hardware.

Eddie was almost out the door when he remembered his face mask. He'd had asthma as a kid, so he was taking the mask mandate pretty seriously. Some of his buddies had been getting together for beers every weekend—no face masks, no social distancing, drinking Coronas as part of the joke—but Eddie wasn't taking any chances. The coronavirus was supposed to fade away in the summer, so he didn't mind wearing the mask for a few more weeks until this whole thing was over. Everything had been closed for two months. Six weeks longer than most experts expected. And apparently all this was happening because of something called a wet market on the other side of the world.

When he walked around the desk to get his mask, he felt his phone vibrate and saw that it was his wife, Kim, trying to hit him up on FaceTime. He put the phone back in his pocket. He'd check in with her a little later.

Kim was an ER nurse, but she hadn't seen a single Covid patient yet. She kept changing her mind about whether or not the virus was worthy of serious panic. The original reports said there might be two million dead Americans before they could create a vaccine, but now they were saying the total might be only 200,000. If Kim didn't trust the reports anymore, Eddie didn't know who he was supposed to listen to. He knew only that there'd been some cases of young guys with respiratory problems who'd died from it. A man to whom Eddie had sold a house about six months before had cystic fibrosis and ended up dying up at UCSF last week. Charlie Ellis. Forty-one years old.

Eddie was only thirty-two, but Charlie's death had scared him. Eddie was lucky he'd gotten Charlie's sales commission before the market started to get fickle. That house was the only one he'd sold in the past year. He was already struggling with business development, and then Covid came along and made things worse. No one was selling.

People were hunkering down. His partner—his boss really—had been paying him to work Sundays and help with marketing, but the Department of Public Health had banned open houses. Eddie needed a commission soon, or Kimberly was going to look at their finances and say they should sell the San Francisco house and move to one of the smaller towns to the south. But Eddie wanted to stay in the city. He'd grown up in the city. He believed it was part of his identity.

So, he got himself a side job.

He liked to bet on games. He'd done it for years and was pretty good at it, but, just like everyone else who liked to bet on games, his career tally definitely put him in the red. He wasn't as bad as a lot of guys, but he knew the racket: if people were making money gambling, all the casinos would be out of business.

Eddie wanted to have the odds on his side for a change, so he became the casino. He was more talented at booking bets than closing deals, but he knew he had to keep his book small. He didn't want Kimberly to find out, and he didn't want to get busted. So, he tried like hell to sell houses, and he booked bets from a small group of screened clients who consistently bet a couple hundred bucks a week. He was netting four or five thousand a month—nothing to brag about, but tax free and enough to help with household cashflow.

At least it did until the pandemic hit, and Fauci cancelled all the games. Nothing to bet on now. Maybe an occasional golf match or Korean baseball or MMA, but that was it. Business was dead, and would continue that way until these assholes at the CDC let the athletes start playing again. The virus didn't seem to affect healthy young people at all, so Eddie didn't understand why they wouldn't just let these players in peak condition run around a little bit, shoot some baskets and swing some bats so that folks could place bets. A little something to do during the lockdown. It didn't seem like too much to ask. And the athletes with asthma could wear masks with the team logos on them. Great marketing.

He adjusted his own mask and jogged across Taraval Street to where he'd parked his Porsche just a few storefronts down from El Burrito Express. Eddie drove a Porsche. Bought it two years ago after he'd sold a three-bedroom place near the Cow Palace—total dump, but it went for

$800k. Having the car was part of the business. If you didn't have a nice ride, people didn't believe you could sell a nice house. He'd explained it to Kimberly a hundred times. He had to have nice clothes and a nice car. They could tighten the budget everywhere else, but he needed that car, and he needed the suits. In San Francisco, the competition was savage, dogfights over every property. And Eddie kept losing.

As soon as he fastened his seatbelt, he could feel his phone vibrating again. He assumed it was Kimberly, but now he was starting the engine and decided he'd call her once he got up to Elmore's Boot at the end of West Portal. He knew there were a couple of guys who owed him money and were sitting at the bar right now. If he didn't catch them today, he might not collect for weeks.

Bars were supposed to be closed, but Elmore's Boot had a back entrance, and it was easy to park around the corner and walk up through the alley without being seen. The front of the bar was boarded up, so as long as people were quiet, Duff would invite small groups and pretend there wasn't a citywide lockdown.

Oaklawn Park in Arkansas was still an operating racetrack, and the bar had a satellite feed, so six or seven guys were supposed to meet to watch the simulcast of the races on the big screen and maybe place a few online bets. Eddie didn't know horses, so he stayed away from that action, but two clients who were supposed to be at The Boot today still owed him money from college basketball games played right before the lockdown, and Eddie couldn't keep putting it off. Until the leagues started up again, he needed to use his time to at least collect from the guys who owed him.

The apartment building on the corner was under construction, so Eddie almost missed a nice parking spot under the shade of the scaffolding. He braked hard after he passed the spot and then backed in quickly as the car driving up behind him leaned on the horn. "Yeah, yeah … bite me," Eddie mumbled and felt his phone vibrating again. Kimberly. Facetime. He checked his watch and decided to take it.

As soon as he swiped over to see her, he felt his jaw lock up. The camera was too close to her face, but it was clear from her red eyes that she'd been crying. Was still crying. When she saw his face, she snorted once almost violently to clear her nose and then shouted in a phlegm-gargled voice, "Just do what they say."

"Kim, what's going on?" he said and heard his voice crack. His body had seized from his groin to the back of his throat, and his sentence sounded like a child banging on a toy xylophone.

"Check your trunk!" she said and the screen went black.

He fumbled with the phone for a moment and got her back on. This time the camera was a little farther away from her face, and there was a shadow obscuring one side of the screen. The other side was bright and washed out, but Eddie could see the barrel of a pistol held to Kimberly's temple. Her cheeks were streaked with tears and strips of matted hair. Her eyes seemed to be straining to leap out of their sockets. "The trunk," she screamed and then took a short breath before she said, "And no cops, Eddie." The screen went black.

Scrambling out of the car, Eddie banged his knee on the steering wheel and hit his head on the door frame. He'd considered popping the trunk with the inside lever, but something stopped him. It was a fairly busy street, and he had no idea what was in there.

He tried to look normal as he limped around to the back of the car and pointed the key fob at the trunk. He looked back up the street toward West Portal and then over the car toward Wawona Street. Nobody. He pressed the button and caught the trunk door before it sprang fully open. Then he bent down into a catcher's stance and peered into the dark space.

Almost immediately, he recognized his golf travel bag. He'd only used it once for a trip to South Carolina, but he knew this was his. Sturdy black nylon. Oversized—big enough to hold his cart bag. It was called the CaddyDaddy. He stood up and let the trunk door spring to its full, open position. The bag, which looked overstuffed and lumpy, barely fit in his trunk. In fact, he could see now that the back seat had been pushed forward to make room for it. And at the very top of the bag, in the farthest corner of the space, near the zipper pull, he saw a yellow sticky note.

He reached in and grabbed it with two fingers. He caught some pieces of thread that were stuck to the adhesive strip and rubbed them off his fingers before he read the message in all caps: "BURY ME."

Michael Duffy was a good cop for about seven years, so good that a gangbanger publicly put out a hit on him, and Duff required 24-hour surveillance for six months. His dad, Elmore Duffy—also a cop—died of a heart attack in the fifth month of young Duff's security detail and left his only son the bar, paid in full. Duff's sister got a duplex in Noe Valley. And Duff's mom kept the house.

Two weeks after Duff's dad's funeral, the gang leader who'd wanted him dead was killed in a drug deal-gone-bad in Oakland. The next day, Duff told the SFPD that he didn't need the surveillance anymore and turned in his badge and gun. He was still young but he'd seen enough violence for two lifetimes. He'd worked undercover in the drug task force and didn't need that kind weight on him anymore. His cowboy days were over. And besides, someone needed to manage Elmore's Boot.

When Elmore first bought the bar in 2003 and put up the new sign, a myth was born that Elmore had spent a good deal of his time as a tough city patrolman, often kicking the crap out of career criminals who liked to resist arrest—hence the boot reference. But none of that was true. Duff's mom, Doris, actually came up with the name after an incident that had occurred just a few months before Elmore had bought the place.

The family was vacationing up at Lake Tahoe, and when they were on the way home, Elmore realized that he'd left his boots on the back porch of the cabin they'd been renting. The Duffys had already been on the road for an hour and half—just clearing Sacramento, almost to Davis—but Elmore insisted they turn around and go back to get the boots. Doris complained the whole way back up the mountain and tormented him ruthlessly for weeks afterward.

About a month later, when Elmore told her she would be granted the honor of naming his new bar, she jokingly said she wanted to call it *Elmore's Boots*. Well, Elmore didn't think it was funny. He knew she wasn't serious, but he was sick of the ribbing by that point. He told her that she had made her choice and that would be the name. She begged him to change it to *Doris' Place* or something like that, but he was a stubborn man, and the name grew on him over the next couple of days, so he dropped the "s" and went with it.

Now Elmore Duffy's son, Mike, was running the place and doing a nice job despite the forced Covid-19 closure. This past Saturday, he made $1,200 selling "Newsom Sucks" t-shirts from a little table he'd set up in front of the bar. Gavin Newsom was the California governor, and all the regulars from Elmore's Boot hated the man for putting San Francisco on the "watch list" and shutting down all the bars. Duff sold out of the t-shirts in less than an hour.

The only image on the shirt was Newsom's famously quaffed mane of hair, exaggerated into a ridiculous, caricatured pompadour, between the words "Newsom" and "Sucks".

Today, Duff had a little private party organized for a few amateur handicappers who'd come in to watch some horse race being run in Arkansas. There was an inquiry in the third race, so all six guys were staring at the screen, waiting to see if the favorite had won, or if the panel was going to take it away from him.

Duff had his eyes on the screen when he heard Wade say, "Here's your man, Eddie Bilker."

Duff turned to see Eddie coming in through the back door and wearing a starched white shirt with one of those tight suits that they wear these days, pants tapered at the bottom. No tie and his hair combed straight back like Governor Newsom's. Duff smiled at the contrast between Eddie and the four guys sitting at the bar, all wearing flannel shirts.

"Duff's brother-in-law's here," said Wade, eyeing Duff from above his beer. "Hold onto your wallets, lads."

The other guys grumbled. They didn't like Eddie.

"He's not my brother-in-law," said Duff.

"Almost," said Wade.

Eddie's suit and hair looked like they always did, but he didn't look right. For one thing, he was sweating too much for a guy dressed like he was on his way to a photo shoot. And there was something wrong with his eyes. They looked tired and alert at the same time if that's possible. He stopped at the end of the bar where he handed an envelope to Bill Sweeny and then collected some money from Doobie Dan and Tommy Garcia before he walked right past Wade and stood at the bar in front of Sweeny.

All the other guys were drinking bottles of Miller High Life, but Duff had started the process of pouring Eddie a Guinness. While Duff was waiting for the beer to surge—he usually let it cascade for over a minute—Eddie said, "Can I talk to you in the back for a minute?"

"Sure," said Duff and nodded back at the Guinness that was still settling under the spout. "Just a second."

Eddie was grinding his teeth. Duff wondered if he'd done some lines before coming into the bar. Eddie was a strange kind of mess today, staring at the Guinness while Duff leaned against the bar and waited.

"Just grab it," said Eddie, but Duff nodded again and gave it a few more seconds. He topped it off and handed it to Eddie, who walked past the bathrooms back to the office.

"Eddie Bilker," said Wade, raised his glass, and smiled at Duff, who ignored him.

Duff pulled a bottle of Miller out of the cooler and went back to the office where Eddie was pacing. The pint was almost empty, and Eddie was wiping, with his thumb and index finger, the Guinness mustache that had foamed up at the corners of his mouth.

"What can I do for you, Eddie?"

"Kimberly's in trouble," he said and swallowed the last of his beer.

Duff liked Kim. He was living with her sister, Marilyn. Like his buddies out there watching the horse races, he didn't particularly like Eddie Bilker, but he'd known him since they were kids, and he played nice for the sake of his relationship with Marilyn. "What kind of trouble?" he asked, adjusting the newspapers and a greasy doughnut box on his desk to make room for him to sit down. He rested his beer on the sports section, which was nearly useless during the pandemic.

"It's not good," said Eddie, who walked over and closed the door to the office. He was still holding the empty pint and didn't seem to know where to put it.

Duff's bartender muscle memory kicked in and he said, "Can I get you another?" as he reached for the empty.

Eddie handed Duff the empty pint glass and said, "This is so messed up, Duff."

"Eddie," said Duff. "Let's get to it. The next race is about to start. How can I help you ... or Kim? What's going on?"

"Can Wade close up for you?" said Eddie, rubbing his hands together now like it was cold in the office, which it was.

"I gotta go with you?" said Duff, thinking he was going to have to jump Kim's car or snake a drain or something that he did not want to do right now.

"I can't do this by myself," said Eddie. "I'm sorry to drag you into it, but this is not good, man."

Duff was still trying to gauge the situation, so he floated a suggestion just to see Eddie's reaction: "Why don't you ask Wade or Doobie Dan?" he said and pointed his thumb in the direction of the guys who probably needed another round of beers about now. "I'm working today."

Eddie stepped up to Duff, uncomfortably close. "Tell Wade to close up, Duff. I got a dead body in the trunk of the Porsche."

Eddie was surprised that Duff didn't ask to look in the trunk. When they got to the car, Duff just said, "Start driving."

"Where?" said Eddie, still shaky but feeling a little better after the Guinness.

"Doesn't matter," said Duff. "Maybe drive like you're going to Sloat Beach. I just wanted to get you out of there. You were acting weird. I didn't want Wade asking questions."

"Will he?" said Eddie.

"No," said Duff. "He'll just drink a bunch of beers and give away a bunch more while I'm gone."

"Sorry," said Eddie.

"Can I see the video with Kim in it?" asked Duff.

For a moment, Eddie didn't know what Duff was talking about as they turned onto Sloat Boulevard at the end of West Portal and merged into the beginning of Friday rush hour traffic heading west. Then Eddie got it and said, "It wasn't a video, Duff. It was FaceTime."

"Explain that to me."

"It's a video chat, man. I look at my phone and see her, and she looks at her phone and sees me."

"So, it was live?" he asked.

"Yes," said Eddie. "This isn't the complicated part, man."

"Eddie," said Duff, and Eddie looked over at him. Duff was wearing a faded green windbreaker with a softball team logo on the back, a pair of old work pants, and Vans—those shoes that skateboard kids wear. He hadn't shaved in a couple of days, and he needed a haircut, but he was a good-looking guy, the way some tough guys can look. He was staring at Eddie now.

"Sorry," said Eddie. "I'm just freaking out, you know?"

"Yeah," said Duff. "I'm watching you. I'd be freaked out, too. But I need to know what happened before I can help you."

"Yeah," said Eddie. "Sorry. It was FaceTime. Live. It was like star trek, man. I could see her when she was talking to me."

"Okay," he said. "I get it now. Yeah, yeah. I just didn't know what it was called."

They were passing by Sigmund Stern Grove where Eddie and Duff had partied in high school. They were closer back then. The only reason they really saw each other was that he was dating Kim's younger—hotter—sister, Marilyn. So, it must have seemed odd to Duff now that Eddie was asking him for help. But Eddie didn't have anyone else to call for something like this. And since Duff was an ex-cop, he probably knew what to do. He'd been in a lot of situations.

"Really think about that Snapchat," said Duff. "There could be a detail in there that could help us find Kim."

"Facetime," said Eddie. "And I can't remember anything. It was just her face. The whole frame was her face."

"I thought you said you saw a gun," said Duff.

"Just barely," said Eddie. "It was pointed at her head." He felt his voice start to crack, but he fought it off.

Duff didn't flinch at Eddie's voice. He looked out the passenger side window like he was trying to pretend he didn't notice Eddie losing it. Then he said, "We're kind of screwed for a while. We can't bury it until the sun goes down. Someone'll see us."

"But I think we're supposed to do it now," said Eddie, picturing Kim's tear-streaked face.

"You sure you don't want to call the cops?" said Duff. "I do know a few."

"She said 'no cops,'" Eddie yell-whispered as if the mere mention of the police would break the deal. If there was a deal.

Eddie was scared that Duff was going to give him that look again, but he didn't. He stared out the window for a moment and then said, "Take the Great Highway." And as they turned onto the Great Highway with sand dunes and ice plants and the Pacific Ocean now on their left, he added, "And don't speed. You don't want to get pulled over. I used to love pulling over guys in Porsches."

"Why?"

"C'mon, Eddie," said Duff.

"What?"

"They're mostly douchebags."

"Guys who drive Porsches?"

"Yeah," said Duff. "Sometimes it would be a good-looking gal in her forties, but most of the time it was guys like you, and I could always figure out a reason to pull 'em over."

"Not that it matters right now as we're in the middle of something," said Eddie. "But it sounds like you're calling me a douchebag."

"Nah," said Duff. "You're okay, Eddie. You're from the neighborhood."

He didn't sound very convincing to Eddie, but he didn't care. Duff was going to help him get out of this. "So, what do we do?"

"Didn't you tell us you were selling a place out near Sutro Park?" said Duff, turning away from the window now and looking at Eddie again.

"That place has been on the market for over a year," said Eddie. "The owner lives in Reno. He won't lower the asking price, and he won't put any money into fixing it up a little bit. It still has his mom's old drapes and wall-to-wall carpeting."

"But the owner lives in Reno, right?"

"Yeah."

"Is there a renter?"

"No."

"You got a key?"

"Lockbox," said Eddie.

"Does the place have a garage?"

"Yes."

"Can you get into the house from the garage?" asked Duff.

"Yes."

"Does it have a backyard?"

"Yes."

"Concrete slab?"

"No," said Eddie. "Overgrown garden. Weeds and rocks."

"Bingo."

This giant piece of luggage—Eddie said it was used to transport golf clubs on a plane—had rollers. He easy wheeled it around the Porsche once they'd parked in the garage of the rundown shack way out on 47th between Geary Boulevard and Point Lobos. The air was salty down there, and you could see the effect on the rusted-out mailboxes and gutters. To the left of the driveway, there was an old palm tree whose roots were wreaking havoc on the pavement, which was buckled just in front of the garage door so that it couldn't close properly. No wonder Eddie couldn't sell this place.

Duff let Eddie do all the work for now. He didn't want to touch the bag until he knew more about what was going on, what he was getting into. He liked his life and didn't want to mess with it, especially for Eddie. Sure, they went back a long way, and the guy was married to Marilyn's sister, but Duff didn't have any desire to get back into all this again. He'd left that life behind for a reason.

So far, all Duff had done was ride over here with a guy he knew. That's it. Now he was watching the man lug this big ass bag up the three stairs of the garage that led into a short hallway and the living room. There was a sliver of sunlight coming from the front window, so Duff walked over and closed the heavy curtains all the way, overlapping the bottoms to make sure.

"What's the ground like out back?" he asked.

Eddie was sweating again, wiping his forehead with the sleeve of his suit jacket and squinting his eyes like he was out in the sunlight though the room was dark. "It's foggy all the time out here, so it's probably wet. Pretty soft is my guess."

"You better take that suit off," said Duff.

"Huh?"

"Unless you want to ruin the suit, you should take it off."

Eddie didn't answer.

Duff walked back into the garage where he'd seen a work bench on the way in. The light down there didn't work, but he didn't want to open the garage, so he was feeling his way around. There was a rake and a hoe leaning against the wall behind some folding lawn chairs from the early 60's. No shovel.

He made one loop around the perimeter of the garage feeling for anything with a handle. The best he could do was an old army pickaxe with a smooth handle and dirt caked on the flat edge of the head. He put both hands on the handle like he was holding a baseball bat, and he liked the feel of it, the heavy weight up top.

When he got back upstairs carrying the pickaxe in one hand and the hoe in the other, Eddie had stripped down to his underwear but was still wearing his shoes. The sight would have been comical if it weren't for the bag in the middle of the room in front of the fireplace. Eddie was sitting on a window bench near the back door, his suit neatly folded next to him. "Do you think we should look in the bag before we start digging?"

Duff didn't hesitate. "Of course," he said. "We need to see what we're dealing with here." There was a moment on the Great Highway during which he was struck with a wave of anxiety as he pondered whether or not it could be Marilyn in that bag—punishment to Kimberly for something she or Eddie had done. But Eddie said that he'd seen black hair caught in the zipper. Marilyn was strawberry blond— she still had freckles almost into her late twenties now. Beautiful girl without trying. Natural. And no black hair. She had a sense of humor like a guy. She loved to cook. Seemed like a person who'd be a good mom.

Eddie walked over and kneeled in front of the luggage. Duff stood behind him, looking over his shoulder as Eddie placed a hand on the side of the bag before moving it to the zipper. He paused for a moment with his fingers twitching and then rubbing the zipper like it was a good luck charm.

"Let's go," said Duff, and Eddie jumped away from the bag.

"Jesus Christ," he said. "You scared the shit out of me."

"Eddie," said Duff. "We gotta keep moving. We don't know what's going on with Kim right now, and we don't know how long it's going to take to dig that hole." He paused for just a second before he added, "Are you sure you don't want to call the cops?"

"She said 'no cops'," he shouted.

"Then open the damn bag," said Duff, who was now trying to put some scale to the oversized piece of luggage. When Eddie was rolling it, the bag was tilted, so it was hard to tell how long it was. But now that Duff was seeing it lying flat on the floor, it didn't look long enough to fit a body in there. It was wide enough, but it didn't seem long enough. From Duff's estimate, it was maybe five feet. Or maybe it was five and a half feet, which *would* make it long enough for an average-sized woman. And if Eddie would just open it up, the mystery would be solved, but he was kneeling next to the bag with both hands on top of his head now, looking like a hostage about to be executed.

"Get out of the way," said Duff, pushing Eddie aside and taking a knee. He pulled the zipper over the tuft of black hair all the way down to the bottom of the bag, like he was field dressing a mule deer. He was ready to extract whatever was inside, wrapped in garbage bags, which had ripped open in places during the packing process.

"Jesus," said Eddie, who had created some distance between himself and the bag, but Duff could feel him inching up from behind now.

The hair was coming out of a tear near the top of the plastic wrap, and Duff could see the outline of the body, forced into a fetal hug of itself in order to fit into the bag. Duff reached for the plastic near where the hair was coming up, but he stopped himself. "Do you want to do this?" he said.

Eddie looked disappointed in himself. "I can't," he said.

When Duff ripped apart the plastic bag around what he took to be the head, the face of a woman was turned to the side. For some reason, the first thing he noticed was that there was duct tape wrapped around her throat, high up near her chin. But then he looked at her face and saw that she was beautiful—not like Marilyn. A different kind. Exotic. Maybe middle eastern. But she could have been Italian or Greek. He was about to turn her head and move to the side so that Eddie could take a look, but he stopped. "Damn it," he said. "I got my fingerprints all over this."

Then he turned to Eddie and saw the man in his underwear, sitting up against the wall. He had his arms crossed over his chest. And here's the strange part: he had his mouth open like he was screaming, but no sound was coming out, and tears were streaming down his face.

"Who is this, Eddie?"

Eddie closed his mouth and his eyes, but the tears kept coming.

"Eddie," said Duff. "Let's go. We're wasting time. We gotta wipe down this bag, get it into the ground, wipe down the house, and get out of here. Who is this?"

Eddie opened his eyes and looked at the bag for a long time. Duff wanted to move this along, so he took the head of the girl and turned it toward Eddie. He spoke softly when he said, "Who is this, Eddie?"

"My girlfriend," he said, sounding like he was in high school—a little whisper that ended in a short cry. Really pathetic.

"You dumb-shit," said Duff. "We can talk about who might have done this later. We need to get the poor gal in the ground now and call these sickos to tell 'em we've..." he stopped himself. "...that *you've* completed the job."

## 5

Eddie didn't look at Angie's face when Duff was zipping up the bag. He couldn't do it. He had pictures of her in his phone. Wanted to remember her that way. He didn't love her, but he sure liked her. She was a fun girl. Dangerous. Was helping Eddie with an easy money play that was just about to hit.

Duff had wiped everything down and even ripped off the part of the plastic garbage bag that he'd touched and put it in his pocket. It didn't matter if Eddie's prints were in the house. This was his client's property. But Duff didn't want any trace of himself anywhere near this place.

Eddie rolled the bag out to the backyard, and Duff came walking outside holding a pick and hoe.

"Where's the shovel?" asked Eddie.

"Keep it down," said Duff, looking up at the houses on both sides and handing Eddie the hoe. "We don't want anyone to hear us out here."

The wooden fences were tall enough to give them cover from the neighbors—both houses being single story ranchers. Duff picked a spot about three feet in front of the small brick patio and said, "Right here." Then he raised the pick and swung down hard into dead grass and dirt.

"Where's the shovel?" asked Eddie again.

"I'm going to pick out the hard stuff on top, and you're going to pull it out with that hoe," he said.

"So, there's no shovel?"

"This might take a while," said Duff.

"Shouldn't we just go out and buy one?" said Eddie.

"Do you want a credit card receipt showing that you bought a shovel?" asked Duff. "Do you want security camera footage of you carrying a shovel to the register at the hardware store?" He didn't wait for an answer. He swung down hard again, pulling up a large wedge of dry turf, and Eddie pulled it away with the hoe.

After about five or six swings, Duff looked at Eddie and smiled. He pointed to the small hole in front of him and said, "Sand," before swinging down with the pick again. "This won't be as hard as I thought. This is all sand down here." Then he said, "Wait a minute" and walked back into the house.

A few moments later, he walked back out with an empty plastic, five-gallon paint bucket and threw it over to Eddie, who let it drop into the small hole. Duff said, "Get goin'," and nodded at the little hole.

"With this?" said Eddie.

"Yessir," said Duff. "Better than a hoe."

Eddie grabbed the bucket and pulled out the first load of sand. Duff was right. It was soft and easy to scoop, but Eddie also knew it was going to be difficult to keep the sides of the hole shored up. "This is going to be like trying to fill up a bucket that has a hole in it," said Eddie.

"Fill up a bucket?" said Duff. "We're doing the opposite here, Ed. We're creating a hole, not filling one."

"Yeah," said Eddie. "The opposite, but the same principle if the sand keeps falling back into the hole."

"Isn't it the opposite principle?" said Duff, just standing there, leaning on the pick, sounding like he was messing with Eddie now. Eddie ignored him and kept scooping out buckets of sand. When he got down beneath those first few feet, the sand was wet, so the sides of the hole were actually holding.

"What's the next step after we bury her?" asked Eddie.

Duff was holding the pick now like it was a baseball bat. He'd been a great hitter when they were kids, and he looked like a natural standing there in his windbreaker and Vans, gripping the handle like he was ready to swing if someone threw something at him. Meanwhile, Eddie was in his underwear, crouched down in the hole, the sand trickling in the back of his undershirt and into his boxer briefs. He was sweating pretty good now and starting to ache a little bit, but he kept going.

Duff was watching him slow down and said, "You want me to jump in, give you a break?"

"What do we do after we have it in the ground?" he said and kept digging.

"We have to call Kimberly's phone and tell these people you did what they asked."

Eddie knew that was right, but then what? This couldn't be all they wanted. This was a message of some sort. "And then how do we get Kimberly back?" he said.

Duff said, "Okay, let me get in there for a bit. You're slowing down."

Eddie climbed out of the hole and inspected his work. It was narrow, but it was already pretty deep. It was just hard to work in there now because you could only dig on one side of the hole and then had to lift the bucket over your head in order to turn around and work on the other side, which is what Duff was doing now. "Sorry," Eddie said. "I should have made it wider."

"Nope," said Duff. "This is good. It doesn't have to be wide, but I want to make sure it's deep enough so the coyotes or dogs don't dig it up."

"The garbage bags and that luggage should help, right? With keeping animals away?"

"I guess," said Duff, working systematically—three scoops on one side and then three more on the other. He was waist-deep now. "Make sure the luggage is closed up tight."

***

They had each taken two more shifts in the hole. It was dark now, and Eddie was shoulder deep. "I think we're done," he said.

Duff was sitting on the little brick patio. "Yep," he said. "Let's throw it in there and get out of here."

Eddie placed the bucket upside-down and stood on it. He put his hands on the ground at the upper rim of the hole and started to pull himself out, but he could feel the earth begin to give, and he pulled his hands back quickly. "Shit," he said. "How am I going to get out of here without caving in the hole?"

Duff got up and walked over to the edge, careful not to get too close. Then he walked back over and grabbed the hoe, which had been virtually useless to this point. "Lean back," he said, and Eddie stepped off the bucket and rested his back against the opposite wall of the hole, sand sneaking in the back of his undershirt again. Then Duff took the blade of the hoe and carefully carved a small toe-sized notch in the damp wall beneath him. He threw the hoe on the ground and grabbed the pick. "You're going to stand on the bucket, step up into that little wedge I just made for you, and then grab the pick, and I'll pull you out."

Eddie stepped back on the bucket and practiced putting his foot onto the little toe notch. Duff was standing up there with the pick held out horizontally so that Eddie would be able to grab it like a water ski rope-handle and let Duff pull him out. Eddie knew that if he didn't pull his toe out of the wedge at the right time and straighten his legs, his knees were going to smash into the bank of the hole, and it would collapse that side into the grave. "Let's go," he said. It had been hours since they arrived at the house. "I got this."

It wasn't a perfect maneuver, and some sand drifted back into the hole, but Eddie jumped out and scrambled onto the mound of sand next to the hole. Duff lied down flat next to the hole and reached down with the hoe handle. He knocked over the bucket, stuck the handle inside, and lifted it up and out of the hole.

"Okay," he said. "Bring the bag over here."

Eddie used the rollers to wheel the bag over to the hole, and he used the momentum to shift the bag sideways and throw it in without breaking stride. Once the bag hit the bottom, Duff grabbed the bucket and started scooping mounds of sand into the hole. Eddie grabbed the hoe, but quickly abandoned that idea, got down on his hands and knees, and pushed in as much sand as he could using his arms and knees and thighs … whatever it took to make this terrible thing be over as soon as possible.

Once it was done and the two of them were stomping on the area that had once been the hole, Eddie said, "I guess I should call Kim now."

"Yeah," said Duff. "That'd be a good idea." Duff was sitting on the bricks again and said, "I don't want to be a pessimist, but even though we did what they asked, that doesn't mean they're going to let her go."

"But at least we followed directions," said Eddie.

"Yeah," said Duff. "There is that."

Eddie pulled his phone out of his pocket and decided to text: *We buried the bag.*

About a minute later, Eddie got a text from a different number: *Prove it.*

Eddie read it out loud and then said to Duff, "How the hell are we supposed to prove it, and why is this a different number now?"

Duff paused for a moment and then said, "Just tell 'em they're going to have to trust us. And they must have switched to a burner phone so we can't trace it."

Eddie texted: *Trust us. It's in the ground.*

*Who's us?*

"Crap!" said Eddie. "I said *us* by accident."

"Huh?" said Duff.

"I texted that they should trust *us*. Sorry."

"God damnit," said Duff. "Just tell 'em you did what they asked."

Eddie texted: *I did what you asked*

*Prove it.*

"Duff, they want me to prove it."

"Ask them how," said Duff.

Eddie texted: *How?*

This time it took a couple of minutes, and then the word *Video* popped up on the thread. He let it sink in before he told Duff, "They want video evidence." He hoped it didn't show, but he felt like he was going to cry again.

## 6

They took turns digging out the dirt from the grave. At this point, Duff was more angry than anything else. He wanted to know what kinds of people they were dealing with. Eddie was sniffling, so Duff decided to be delicate with him.

When they'd gotten about halfway down to the bottom of the grave, Duff asked, "Do you have any idea who might be doing this to you?"

Eddie was holding the bucket in front of him with both hands like it was a tub of vanilla ice cream. "I don't run with the kind of people who'd do this, Duff. You know that," he said and scooped out another layer of sand.

"Yeah," said Duff. "But we gotta start somewhere."

"I know it," he said. "But I'm telling you, I can't think of a single person who'd go to this kind of extreme to punish me like this."

"Okay," said Duff. "Let's start with your jobs." He was sitting on the patio again, but his knees were starting to cramp up, so he stood and felt good pacing and thinking. "Have you screwed over anyone on a real estate deal?"

"I haven't *made* any deals in months, man. So, I can't imagine anyone being pissed at me over real estate. Except maybe my boss because I'm not closing."

"How about more than a few months ago?" said Duff. "Have you *ever* screwed anyone over on the sale of a house?"

Eddie looked like he needed a break. He shoveled one more scoop out of the hole, then climbed out and sat on the bucket. "Believe it or not," he said. "I take my job really seriously. I actually try. I just haven't been very good at it lately."

Duff got up, walked over to Eddie, and pointed at the bucket. Eddie handed it to him, and Duff got back to work on the hole. It was really dark now. The fog had rolled in, and it was thick and low. Eddie had been in his underwear out here for almost five hours now, and he was shivering.

"What about your other gig?" asked Duff. "Do you owe anyone money?"

"I got more people that owe me money than the other way around."

Duff lifted out another scoop and said, "Answer the question."

"A few small-timers. I don't even think they know they're owed. They just like to bet to say they bet when they're at the bar."

"Any big-timers?"

"Al Young," said Eddie.

"The sheriff? Big black dude?"

"That's the guy," said Eddie. "PGA."

"Huh?"

"The golf tournament, Duff. At Harding Park."

"Yeah?"

"Because of the lockdown, there's just not a lot to bet on, so everybody bet on the golf."

"Okay," said Duff. "But you usually do well when a lot of people are betting, right?"

"Did you watch it?"

It was played in San Francisco, so Duff took a passing interest but couldn't remember what happened on Sunday. "I only watched a bit," he said.

"Well," said Eddie. "A twenty-three-year-old Japanese-American kid who went to Cal won it."

"Yep," said Duff. "Now I remember."

"He was a 30-1 longshot," said Eddie. "And Al Young put a thousand bucks down on him."

The math was pretty easy. "So, you owe Al Young thirty thousand dollars."

"I do," said Eddie.

Duff's back was killing him, but he wanted to get this done, so he went hard without talking for about two minutes and made some real headway. Then he climbed out of the hole and handed the bucket to Eddie. "I assume you don't have that kind of money."

"I do not," said Eddie and jumped back in the hole. His white undershirt was filthy, and he somehow looked smaller than he did when he walked into the bar earlier that day in the fitted suit. But he must have had the same idea as Duff, because he was working almost violently now, shoveling out scoop after scoop without pausing in between.

After a few minutes, he stopped, panting like a dog, and said, "I think I just hit the bag."

"Good," said Duff. "Just clear off enough dirt so that we can show that it's the bag." Then he got up and looked down at Eddie. He took out his phone and shined the flashlight on the bottom of the hole. Eddie was working with his hands now clearing enough dirt off to show the CaddyDaddy emblem.

When Eddie turned his head toward Duff, he looked like someone who'd tunneled his way out of some kind of detention camp, or a miner being saved from a collapsed shaft. "Can you see it?" he said, his voice dry, almost a whisper.

"Yep," said Duff. "Give me your hand."

Eddie placed the bucket on the luggage, stood on it, and reached up to clutch Duff's forearm. For a brief moment, Duff had a flash of a memory of the two of them as kids engaged in a grade school handshake, during which one component involved the two of them clutching each other's forearm, just like they were doing now—only back then Eddie wasn't standing on a dead girl. Duff pulled hard and lifted Eddie out of there. Then he shone the flashlight back down at the bag: the CaddyDaddy label was visible.

"Grab your phone," said Duff. "Make sure to use the flash. And don't let me be in the frame. You did this by yourself."

Eddie nodded and videotaped the hole and the bag at the bottom. Then he leaned down, still filming, and with his forearm, moved a mound of dirt into the hole. He did that one more time and then stopped the video.

"Done," said Duff.

"Let's go in the house and send it," he said.

"Do you think Al Young is behind this?" asked Duff.

Eddie just shrugged as if he were too tired to even talk anymore.

When they got inside, Eddie sent the video. "What now?" he said.

"We wait and see what they want you to do next." It was warmer in the house, but it was still cold—typical summer weather in the city. Duff assumed Eddie would want to put his clothes back on, but he left them folded on the window bench. He stared at his phone.

"You want to get in the car and start driving back?" said Duff. "I think we should get out of here."

"I don't want to miss the call," he said.

"Don't worry," said Duff. "We can pull over if they call."

"Okay," he said, and Duff felt like he could suggest anything at this point, and Eddie would go with it. The man's brain was fried. "Can I just sit down for one minute?" he said.

"Absolutely," said Duff. "And we can talk about Al Young in the car. And the girl. We need to talk about the girl."

"What girl?" said Eddie.

"Jesus, Eddie," said Duff. "The girl in the hole."

"Angie," he said, as if he were calling out to her or singing the old Stones song, like she was in the other room and was going to come out holding beers for everyone.

"Yeah," said Duff. "Angie."

"So, she's gone," he said, still staring down at the phone, sounding like he was hypnotized now.

"How long were you two together?" asked Duff.

"Too long, I guess."

## 7

In the car on the way back to the Sunset District, Duff wanted to know more about Al Young. He'd met Al a few times over the years and didn't like him. He was the worst kind of blowhard: the loudest guy in the room but rarely had any idea what he was talking about. He'd been a San Francisco sheriff since he was in his early twenties, and now that he was in his fifties, he'd run every possible scam on the city and landed a captain's position where he didn't have to do any work. He just had to make sure his immediate underlings were happy. And he did.

He enjoyed bragging about all the ways he'd manipulated the system to score piles of taxpayer cash. He was actually referenced in the *SF Chronicle* just a few weeks back as making more in overtime pay than in his actual salary. The paper did an article on this kind of nonsense every year, and Al was almost always on the list. Most of that OT was earned sitting on his ass at home, being "on-call". Total scam.

There were a hundred different ways for city employees to cheat the system, and a lot of guys did. There was a school security guard a couple years back making over $300K a year because of all his overtime. Every time the school burglar alarm went off at night, this guy got four and a half hours pay for going in to shut it off. Well, one night he got caught on security camera setting off the alarm himself. They don't know how many times he'd done it, but you can bet more than just the once.

Most of these grifters kept their mouths shut about it. Not Al, though. He liked to shove it in everyone's face. He had short legs and a huge belly. Some people called him "The Penguin", but he was still strong. He'd been a great running back in high school. Liked to brag about that as well.

"You need to decide whether or not Al could be behind this," said Duff as they drove east on Geary.

Eddie had been very quiet since they'd gotten in the Porsche. He was still in his underwear, which seemed ridiculous, but his face was serious—now some kind of combination of rage and fatigue. "I guess so," he said, turning onto 25th Avenue and heading south toward Golden Gate Park.

"Did he threaten you when you told him you didn't have the money?"

"Yeah."

This was like pulling teeth. "What did he say?" asked Duff.

"It was a long speech," said Eddie. "Really annoying to have to sit there and listen to it." They slowed to a stop at Balboa Street and watched an ancient Chinese woman in a Niners beanie push her cart across the street. "The fat asshole spent fifteen minutes lecturing me about all the cheap screws he'd known that ended up with permanent scars because they didn't make good on their debts."

"How did it end?"

"He told me he expected at least $3,000 a week for ten weeks. Said something bad would happen if I was late."

"It's usually the other way around," said Duff.

"What is?"

"Aren't bookies usually threatening the betters?"

"I don't really consider myself a bookie," said Eddie.

"No," said Duff. "You're a real estate agent who takes bets."

"Whatever," said Eddie. "The prick wants his money."

"Where did you have this conversation?"

"He made me meet him down at Lake Merced in the parking lot so we could actually see the golf course, and he showed up in a city cruiser. He was wearing a suit. I guess the sheriff's office brass only wear their uniforms when they're on TV."

Duff didn't want to mess with Al Young. Al was just the type of guy who thought he could do whatever the hell he wanted and get away with it, but killing Eddie's girlfriend seemed like a lot. "Were you late on a payment?" he asked.

"Last week," said Eddie, as they drove across Fulton Street and into the park. "I only had $2,000. I put it in his hand and told him I'd give him $4,000 next week, but the fat son of a bitch slapped me across the face. You ever been slapped in the face, Duff?"

Duff just stared at Eddie who was focusing on the road as they merged onto Crossover Drive, a blur of red taillights in front of them, dancing in the fog.

"I'd rather have a guy hit me in the head with a baseball bat than slap me like this asshole did. Don't ever get slapped, Duff. I know you been in plenty of fights, but I'm telling you, don't ever let anyone slap you. I can actually still feel it in my cheek when I think about that fat piece of shit."

His voice was breaking a bit, so Duff interrupted: "Did he say anything after he hit you?"

"He *slapped* me, Duff. It's different."

"Yeah," he said. "I got that. After he *slapped* you, did he say anything?"

"He told me it was unacceptable."

"That's it?"

"That's it," said Eddie. "Then he got in the cruiser and drove off. I'm surprised he didn't use the siren."

They were coming out of the park now onto 19th Avenue, and Duff was trying to figure out if he wanted to be in this anymore. "You coulda come to me for the money," said Duff. "Why'd you want to mess with this son of a bitch?"

He pulled into the bus stop in front of the French school near Ortega Street and put the car in park. He took a deep breath and said, "I didn't think the guy would make a big deal out of me being short one week." He put his hand through his hair and shook his head, sandy dirt spraying onto the dashboard. "He knew I'd eventually get him his money. I never thought he'd do something like this."

Duff was uncomfortable sitting in a car with a guy in his underwear on 19th Avenue—three lanes of pretty heavy traffic moving past the Porsche, the fog lifting a bit now, making it easier to see inside. "How 'bout now? Do you think he did it?"

"It still doesn't seem possible," he said. "How did he even know I was seeing Angie?"

"That depends on how many other people knew."

"I thought it was a secret," said Eddie. "We were pretty good about it."

Duff wanted to get moving again. "Do you want me to come to your place and wait until he calls?"

"What's he waiting for?" said Eddie. "We sent him the video. We did what he said."

"Why don't you take me up to the bar," said Duff. "I'll pick up my car, call Marilyn, and tell her I'll be late. Shit. She probably thinks I've been in the bar with those guys drinking all night." He wondered if Wade had locked up yet, or if those guys decided to make a night of it after the races were over. He was almost certain there'd be no more Millers in the cooler. "I'll drive up to your place and wait with you for the call," said Duff. Eddie was quiet. "I won't tell Marilyn yet."

"Thanks, man," he said and pulled the car back onto 19th.

"While we're waiting, you can tell me about Angie," said Duff. "If it's not Al Young, maybe this has something to do with her, and we can try to connect the dots."

"I don't even care," said Eddie.

"I think you better start caring."

## 8

Duff tried to sound casual on the phone, but he could tell Marilyn was on to him. She knew he was keeping something from her. She'd made sure to tell him not to drink and drive. *Just call Uber, or I'll come get you.* He'd assured her that he was just helping someone out. He knew he was going to have to explain all of this to her at some point and that she'd be mad he didn't inform her right away. In fact, he'd made up his mind to tell her everything as soon as he got home, regardless of what kind of progress he and Eddie had made in finding Kim and regardless of whether or not he had to wake her up.

He knew this could make her an accessory after the fact, but he wasn't even sure if they'd committed a crime. They'd buried a dead person to save a live one. And Marilyn would never talk to him again if he kept this from her.

Eddie lived in a little area that was almost part of the Sunset District, but a little different. There wasn't really a Sunset District street that led to Country Club Drive. You came in by taking Ocean Avenue across Sunset Boulevard, and you were in. There were no stores or businesses. There was no country club either. It was strictly residential. Maybe a bit nicer than the houses in the areas adjacent to this little sliver of fog-covered land just east of the zoo, but not much. But it did have privacy. If you weren't going to your house, there was no reason to be on Country Club Drive. It didn't lead to anything else.

When Duff pulled up in front of the house, he could see that Eddie had left the Porsche in the driveway, the front left tire partially on the grass. Duff was hoping that when he got to the front door Eddie would open it with a smile on his face and say *She's home!* But he knew that was wishful thinking.

He climbed the stairs two at a time and arrived at the top to see that the door was ajar. He hesitated. There was a chance that Al Young or someone else was in there with guns or brass knuckles—or maybe just an open hand slapping Eddie in the face a few more times.

Duff poked his head in and listened. Nothing.

For a moment, he considered calling the cops. Maybe now was the right time regardless of what Eddie had been told. This really was a police matter. Duff was thinking all this as he was creeping into the house, still listening. He didn't want to call out to Eddie because he had no idea what he was walking into.

From the hallway, he was hearing something now coming from the kitchen. Maybe a hiss, like a broken radiator. Then it turned to a low whistle and eventually what sounded like a Piccolo Pete. Duff walked into the kitchen and saw Eddie sitting in a chair in front of the stove. He was staring at the tea kettle but not making any move to turn off the burner.

Duff turned it off and Eddie looked at him, just noticing that Duff was in the room. "You're making tea?" asked Duff.

Eddie was out of his stupor now. "I thought you might want a cup."

"I guess," said Duff, walking over to the cabinet and pulling out two mugs. "Anything in the house look different?"

"I ran around to every room," said Eddie. "And everything looks normal." He shrugged. "These guys must be pros," he said and pulled a variety pack of tea out of a drawer in the kitchen island.

They both poured their tea and then sat on stools at the island, kitty corner from one another. Duff blew on his and said, "Tell me about Angie."

"What do you want to know?"

"Were you just nailing her, or was there something else going on?"

"At first, I was just nailing her," said Eddie. "But then we kind of went into business together."

"You're telling me you were into something else besides real estate and sportsbook?"

Eddie took a small sip of tea and said, "It was related to real estate."

"Was it legit?" asked Duff.

"She was basically going to be a client after she inherited a big place in St. Francis Wood. Huge commission for me."

"Really," said Duff, wondering who was bequeathing the house to her. "Something doesn't sound right about that."

"What's the problem?"

"Let me guess," said Duff. "The homeowner is *not* Angie's relative ...." He let that float for a moment. Allow Eddie to absorb the fact that Duff wasn't a fool.

"She's not really related to the guy, no," said Eddie.

"What's the scam?" said Duff.

"The old-timer's got cancer," said Eddie. "Angie made friends with him and got him to leave the house to her in his will."

"Jesus," said Duff. "This guy have any relatives?"

"He does," said Eddie. "But they live in Ohio and Indiana or some shit, and they never call this lonely old bastard. So, Angie's been taking care of him."

"Is she a nurse?"

Eddie let out a short, snort of a laugh. "She took care of him, Duff," he said. "Helped out around the house."

"Did she live with him?"

"She stayed over once in a while."

"Christ," said Duff. "Is this one of those *sweetheart swindles*? Is she a Gypsy? One of those Irish Travelers? What's her game?"

"She doesn't have any game anymore, Duff. We just put her in the ground."

"Is her family involved in this?"

Eddie took a deep breath. Then he took a sip of his tea. "She does have family that's done some work for the old man," he said, serious, like he was trying to convince a jury.

"This sounds like one of those Gypsy deals," said Duff. "How do you get yourself into this kind of shit, man?" Duff stood up and poured the rest of his tea into the sink. It splashed out onto the counter. "We might have to think about calling the cops. This is beyond what I think I can do. These Gypsies are ruthless."

Eddie said, emotionless, "Kim said not to call the cops."

Duff wanted to go over and punch him in the face. "Is there a chance the old man's family could have figured out what was going on and killed this gal to protect their inheritance? Brought you in to do some of the dirty work because they know you're in on it?" He was leaning on the island now, both hands gripping the granite, staring at Eddie, trying to wake the man up to what was happening here. "If the house is in St. Francis Wood, it's gotta be worth at least a couple mil, right?"

"We'll list it at 3.5, but we'll get multiple offers, hopefully a little bidding war."

Eddie was starting to sound like himself again, a smarmy real estate agent. "So, if he's got two or three kids, that's life-changing money for people in the Midwest. Something to fight for. Maybe something to kill for, if you think some con artists have screwed you out of your inheritance."

"Yeah. I agree with that, but I've never met Carl's kids. They might be soft."

"There's no chance the old man, Carl, coulda done this, right?" asked Duff, trying to picture the kind of elderly guy, who'd lost his wife and was losing his mind—just waiting for the cancer to take him. Maybe sitting around watching a lot of CNN or reading the paper cover to cover.

"Actually," said Eddie, "he's probably not what you're thinking. He's kinda tough, always walking around in tight t-shirts, maybe ex-military."

"Are you serious?"

"Yes. He can probably do a hundred push-ups, this guy."

"Why did Angie pick him?" asked Duff.

"I can't tell you that."

"Why not?"

"'Cause I don't know, dude. Never asked. She'd already been working the guy for a month when I met her."

Duff walked over to the fridge and grabbed a beer. Then he put it back and walked into the dining room, where Eddie and Kim had a small bar set up in the corner. Duff grabbed the bottle of Jameson and brought it back into the kitchen. He pulled his mug out of the sink and then threw in a couple of ice cubes before filling it halfway and taking a nice pull. "I can't believe there's *two* people who might want to screw with you bad enough to kill your girlfriend and make you bury her."

"I can't believe it either," he said and reached for the bottle.

Duff pulled it away. "Nothing for you," he said. "You gotta be really sharp when Al or Carl or whoever these sickos are call you with the next instructions. I'm hoping this is almost over. Message received. Give us back Kim. But it doesn't feel that way right now."

Eddie finished off his tea. "I didn't consider Carl until just now."

Duff finished off his whiskey and looked at the clock. "I think we need to go see Carl."

## 9

They left the Porsche in the driveway and took Duff's pickup to Carl's house. It was almost ten o'clock, but they had to give it a try, see if the old man was awake. As they drove up Sloat toward The Woods, Duff turned off the radio—the news was doing county-by-county Covid death counts, and Duff didn't want to hear it.

There weren't any homeless tent encampments in this part of town, but there were plenty of campers parked in residential neighborhoods all over the place, and Duff saw three in a row parked by the reservoir before they crossed over 19th Avenue and then Junipero Serra Boulevard and into St. Francis Wood.

"It's the big grey house on the left with the pillars in the front," said Eddie.

"Nice place," said Duff, pulling over a few houses away. "Hate to be his gardener." Carl's house had a big front yard with a manicured lawn and intricate landscaping around the perimeter.

"He does it himself," said Eddie. "He tried to get Angie to help one time, but she didn't want to ruin her nails, so she went back inside and watched TV while the old-timer was out here pruning bushes." He pulled a Covid mask out of his jacket pocket and said, "We better put these on."

Duff sighed and put his mask on as they headed up the long brick walkway. Duff had his head on a swivel, making sure no one saw them, though his old pickup was pretty recognizable parked just a few doors down. When they got to the door, he used the knocker and looked over at Eddie, who had changed into a blue tracksuit.

Carl opened the door without asking who it was. He was wearing only a white undershirt tucked into a pair of tighty-whities. The effect was that he looked to Duff like a high school wrestler. "You two here to rob me?" he asked.

"No, sir," said Duff.

"Then take off those masks," he said. "I don't want my neighbors thinking I'm hosting some kind of gay orgy over here."

Eddie said, "The governor—"

"Stop it," said Carl, not letting Eddie finish the thought. "I'm sick of all the Covid bullshit. First time in history we quarantine healthy people. It's never been done."

"Got it," said Duff, holding his mask in his hand now.

Carl leaned in closer to Duff and began sniffing at the air. "You a gardener?" he asked.

Duff thought about all the digging he'd done a few hours ago. "No, sir," said Duff. "I own a bar."

"You smell like a gardener," he said, staring at Duff like he was trying to catch him in a lie.

"Oh," said Duff. "I planted some flowers for my girlfriend today. Haven't had time for a shower."

Carl nodded. "What do you guys want?"

"We're friends of Angie," said Eddie.

"Oh yeah," he said. "What did she do now?"

Duff couldn't read the man, standing there in his underwear. Short. Maybe 5'7". Like a gymnast—a compact network of muscles. Tight skin around his cheeks and eyes. Grey hair cut military style. Bare feet spread apart like he'd just landed a perfect dismount. "She's gone missing," said Duff. "We were hoping to talk to you a bit, see if you could help us locate her."

"Come on in," he said and started walking toward a beautiful staircase about thirty feet in front of them. "You guys go in there," he said, not turning around, but pointing to a small office just to the left of the front door. When he got to the first stair, he said, "Let me put on some clothes."

Duff and Eddie were both sitting in leather chairs that made farting noises every time one of them moved. Carl came walking into the room almost immediately after he'd left them to go up the long staircase. Duff thought Carl had to have run to make it back down so quickly, but the man was not out of breath. In fact, he walked in very calmly. The only changes to his wardrobe were a pair of Balboa High P.E. shorts and a faded old pair of moccasins.

"Okay, guys," he said. "Let's get to it. I can tell you're not family. You kids both look Irish to me and Angie's Romanian, olive colored skin. I've met some of her family, and they don't look like you two." He walked behind a fancy desk and sat in a leather swivel chair that didn't make synthetic flatuence.

Duff was trying to figure out how to do this. He didn't want to go down the wrong path. He decided to start with, "Do you know of anyone who would have reason to hurt Angie?"

"Not specifically," he said. "But I can imagine there's plenty of fellas who'd want to take her down."

"Why's that?" asked Eddie, shifting in his seat, sending out more fart noises.

"If you guys don't know," he said, "then you're not really friends with Angie."

Duff and Eddie looked at each other, and Duff could see that Eddie didn't know where to go next, but there were time considerations here. They hadn't heard back from anyone regarding Kimberly since they sent the video hours ago, and they couldn't waste time with this guy if he wasn't in on it or couldn't help them. "Okay," said Duff. "We know she's done some stuff, but we didn't know that *you* knew."

"Yeah," said Carl, holding a letter opener now and spinning it around in his hand. "She thought she was getting over on me, but I'd figured out her game the day I met her."

Now Eddie was sitting all the way at the edge of his seat. "So why did you keep letting her come over here?"

Carl looked at Duff and pointed his thumb in the direction of Eddie. "Is this guy some kind of idiot?" he said. "Have you ever *seen* this girl? She looks like the best-looking Kardashian only she doesn't have the gigantic ass. Actually, she looks like a young Cher Bono, you catch her in the right light."

Eddie seemed to be taken aback by the epithet and just sat there staring at the old man behind the desk, now tapping the letter opener on the blotter. "Who's Cher Bono?" he finally asked.

"You don't know Cher from *Sonny and Cher*," said the old guy.

"Is that like Cher, the singer?" asked Eddie.

"Yeah," said Carl. "Only she used to do a variety show, come out in all these outrageous costumes, lots of skin. Beautiful woman before the plastic surgeons got at her face."

Duff said, "So you *knew* she was ripping you off, but you let her hang around because you liked the way she looked?"

"She *wasn't* ripping me off," said Carl. "She *thought* she was ripping me off. And she was more than just hanging around."

"Explain," said Duff.

"Well," he said, standing up, scratching at his elbow, showing his bicep now in his tight undershirt. "She thinks I put her in my will."

"And you didn't?" said Duff.

"I don't have Alzheimer's," he said. "I'm fit, mind and body. These dumbshit Romanians think anyone over the age of sixty is losing his mind. I'm not."

"Jesus," said Duff. "So, you were conning *her*. For sex?"

"That's an ugly way of puttin' it," he said. "I have a darn good thing going, but I'm not hurting her, and even though you guys won't believe me, it ain't all that bad for her anyway." He was smiling now when he said, "I pop a few blue pills, and I know how to get this chick going. She never leaves here disappointed. I guess you could call me a generous lover."

Duff didn't look over at Eddie, but he could imagine the look on his face. "So, what was your exit strategy?" Duff asked. "It sounds like the girl's put in some sweat equity. How were you planning on ending this without any consequences?"

"It's not like they didn't get anything out of me," he said. "I let her brothers or cousins or whatever the hell they are do some bogus repair work around the house, and I paid them well. They did shit work on things that didn't need fixing."

"So that's what you paid to have sex with Kim Kardashian?" said Duff.

"Cher Bono," he said. "Yeah, I guess you can look at it that way." Then he paused and smiled. "But remember, she never went away unsatisfied. I'm serious about that."

"Okay," said Duff. "But you never explained your exit strategy."

"I'm a smart guy," he said. "But I've been thinking too much with my pecker. You start getting that steady poontang, boys, and you never plan much past the next roll in the hay."

Duff could tell that Eddie didn't like hearing any of this, and he was standing now as well. He had an easy six inches on Carl, but somehow Carl looked like a man and Eddie a child as they faced each other in Carl's office. "So, you don't have an exit plan," said Eddie, sounding like he was challenging the old man. Then he paused and Duff could tell that he was trying to get his words right. "You're just going to tell her at some point that she's out of the will?"

"I'll figure something out," he said and shrugged, like he'd done this before.

"Why did you tell us all this?" asked Duff. "What if we were cops?"

"Did I break a law?" he said.

"I guess not," said Duff.

"If lying was a crime," he said, "all those assholes on cable news would be in jail."

"So why did you tell us?" asked Eddie, looking really tired now.

"I guess I figured the jig was up anyway," he said. "I couldn't keep going like this for much longer. They were getting impatient. I guess they could try to expedite my demise. But, hey, you guys are right. I need to work on my exit plan. Maybe bring my son into it. He's got a company in Indiana, manufactures plastic beach toys, shovels, and buckets and what not. He does pretty well, but I don't hear from him much. Might have to give him a call, let him know what I've been doing."

"I think that's a good idea," said Duff. "And if you think of any reason someone might want to hurt Angie, will you please let us know. We know what she is, but we don't want to see anything bad happen to her."

"You sound like a cop. What's your name?" he said to Duff.

"Michael Duffy," he said.

Carl looked like he was seeing Duff for the first time. "Your dad Elmore?"

"That's him," said Duff.

"You running The Boot now?"

"I am."

"So, I need to get a hold of you, I can find you there?"

"Yep," said Duff. "Nice to meet you, Carl."

"Your dad was a good cop," he said.

"So, I've heard. You two work together?" asked Duff, wondering why he'd never heard his dad mention a Carl before.

"No," said Carl. "I guess you could say I worked against him?"

"You a criminal?"

"Criminal *defense*," he said, smirking again like he did when he talked about his carnal adventures with Angie. "I cross-examined him a few times over the years. He made a lot of arrests, so he spent a good deal of time in court back when juries in this town used to convict people once in a while."

"I'd think a defense attorney would appreciate the emptying of the prisons."

"No, no," he said, his hands clasped in front of him now. "It's not like that. You see this nonsense going on up in Portland and Seattle? I can't watch the news anymore. Anarchists."

Duff and Eddie were both nodding.

"I did my job trying to get my clients off," he said. "But I never would have represented any of these so-called antifa types." He shook his head but then smirked again. "I used to represent criminals who committed crimes for a reason."

## 10

Duff and Marilyn lived on 47ᵗʰ Avenue. There's no 48ᵗʰ. Just the Great Highway and then the beach. It's kind of a shitty setup in that, because of the four lanes that make up the two directions of the Great Highway, there's no beachfront property from Sloat Boulevard all the way up to the Cliff House. It always seemed like a waste to Duff even though the weather made the beach useless most of the year if you were into sunbathing.

Regardless, Duff and Marilyn rented a one-bedroom bungalow on 47ᵗʰ, and they could see Ocean Beach from their front porch—a quick jog across the highway with their boogie boards if they wanted to swim. It was almost always foggy except for September and October, but they loved the neighborhood, a short walk to Java Beach for a coffee and the Wawona Gates for some beers. And they had funky neighbors who left them alone.

Duff pulled the pickup in front of the house and took a deep breath. He knew Marilyn was going to be upset, primarily about the danger her sister was in, but also about Duff's withholding of the information for so long. It was 11:30, and she was probably asleep because she had Zoom school tomorrow morning for a bunch of little kids who'd be taking the class from their living rooms because of the shelter-in-place order. She was a kindergarten teacher, and she was almost irrational about having everything set up perfectly before the kids arrived. Duff knew this because she'd invited him to come in as a volunteer several times, and she had just about the coolest kindergarten class you could imagine. And when she was teaching, it looked like everything was spontaneous, but it wasn't. She prepared.

It was like the great basketball coach, Bobby Knight said, "The will to win is not nearly       as       important       as       the       will to prepare to win. Everyone wants to win but not everyone wants to prepare."

Duff's high school coach had made the team memorize the quote, and they would recite it before practice. Duff still remembered every word. To him, it worked with all aspects of life. When he was doing undercover, if he didn't do his prep work, he could have gotten himself killed. Even with the Boot, to a certain extent, any success he had was from preparation—make sure the place is stocked, the fruit cut, the bathrooms clean, and the Gonzaga group has their hot dogs on game nights. All that little shit matters. Obviously, the cop stuff was more serious, but Duff believed in that quote. It was his mantra.

That's why he was struggling today. There just wasn't any way he could have prepared for the past seven hours. He never panicked, and he felt like he was making the right decisions for the situation, but Kimberly was still out there somewhere, and now he had to tell her sister, whom he loved, that he couldn't find Kim. At least not yet.

There was a moment in the truck when he considered taking his clothes off in the living room and bringing them into the laundry room before Marilyn could see how dirty he was. See if he could slip into bed without waking her up and then tell her in the morning. His muscles and his brain were both throbbing, and there was nothing he could do for Kim tonight anyway. Why not get a little bit of sleep and talk to Marilyn in the morning? But as nice as that all sounded in his head, he knew it wasn't going to happen.

The door to the bedroom was barely ajar, but he could see the blue-grey flicker of the TV through the crack. He was in only his boxer shorts now. Marilyn had bought them for him. They were black with white whales, all swimming in the same direction. And right now, there was sand in the waistband. Before he opened the door, he pulled the elastic fabric away from his body and heard the dirt dusting the hardwood floor between his feet.

He pushed open the door gently. If Marilyn was awake, he would tell her he was going to take a shower.

She was awake. Staring at him. Eyes squinting, the hints of a grin at the corners of her mouth.

"Sorry," he said. "I'm taking a quick shower."

"Get in here," she said, smiling. She was sitting up with the comforter over her legs, her faded, oversized Neil Diamond t-shirt with the sleeves rolled up showed her tan arms when she looked at her watch. "What the hell's going on?"

He paused. He really wanted that shower and a few moments to collect his thoughts, but he knew that wasn't going to happen.

"This is not good," he said and walked over to the corner of the bed, where he sat down and felt the ache in his back and arms and hamstrings and knees.

***

"Who *are* you?" she said. "You knew what was happening to Kim at what time?"

"Sometime this afternoon," he said. "But it was immediately kind of crazy, and we didn't have time to screw around…"

"So, telling me would have been *screwing around*?" she said.

"That's not what I mean," he said, thinking this was almost exactly how he imagined this conversation would go down, like he'd dreamed it. "I was trying to help Eddie, and I thought that if we quickly did what these people asked, we could get Kim, and you wouldn't have to go through all the worry."

She was staring at him now, her mouth open just a little bit, her long hair covering one eye. Duff was wishing that both eyes were covered because she was looking like she hated him right now. And then he saw the tear run down her cheek. She didn't cry much. It wasn't her thing. But this situation did seem to call for it.

"Don't you think we should be doing something?" she said. "Don't you think you maybe should've called the cops in the first place."

"I am a cop," said Duff.

"C'mon, Michael," she said. "You don't want to be involved in this kind of shit anymore. We need help."

"She told Eddie no cops," he said. "But you might be right."

"Isn't there something where if someone is missing for more than forty-eight hours, then it's like impossible to find the person afterward?" Her nose was running, and she was wiping it with her forearm, still staring at Duff, her hair pulled behind both ears now. And she sounded a little crazy.

"Um," he said. "That's not true."

"Okay," she said. "Then what's the plan to get my sister back?"

"We have some leads," he said.

"And?"

"Well, we actually have just one now," he said, standing up and moving closer to her. "We checked the other one out already, and it didn't really pan out."

"You smell," she said. Then, "What's the actual lead?"

"Eddie owes someone money," he said. "And he's late on the payments."

"That piece of shit," she said. "And he was cheating on my sister? If we don't find Kim, my dad's going to kill him. I'm not just throwing that word out there, Michael. My dad is literally going to murder Eddie Bilker." She paused for a moment and let that sink in. "And then you and my dad are going to have to go out in some backyard somewhere and bury him like you did with that girl today."

Duff nodded, half believing what Marilyn was saying. Her dad was some kind of politico—he ran a lot of campaigns in the city and knew a lot of important people. And Duff knew that Marilyn's old man had probably done some shady stuff over the years to get people elected. But murdering his son-in-law seemed like it might be beyond his expertise.

"Well, your dad's going to have to dig the hole," said Duff.

## 11

Marilyn never had trouble getting guys, but she had to work hard for Michael Duffy. They met about five years ago. For two hours, they sat next to each other on a couch at a New Year's party, and Michael never put a move on her. He was sitting at one end of the couch, drinking a can of beer and had a second and a third in the pockets of his jacket. Marilyn was sitting in the middle chatting it up with a girl from Denmark who occupied the third seat cushion. Michael seemed content to sit there drinking his beer and talking to people, who would stop by and shoot the shit with him for a few minutes and then move on.

At one point, Marilyn moved closer to Michael to make room for a fourth person who wanted to sit down between her and the girl from Denmark. Marilyn was nearly sitting on Michael's lap when she said, "Oh, sorry."

"That's all right with me," he said, and she thought he sounded a little bit like a character in a western, and she liked it. But he didn't say anything else. Didn't even tell her his name. Just smiled and nodded and took another sip of his beer.

But that was it. Two hours he sat there next to her, but never said anything else, and she eventually got up to leave. Almost immediately, a girl wearing a tank top in January sat down next to him, and the two started a conversation.

Marilyn and Michael bumped into each other a few times over the next few months, and he finally asked her out. She'd been seeing someone else, but she said yes without hesitation.

After they'd been going together for a while, she asked him about that first night at the New Year's party. "Sure, I noticed you," he'd said.

"Then why didn't you say something?"

"I was waiting for the right moment," he said.

"For two hours?"

"Yeah," he said. "Maybe I was a little nervous."

"And what was with the beers in your pockets," she said.

"I didn't want to have to get up and maybe lose my spot next to you," he'd said, and that was all it took. She knew he was the one.

He was still a cop back then, and she didn't like that much. There was the whole thing with this gang leader putting a bounty out on him because Michael had arrested the guy's brother or some nonsense. It was crazy. They had cops parked outside their house for months, and one would drive her to school in the mornings. It was in the paper and everything. Her dad wanted her to move out, but she saw this as a test. If they could make it through something like this, they were meant to be.

But now here they were in something else, something worse.

They were sitting at their little table now in the little kitchen. Everything in this house was small, but it was clean. She and Michael had a lot in common. They both liked a clean house. All their stuff was old and chipped and scuffed and faded, but it was really clean—scrubbed and swept and polished. They liked it that way. It worked for them.

They both had plates with English muffins this morning, but neither one of them was eating.

"First you fell asleep while I was talking to you," she said. "And then you snored for a couple of hours."

"Sorry," he said and picked up his muffin but didn't do anything with it.

"I wanted to know about the girl …." She just let it sit there, but Michael didn't respond right away. "What?" she said. "Is this some kind of guy code where you're not going to tell me about this girl Eddie was screwing?"

"Whoa," he said, putting down the English muffin. "I was just thinking where to start. You know I don't really give a shit about Eddie, right?"

"Sorry," she said. She was so upset last night that she'd cried until the sun came up. She couldn't sleep knowing Kim was out there somewhere, and she and Michael and Eddie weren't doing anything. "What's the story with the girl?"

"Angie," he said.

"Yeah?"

"I think she was some kind of professional con artist," he said, his elbows on the table, his hands clasped as if he were in prayer.

"What do you mean?"

"You ever heard of a sweetheart swindle?" he said, looking at her now with those pale blue eyes that could get squinty when he smiled. And he'd been smiling a lot lately. Much more than when he was a cop. He was happy when he was a cop, but it was a different kind of happiness. It was intense, an adrenaline rush. And his smile was different back then. He didn't do drugs, but he'd had a tight-lipped smile like a cocaine user, always looking for what's next.

His current smile was easy, relaxed. Not toothy, but natural. And she liked it. It was almost a lazy kind of happiness. Not that he was lazy. He worked hard to make the bar successful, but there certainly wasn't anything dangerous about it. He was over the danger. He was a guy who enjoyed reading the paper now. He even wrote funny letters to the editor. He was in the water a lot more now, hanging out across the street with neighborhood surfers on nice days. It was better, but she needed him to get a little bit of that edge back right now.

"Sweetheart swindle?" she said.

"These young gals make friends with old people and then try to rip 'em off," he said. "Some of the old-timers lose everything, all their retirement, their houses—"

"That's disgusting," she said. "There's a special place in hell for that kind of awful human being."

"Well, maybe she's there now," he said.

"What was Eddie doing with her?"

"It sounds like he was just screwing her," he said. "But she might have been conning him, too. You never know with these people."

Marilyn took a bite of her English muffin. She still felt terrible, but she always ate when she was listening to Michael's stories. "Disgusting," she said.

"You ever heard of the *Foxglove Murders*?" he said.

Marilyn shook her head.

"That's right," he said. "You're younger than me." He closed his eyes for a moment, then said, "My dad worked on the case back in '96 or '97," he said. "So, I was just a little kid, but I remember the talk around the house about Gypsies stealing from old people."

"What even is a Gypsy?" she asked. "I thought they were just like fortune tellers in old movies."

"I'm no expert," he said. "In fact, I think there's actually Irish gypsies, too. Called travelers. Maybe that's all it is—people who travel around."

"But the ones you're talking about are criminals."

"Yeah," he said. "They do scams, mostly on old people."

"So why did you say foxglove?" she said. "What's that?"

"It's what they called that case my dad worked on," he said, and then he started nodding. "Yeah. That was the name of the poison. Foxglove. They would get in these people's wills and then start to slowly poison them. Jesus. Now that I think of it as an adult, it's really brutal stuff."

"So, you think Gypsies have my sister?" she said, really scared now, believing these people sounded ruthless.

"I don't think so," he said. "The people who have Kim also killed Angie, right? And they stuffed the body in the trunk of a car. I don't think these people would treat one of their own like that."

"But what if Eddie and Angie tried to double-cross these people, and they killed her?"

Michael was holding his English muffin again, but now he set it down on his plate. "I think the whole deal is that these people are fiercely loyal to their own," he said. "I can't imagine Angie betraying her family."

"Unless she broke some kind of code by doing business with my brother-in-law."

Michael stood up now, slowly, like an older guy, not straightening his back all the way. Then he walked into the bathroom. When he came out, he'd washed his face, and his hair was wet. He could use a haircut. When he was a cop, he always had a buzz cut. Marilyn didn't even know he had blond highlights until he let it grow out. She liked it this length, but if it got any longer, it would start to look like he didn't care about his appearance, and that would be accurate, but she didn't want everyone to know.

"I'm supposed to check on this other lead with Eddie this morning," he said. "Then we can look into the gypsy theory."

"I'm going with you," she said.

"You really want to go watch me talk to a fat sheriff?"

"Michael," she said and swallowed. "It's my sister. Of course, I'm coming to watch you talk to the fat sheriff."

"I don't think you should," he said.

"Why not?"

"From what I've heard, this guy likes to slap people."

## 12

Carl didn't sleep well. He was a little worried about Angie. Not a lot. She *had* been trying to steal from him. But she was just a kid, and the two of them had shared some moments together that he would swear were genuine. His days in court made him an experienced lie detector, and either she was really good at it, or the two of them had an odd kind of connection. Either way, he didn't want anything horrible to happen to her, but her line of work certainly led to the bad stuff. He'd represented a lot of people who'd been good-hearted at some point in their lives, but they got caught up in some garbage and backslid into their more primal selves. That's when they got into trouble. The greedier they were, the worse the trouble.

Carl was always amazed at what humans were capable of doing to each other, and he was aware that he might be in the middle of something with these gypsies, so he set up a zoom session with his son in Ohio and his daughter in New Mexico. The two of them were worried about the cancer, but this new situation could be a lot more dangerous.

Angie's crew was rotten. They hadn't fooled him. But when he was honest with himself, he had to admit that at one point, he actually did consider putting her in the will. If she was willing to be with him and nurse him when he was dying in the next six months, it was almost worth it. But he couldn't do that to his kids. They were doing fine, but the money would help them out—make sure the grandkids could go to private school. Maybe they could take the families to Europe or something. They deserved it more than Angie.

His daughter, Tess, had some kind of tropical forest behind her.

"Where are you?" he said, laughing.

"It's a fake background, dad," she said. "I'm still in Las Cruces."

It looked like Dan was at his office. He was wearing a sports shirt with the company logo on it, and there was shelving behind him. "How are you, Dad?"

"Well," he said. "That's why I wanted to have this call."

"Is it something about the chemo?" asked Tess, and she almost immediately started to cry, the bottom lip quivering as she wiped the corners of her eyes with a knuckle.

"No, no," he said. "I quit the chemo months ago. It wasn't going to cure me and getting off of it bought me a few months of feeling almost normal. Totally worth it."

"I get it, Dad," said Dan. "I respect that choice, but I wish you'd have told us before you decided on that."

"Okay, yeah," said Carl. "So, this is what I really want to tell you guys. And it's going to sound crazy, but I haven't lost my mind yet, so please believe me."

"Dad?" said Tess.

"Here it goes," said Carl. "A group of Gypsies is trying to scam me, get me to sign over my last will and testament."

"What the hell?" said Dan.

"And I've been sleeping with the sister of these people."

"Daddy?" said Tess.

"I know," he said. "I'm sorry. No disrespect to your mom. The people were trying to scam me, so I decided to scam them right back, and I got caught up in it. It was stupid."

"So how does this end?" asked Dan. He had his elbows on his desk and he was holding his face in both hands. The man was busy. He didn't have time to deal with his dad's shit, and Carl didn't want him to.

"There's something else," said Carl, shifting his eyes back and forth between his two kids. "Apparently, the gal with whom I was cavorting has gone missing."

"Jesus, Dad," said Dan. "You didn't have anything to do with it, right?"

"Danny," he said and sighed.

"Sorry," said Dan. "I guess I should ask if the Gypsies … is that the word you're saying—Gypsies? Are they gonna *think* you have something to do with it?"

"I don't think so," said Carl. "They probably think I'm too old and senile to do anything. Maybe I am," he said and looked hard at himself in the computer screen. He was in the den with the lights low, so his picture was a bit fuzzy, but aside from the deep crow's feet, probably brought on by all the gardening, he thought he looked pretty damn good. And he still felt good, even though he knew he might only have a few more weeks of that. "And who knows how many other jobs these people got going? They might have twenty people they're looking at right now."

Tess said, "Do you think Dan should come out there?"

Dan said, "Ah, yeah Tess, I'm trying to run a company here, but, yes, I guess I can get out there if you need me, Dad. Do you think you're in danger?"

"I don't want you kids coming out here," he said. "There's an ex-cop named Duffy, who's helping me out with this. I think I'll be safe." He felt himself nodding at the computer screen to let them know he was okay. He was starting to wonder why he'd even decided to tell them any of this. "I just wanted you to know that you both will be taken care of when I'm gone," he said. "I wanted you to have some idea about these people in case they try to pull something."

"Dad," said Dan. "Why don't you call the real police?"

"Good idea," said Carl. "I'll do that as soon as we're done here." But Carl knew he wasn't going to do that. He wanted to see where this was going. What were the cops going to do anyway? No real crime had been committed yet. And Carl felt like he needed this. One last bad idea before the cancer started eating away at him like it had done to his wife just a few years before.

He wouldn't mind working with that kid, Duffy. See how far the Gypsies wanted to go with this. See if he was even on their radar. For all he knew, Angie went to Vegas for a few days with some other old-timer with a barely-working pecker and a pocket full of poker chips. And she forgot to check in with the bosses. It could be anything. Sure, he'd lied to her about the will, but she didn't know that yet.

\*\*\*

Carl had fallen asleep watching an old Sugar Ray Leonard fight that he'd seen many times before. He woke to the sound of the phone ringing just a few inches from where he was sitting. He wondered how many rings it had been, but he didn't reach for the phone. And when it stopped ringing, he waited for the message. Very few people called his land line, and he thought it might be Dan, calling him now, without Tess on the line, to talk about Gypsy con artists.

The caller left no message, so Carl checked the caller ID and memorized it. He walked over to his desk, opened the top drawer, and pulled out a stack of business cards bound by a rubber band. He shuffled through until he found the bullshit company *City Builders*, and he read the phone number aloud. Same number. These damn Gypsies were looking for him.

They'd broken his water heater, charged him an arm and a leg to install a new one, and put in a bargain brand replacement. They'd told him he should put in double-paned windows on the west side of the house to prevent mold. Then they installed some used windows they'd bought from some scrap yard. These guys were filthy bastards taking advantage of him, and he was banging their sister, who thought she was taking advantage of him as well. It had been a fair trade for a while, but it was time to get out one way or another.

He walked down to the garage and had to move all the tubs of Christmas ornaments and his old army footlocker to get to his camping gear. He could almost smell the lake when he got to his fishing tackle box. He pulled it out, wiped off the cobwebs, and looked at his name stenciled on the side. He made sure the latch was on tight, and then he packed it across the floor. Before he brought it upstairs, he noticed that his hands were shaking.

He sat on the bottom stair and opened the box. He picked up an old lure and felt the weight of it in his hand, and then he lifted the top tray to see what was underneath.

## 13

Al Young was wearing his light suit, a powder blue summer look, with loafers, no socks, no tie. It was probably about 70 degrees, zero wind. He would have normally felt good—really good—on a day like this. But he had to meet with Rick Cardenas today to talk about the video.

Rick was a former public defender, who got sick of apologizing for lowlifes and started chasing ambulances instead. He was loaded now but still liked to deal. He was unofficially working on behalf of a young, female member of the San Francisco Sheriff's department, and Al was ready to play but not confident he could win this one.

Al parked near Saints Peter and Paul Church by Washington Square and walked through the park to get to Original Joe's. When he was about halfway, he was sweating, and his loafers were chafing his heels. He was out of breath and wanted to take his mask off, but he wasn't in the mood to get yelled at by the middle-aged women doing yoga on their mats in the middle of the park. So, he huffed his way toward the restaurant and saw Rick sitting at one of the curbside tables. The inside of Joe's was still closed because of the state mandate, but today was a perfect day to be outside anyway.

Rick was wearing a pair of old school wayfarers, and he still had great hair—salt and pepper, but thick and wavy, brushed straight back. "Albert!" he called over and waved as Al crossed Union Street and nodded to the valet leaning on a podium.

Al put his mask in his jacket pocket, pulled out a chair, and sat down without shaking Rick's hand.

"So, we're not going to be cordial?" said Rick, big smile—looking a little like George Hamilton, leaning back in his seat, legs crossed.

"I've got a rule," said Al. "I don't shake hands with a guy who's got me by the balls."

"That rule is foolish," said Rick.

"Oh yeah."

"Yes," he said. "In order to shake your hand, the man has to let go of your balls, no?"

Al didn't have time for this bullshit. "It's not really a rule," said Al. "And you don't really got me by the balls."

"I don't?" he said, smiling even wider and motioning with two fingers to the waiter. "How about something refreshing?" he said to either the waiter or to Al or to himself. "What's that Italian cocktail that tastes so good on a summer day?"

"Aperol Spritz, sir?" said the waiter.

"Ah, yes," he said. "That's the one. Bring me one of those." Then he looked at Al and said, "Perhaps my friend will have his usual." Then he paused for dramatic effect and said, "Vodka-prune juice?"

The waiter raised his eyebrows at Al, who didn't smile. He shook his head and said, "Jim Beam over."

"Right away," said the waiter and rushed up the sidewalk to the main entrance.

"How are we going to resolve this?" said Rick, leaning forward now, trying to look relaxed, but turning the corner now. No more cool-guy act. He was ready to go.

"I don't really know what you have," said Al.

"Oh?" he said. "I thought Brianna told you."

Al closed his eyes for a moment and took a deep breath. When he opened them again, the drinks had materialized on the table, and Rick was reaching for his fruity, orange, Italian thing. He actually used the straw and made one of those gaspy sounds as he put the glass back down on the table.

"She said she's got video of her and me getting out of a car in an underground parking garage," said Al.

"Yes," said Rick. "I've seen it."

"And that's illegal?"

"Of course not, Albert," he said. "But she does work for you, yes?"

Al took a nice swallow of the bourbon and waited until the burn stopped and turned into a warm sensation in his chest and belly. "Still not illegal," said Al.

"Yes, yes, yes," he said, enjoying this, taking another dainty sip from his drink. "This is your retirement year, correct?"

"Correct," said Al, looking down at his bourbon now. He didn't want to look at this guy anymore. He was feeling out of breath again, just sitting there, not even doing anything. He knew he was out of shape, but he shouldn't be winded from sitting.

"Would you like to see the video?" he said finally and pursed his lips like he was going to blow Al a kiss.

"Not particularly," said Al. "But I guess I should see what we're dealing with here."

Rick was looking down at his phone now, poking and scrolling like he was playing a video game. "I'm going to hand you my phone," said Rick. "But please don't destroy it. I have a copy of the video, and Brianna has a copy as well."

Al finished his drink in one swallow and took the phone from Rick, who had the video all set to go. Al breathed in through his nose and pressed play. He'd been with Brianna so many times, he didn't know what he was going to see.

The video is dark and a little grainy, but it's clearly his car, and that's him getting out of it, and then helping Brianna out. Oh, man. Now he's tucking in his shirt. Jesus, he looks fat. And now here's Brianna straightening her skirt.

This wasn't good, but Al didn't look away.

Brianna is putting on some lipstick, and Al is leaning up against her. Can he really be that fat? She's laughing and pushes him away. He steps around her and reaches in the car to grab his sport coat.

It was bad. Really bad. But he still thought there might be some wiggle room.

The two of them walk toward the elevators and Al puts his hand on Brianna's ripe ass. She pushes it off, but she also leans in toward him so that their shoulders are touching when he pushes the button for the elevator.

Al almost handed the phone back, but he decided to wait until the elevator doors opened. He didn't fully remember any of this, but it was starting to come back to him, so he kept his eyes on the screen.

The doors open and the two of them step inside. And here it is. Al has her by the waist and pushes her up against the elevator wall. Brianna is wrapping her leg around him just before the doors meet in the middle.

Al felt his cheeks fill up with air, and he blew out a long sigh but held onto Rick's phone.

"Albert," said Rick. "This video looks bad for you, yes?"

"What does she want?" Rick didn't hesitate. "It's still $50K, Albert."

"Even though it was consensual?"

"You know that does not matter, my friend."

"It should," said Al.

"Perhaps," said Rick. "But you were her superior. I believe you're aware of what this could do to your reputation, not to mention your pension."

Al felt his stomach tighten. He hadn't eaten anything, and he drank the bourbon too fast.

"Surely, the fifty thousand is worth the hundreds of thousands you'll save in your retirement fund," said Rick, swirling the ice in his girly glass.

"Yeah," said Al. "I get that. But what's to stop her from holding on to the video and pulling this shit again?"

"I have a reputation to uphold as well," said Rick, frowning, like he was disappointed that Al would even suggest something so unpleasant.

"And you'll prevent this from getting out if I can get you the money?"

"I give you my word."

"What's your cut?" asked Al.

"Please, Albert," said Rick. "Let's try to remain professional."

"When does she want the money?" asked Al.

"Tomorrow?" said Rick, running a manicured finger around the rim of his glass.

"I'm a little short," said Al. "But I got a big payoff coming in over the next few weeks. I won a lot on the PGA out at Harding. Dude that owes me the money's screwing me right now, but I think he's ready to cough it up." He paused and thought about Eddie Bilker for a moment. "I put a pretty good scare into him."

"I wish I could help with that," said Rick.

Al wanted to slap Rick across the face. He'd developed a taste for a good slap. But he couldn't. Instead, he placed the man's phone on the table. Then he picked up his tumbler, poured the ice on the sidewalk, and brought the bottom of the glass down hard the phone, which shattered immediately. Next, he took off his loafer, smashed the phone two more times with the heel, and then put the phone in the pocket of his jacket.

"Copies," said Rick.

"Yeah," said Al, putting his shoe back on and standing up. "Had to take the shot you were bluffing, though."

"Of course, Albert," said Rick, leaning back now and crossing his legs. "Tomorrow?"

Al didn't look at him. He just walked away from the table. By the time he got to the curb, he heard Rick ordering another Apple drink. And then a jogger ran by and yelled at Al, "Put on a mask."

Al wanted to slap her as well.

## 14

"Do we need to go over the game plan?" Duff asked, looking over at Marilyn, who was staring out the windshield toward the foggy curve of Country Club Drive. It was so thick this morning that they could see only about four houses down. The rest of the street would appear and disappear depending on the wind.

"No sitting around bullshitting, right?" she said, looking back hard at him now and somehow freezing the moment.

Duff thought she was beautiful, but he wasn't the kind of guy to stare deeply into a woman's eyes. It was an uncomfortable moment for him. He preferred sneaking looks at her when she didn't know. It sounded kind of creepy, but he wasn't looking at her that way. He would watch her face, the bone structure, the coloring, the way her nose crinkled when she smiled. But he didn't like to look deeply into her eyes. But he was doing it now.

"Exactly," he said, finally. "The clock's ticking."

"And we're calling the cops right away if he has no leads."

"That's the plan," he said and gave her knee a squeeze. "Let's go."

She took a deep breath, and Duff could tell she was holding back tears. She cried only when she was angry or frustrated or desperate. In this case, she was probably all three, but she was holding it together when she gave Duff a nod of determination.

***

They were sitting on the same stools that Duff and Eddie had used the night before. The empty mugs were still on the counter.

Eddie looked like shit. Pasty. He'd put on a pair of khakis and a light blue oxford shirt, but he was barefoot, and the collar of the shirt was wrong. It was starched stiff, a clean triangle on one side but was limp and curled under on the other. "They contacted me," he said as soon as everyone had a stool. His voice was hoarse and had the crackle of phlegm that he seemed too tired to clear.

"Yeah?" said Marilyn, impatient.

"Same deal," he said. "The video was up really close, so I couldn't see much of anything except her face." He shrugged as if to say sorry. "I did what you said, Duff. I tried to see something, anything, but all I could catch was a blur of red when the camera moved for a second."

"You mean like blood?" said Marilyn.

"No, no," said Eddie. "The red wasn't on Kim. She looked okay except she was crying. The red was in the background, but I only saw it for a second when the camera was wobbling."

Duff was getting frustrated. "Just tell us what she said, Eddie."

"Yeah, yeah," he said. "She told me, keep the cops out of it, or she's dead. And she looked like she meant it."

"What does that look like?" asked Duff, about ready to grab him by the shirt and shake the information out of him.

"What?"

"You said she looked like she meant it."

"Oh yeah," said Eddie, his hands shaking a bit. "She looked like she *believed* it. Like if we do what they want, she'll be okay. Like maybe she wasn't even scared." He was cleared-eyed now, assuring them with his stare.

"You could see all that on your phone?" said Marilyn. "The hell with this. We gotta call the cops while she's still alive. How long ago did they call?"

Duff put his hand around her waist but kept his eyes on Eddie, trying to figure out if the man was making any sense. "So, what do they want us to do now?"

"Didn't say," said Eddie and then looked to Marilyn. "And they called about fifteen minutes before you guys got here."

Duff held Marilyn tighter and said, "So, they didn't say what they want us to do? They just said what they *don't* want us do?"

Marilyn twisted out of Duff's grasp. "Again," she said. "Enough. We need to get the police involved now. Because if we don't, and all we can do is sit around on our asses and wait for them to call again, I'm gonna lose my shit, you guys."

"I'm so sorry," said Eddie in a whisper, perhaps half-hoping that no one would hear him, but he'd still get self-credit for saying it.

Duff was waiting for this to happen. Marilyn and Eddie were going to have it out at some point. Duff just didn't think Eddie would be the one to start the conversation.

"I hope you're sorry," said Marilyn. "Because if she's dead, it's your fault, you brainless asshole."

"I just talked to her," he screamed, sounding like he was trying to convince himself that she had to be alive still, even as they sat there staring at each other, helpless.

Duff walked around to Eddie's side of the island so that he would be looking at Marilyn for the rest of this conversation. "I know Kim is your wife, but since you're the one that messed up so royally, Eddie, Marilyn's going to make the decision on whether or not we should go to the police."

Marilyn's eyes widened.

"Unless you don't want to," he said, quickly. "Either way, you get to decide what happens next."

She got that look again, like she was holding back tears, and she used the same strategy she used in the truck. Deep breath. "This is what I decide," she said. "We try to figure out a plan. If we got nothing, we have to call the police." Her shoulders were slumped, and she walked over to stand next to Duff, so he'd put his arm around her, which he did. But it was a strange scene, the three of them on the same side of the island, looking out the window toward the zoo.

~15~

Derek and his brother, Alex, were still fairly new to the organization, and neither of them was sure what Club Vulpe was ever used for except Cristian's business meetings. The ornate two-story building in the Mission District included a dark bar with strange green lighting and paintings of naked women on the walls. There was a banquet room with tables and chairs from the 1970's, and several private rooms scattered throughout the old building. Derek imagined all the satellite rooms had leather furniture and extravagant ashtrays, but he'd never been inside any of them.

Cristian always met him and his brother in the private bar.

Today, Cristian looked tired. The weathered skin on his cheeks was just barely hanging on to his drooping bones. He pointed to two low chairs at a tiny cocktail table. Derek and his brother waited for Cristian to sit down, and then they took their seats.

"What's with the hair?" said Cristian in his smoker's cackle, just barely revealing his skid row teeth.

Derek had been shaving his head for over a year. He liked the look better than the receding hairline. But he didn't like that his brother had recently copied this look. They were only a year apart and now appeared almost identical to most people.

"You look like a set of hairless testicles," said Cristian and laughed to himself. That's the only time he laughed—when he thought *he'd* said something funny. And it wasn't really a laugh at all. He didn't even open his mouth or make a sound. His face looked like he was about to whistle. Then he'd close his eyes and bob his head like a marionette. Derek always thought that when the boss laughed, he looked like a guy with a bad toothache.

"Yeah," said Derek. "I didn't know Alex was gonna do that."

"What?" said Alex. "You're the only one can have this haircut?"

"It's fine," said Derek. Cristian didn't want to listen to this bullshit, and Derek had decided to grow a goatee to set him apart from his brother. It wasn't coming in as quickly as he wanted, but it would be fine.

"So, tell me, Derek," said Cristian. "On what projects is your wife currently working?" Then he dropped his chin into his chest and sat staring at Derek.

"She was working two old ladies in the Marina," he said, and then removed a small notebook from the inside pocket of his jacket and flipped through the pages. "Yeah, two ladies in the Marina, a gentleman in a nursing home out on Silver, where she's about to close the deal, and the old guy in St. Francis Wood, who already has her in his will."

"You shouldn't have that notebook," said Cristian.

"The notebook?" said Derek.

"Yes," he said. "That's evidence, you gogoman." He was mad but still sat with his old, wrinkled hands encasing his hard face now, his red-rimmed eyes squinting through a pair of tortoise shell glasses. "It should all be right here," he said and used one finger to point at his temple. "Get rid of that thing."

Derek stood up to throw the notebook into the garbage behind the bar, but Cristian slammed his fist on the table. "Not now. Memorize the contents and dispose of it on *your* time."

"Sorry, sir," said Derek, and he could feel the blood rushing to his face. He didn't look over at Alex, but he could feel him smirking.

Cristian walked over to the bar and used the cobra to pour himself a short glass of club soda. He did not ask Derek or Alex if they wanted anything. Then he returned to his chair and asked, "Before she went missing, what was Angie doing to expedite the completion of her projects?"

"She's microdosing the two old ladies," he said. "Shouldn't be long."

Cristian nodded, pleased.

"No reason to do anything with the nursing home guy," said Derek. "The family started hospice, and Angie is the life insurance beneficiary."

"Yes," he said. "And the last man?"

"She's been working on him the longest," said Derek. "He still looks like he's in good shape."

"Are we wasting our time?" said Cristian.

Alex broke in. "We've generated some construction work from this guy," he said.

"Decent money, so far," said Derek. "But Angie's playing the long game on this one. He's pretty smart, but she's already gotten him to leave her the house."

"Relatives?" said Cristian.

"Out of state."

"How old is he?"

"Stage four cancer."

"Wonderful," said Cristian. "So, where is she?"

Angie was worth a lot of money to the organization, and even though their marriage was arranged by Cristian as a strategic initiative for business development, Derek had fallen for her, and now he just wanted to find out where she was and bring her home.

"That's why we're here," said Derek. "She's never disappeared like this before."

"How long has she been gone?"

"Two nights."

"Does she sleep at other houses sometimes?"

"Yes, but she always checks in with us when she's not going to make it home," said Derek. "Always."

"Is there a chance that one of the targets has made her?" said Cristian. "If she got caught, that's okay. We can help her." He took a tiny sip of his club soda. "But if she runs off, it won't end well for her."

"We understand," said Alex, nodding confidently, and Derek wanted to punch him in the mouth.

"It just doesn't sound like her," said Derek. "She knows to come to you if she's in any trouble. She knows that."

Cristian took another tiny sip of club soda, and then he put the glass down for a moment before he picked it back up and threw the club soda in Derek's face. Then he popped up into a surprisingly athletic stance, stepped back to create space, and threw the glass at Alex. It grazed his head and ricocheted off a barstool, crashing on the floor and splintering across the hardwood.

Derek dabbed at his face with the sleeve of his jacket. His eyes were burning a bit, but he didn't blink. He was impressed that his brother didn't even flinch.

Cristian grabbed the little table with two hands and flipped it. It missed Alex completely but hammered down hard on Derek's thighs before it spun to the side, hit the floor, and twirled like a dreidel for a few seconds before anyone moved. Then Cristian grabbed the back of his chair. Derek thought the old man was going to pick it up and slam it over his head. He would not have resisted. He might have put his arms up, but that's it. Fighting the old man would not be advisable. The organization was vast. Derek would not last long if word got out that he showed disrespect to Cristian.

But it didn't matter. Cristian simply turned the chair around and straddled it backward, looking a lot younger now than he did just minutes before. "You two dodos need to find that girl today," he whispered.

The brothers both nodded.

His hands were folded over the back of the chair, and his chin was resting on his hands. "There are many possibilities here," he said. "She could have run …." He let the words trail off and smiled like he was looking at a couple of dogs that'd just chewed through the sofa cushions. "She could have been taken," he said and let the smile turn into a frown. "Or she could have been picked up by the police."

"I'll check into everything," said Derek.

"People have already checked," he said, shaking his head. "She is not with the police."

"That's good," said Alex, a small welt swelling up on the side of his head, looking like something small and angry was trying to get out.

"She was your responsibility," said the old man, dropping his head now as if he were in prayer. "You've disappointed me."

"We'll make it right," said Derek.

"You will," said Cristian, looking up now, staring at the brothers, challenging Derek to look away. But Derek knew he couldn't. He needed to show confidence, or he and Alex might not make it out of the club today.

"We'll get on it right now," said Derek, happy that his voice sounded almost cocky.

"Which one of these marks would have the wherewithal to make Angie and decide to do something about it?"

Derek and Alex looked at each other. Alex was doing his best to look like a badass. He'd done a nice job after the glass had hit his head, but he looked like he might break now. He was slouching in his chair, looking nonchalant. But Derek saw in his brother's eyes the look of a rabbit—frozen in fear, hoping the coyote wouldn't see him.

"I think just Carl," said Derek.

"Who's that?"

"The old-timer from St. Francis Wood."

"You think he's onto her?"

"I'm going to find out." said Derek.

## 16

When Eddie offered to drive to the police station, Marilyn said, "I'm not riding in that car." She couldn't do it. It wasn't as bad as one of those giant pickup trucks with four rear wheels or, God forbid, a Prius, but she didn't want to be in the Porsche with Eddie.

"Marilyn," said Michael. "We can't all fit in the Ranger."

"Then let's take two cars," she said. She was so mad at Eddie that she didn't care what he thought of her anymore. She, of course, thought he was an asshole of the highest order. And no matter what happened with Kim, this was the end for Marilyn and Eddie. After they got Kim back, she never wanted to see this man again.

"We can take Kim's Jeep," said Eddie. "I'll pull it out of the garage and meet you guys out front."

Once Michael and Marilyn were standing on the sidewalk, Michael said, "I know you hate him, but just cool it until we find your sister." He put his arm on her shoulder and said, "We need him to help if we're going to find her."

Eddie pulled out of the garage in Kimberly's red Jeep—SPESHLK vanity plates. He stopped in front of Michael and Marilyn. Michael got in the front. Eddie said to him, "Taraval Station, right?"

Michael said, "I know more guys at Ingleside, but if she got abducted from the house, then we should go to Taraval. It'll be their case, and they'll probably call in some specialists."

It was about a mile to the station, and the short ride was silent until they passed Eddie's office and El Burrito Express. Then Michael said, "It's only eleven-fifteen. We said we wouldn't go to the cops until noon."

From the back seat, Marilyn said, "If we haven't come up with anything all morning, why do you think we're all of a sudden going to figure out a plan now?"

"I'm just pointing out that you originally said noon."

"Yeah, well …"

"Park across from Kentucky Fried Chicken," said Michael. "And we can sit in the park until noon. Let's stick with the timeline."

After they parked the Jeep on 22$^{nd}$ Avenue, they walked up the grass hill to McCoppin Playground and sat on the bench in the first base dugout, looking across the field at the police station.

Marilyn was trying not to bite her cuticles. She felt like there was no reason to wait. What was happening to her sister right now while the three of them sat there not even saying anything? She was focused on the sound of the L Taraval streetcar rumbling past the park when Michael finally spoke.

He said, "Your phone's charged, right?"

Eddie patted himself down and pulled the phone out of his pocket. "Eighty-six percent," he said and exhaled.

Marilyn checked her watch. "I guess let's start walking over there," she said. She knew nothing was going to happen by noon, and she was sick of sitting around. So, she got up and walked around the backstop. Eddie and Michael followed. They passed the old green bleachers behind the third base dugout and walked along the narrow concrete path with trees and bushes on their left.

Marilyn was still hoping something would happen before they got to the police station. It was her decision to go against the kidnappers' orders, and she knew it could result in her sister getting hurt. Marilyn wanted to know what these creeps wanted in exchange for Kim. Marilyn felt like they were baiting her into reporting this to the police so that they'd have a reason to kill Kimberly. She was about to say this out loud, when, out of the corner of her eye, she saw something flapping from behind one of the trees. It was yellow and green and sounded like one of those cheap nylon kites she played with as a kid.

When she looked over, she saw that it was a tent, and a short, stocky guy was emerging from the opening, holding a bucket of Kentucky Fried Chicken. He didn't look nearly as dirty as most of the tent people scattered across the city, but he looked tired, and she could smell him from ten feet away.

"Duff," he said and took a few steps toward them.

"Jerry?" said Duff.

"How you doin'?" he said.

"We're okay," said Michael. "You remember Marilyn."

"Hell yeah," he said. "Lookin' good, Marilyn."

"Thanks, Jerry," she said and waited for Michael to introduce Eddie, but he didn't. It was unlike Michael to look so uncomfortable, stretching his neck to get a look at Jerry's campsite. Marilyn hadn't seen Jerry in months. He'd put on a lot of weight, lost more hair, and somehow looked shorter, but he wasn't any less attractive to her than he was the last time she'd seen him, glassy-eyed and staggering out of The Boot the night before Thanksgiving.

"How long you been here?" asked Michael.

"Just a couple of weeks," he said.

"Your mom still live on 25th?"

"Yeah," said Jerry. "She gave me some money for rehab and kicked me out."

"Let me guess," said Michael.

"Yeah, yeah," said Jerry. "Spent it all, and now I'm here. But it's not a bad spot. No other campers, and the KFC's right there." He was holding a drumstick now and using it to point down toward Taraval.

"Okay," said Michael, putting his hand in his pocket and pulling out some bills.

"No, no," said Jerry. "I'm good."

"Just for some food," said Michael holding the money out toward Jerry.

Jerry took a step back and said, "Charlisse at the KFC lets me have all the overcooked chicken and the cold slaw before it goes bad. For free. I'll be okay."

Marilyn was pulling Michael's arm back now, trying to help Jerry preserve what little dignity he had left. Then Eddie yelled, "Shit. It's them!"

He was holding the phone way out in front of him, like he was far-sighted, but, when he looked over at Marilyn, she realized he was making room for her to squeeze in and see the screen. Michael was standing behind her when Eddie swiped the FaceTime into action.

Jerry said, "What's going on?" right at the same moment that Kim started yelling, so Marilyn didn't hear what she said. At first, she thought it was "crash", but then she realized Kim was saying "cash".

"Get as much cash as you can," she screamed. "And they'll let me go."

Then Kimberly must have seen Marilyn, and she immediately started crying and insisting she was okay. "They're not hurting me, Marilyn. I'm fine. I'm going to be fine. Please don't worry." Then she gave a Hollywood smile and said, "See? I'm okay."

Marilyn whispered, as if she could keep a secret from the abductors, "We're right by Taraval Station."

"No," shouted Kim, the smile vanishing. "Do not involve the police. I repeat. Do not involve the police!"

"Okay," said Marilyn, who was crying now, tears rolling over her freckles as she looked back at Michael for help. She wiped at the tears with her sleeve and nodded at Kim. She was mouthing the words *I love you* and waiting to find out what to do to get her home.

"Eddie," said Kim. "This has to be fast. Go get as much cash as you can and wait for further instructions. And do not involve the police. I'll be fine if you don't call the police."

Then the screen went dark.

Marilyn closed her eyes for a moment, trying to interpret what she'd just seen, wondering what on Earth they were doing to Kim.

"Did you guys notice anything in the background?" asked Michael. "Maybe something that could help us figure out her location. Even something really small."

"The camera was right up against her face," said Marilyn.

"Could you see any background?" asked Michael.

"Yes. It was different," said Eddie. "It was just plain, like whitish, but remember last time I saw some red."

"That's something," said Michael. "They've either moved her, or that red could have been a piece of clothing or curtains or something. What else?"

"She didn't look like she did last time," said Eddie.

"Eddie," said Marilyn, still so absolutely disgusted by her brother-in-law. "How could she look different? She's your wife. The camera was right up against her face. How could she look like anything other than herself?"

Eddie stood there for a moment, looking at the phone as if Kim might reappear and settle the argument that his brain was having about how she looked during the last FaceTime. Then it came to him. "I got it," he said. "This doesn't make sense, but she had makeup on."

Michael looked at Marilyn to confirm.

"Yeah," she said. "Kim always wears makeup."

"But she didn't in the last call," said Eddie. "I can't remember the first call because I was panicking and not thinking about anything except finding her. But the second time, I was paying attention. That's the time I noticed the red backdrop. And I'm telling you, she didn't have makeup on the last time. I made a mental note."

Marilyn was trying to figure out what this could mean or how it could help but couldn't come up with anything. And then Eddie broke in again.

"Did she have a ponytail?" he asked Marilyn.

Marilyn nodded. She did notice that. That was easy.

"Well," said Eddie. "She didn't have a ponytail last time." He was smiling as if this detail was the answer to their prayers.

"So what?" said Marilyn and noticed that Jerry had thrown his chicken leg in the dirt and was rummaging through the bucket for more.

"Duff told me to try to memorize what I saw," he said. "I'm just telling you what I memorized."

"No," said Michael. "That's good, Eddie. Did you see her clothes at all?"

Marilyn and Eddie both shook their heads, and Marilyn noticed that Jerry was shaking his head as well. She shot him a look.

"What?" he said. "I *didn't* see her clothes."

"Okay," said Marilyn. "We gotta get moving. Good to see you, Jerry."

"You know where to find me," he said, and with a greasy chicken thigh in his hand now, he saluted her and climbed back into his tent.

After he'd gotten all the way in, he yelled out to them, "You guys should really be wearing masks."

## 17

Yesterday, Eddie felt like he was fighting to keep his life on course, but today he had *literally* let go of the steering wheel. Duff was driving Kim's jeep. Marilyn was sitting next to him up front, and they were all headed up to The Boot to see where the road would lead. Duff said his brain worked better in an empty bar, and that was okay with Eddie.

When they stepped inside, despite the fact that the bar was closed, Wade was sitting on the same stool as he was yesterday when Eddie and Duff had left. Now he was sipping a cup of coffee. He was reading the Sunday paper and had CNN on the big screen.

"Take a hike, Wade," said Duff.

Wade looked at Eddie and Marilyn, folded up his paper, and made his way to the door. "How you doin', Marilyn?" he said.

"Been better, Wade," she said and smiled at him.

Duff had walked back to his office and was returning now with a yellow legal pad. He ducked behind the bar and placed the pad and a pen in front of Marilyn. He put a pint glass under the Guinness tap and then grabbed another pint glass and filled it about three quarters up with ice, orange juice and cranberry juice. He was holding it out toward Marilyn and said, "You want anything in it?"

"Just a little Tito's," she said. He grabbed the vodka and provided a generous pour.

He put it in front of Marilyn and then tended to the Guinness, which he then slid in front of Eddie. Eddie instinctively put both hands on the pint. Muscle memory. Like this was a normal day. Like this was a normal year. But it wasn't. The windows were boarded up, and Marilyn had a pen and paper ready to write down a plan to save his wife. This wasn't normal. Maybe things would never be normal again.

Duff grabbed a bottle of Jameson and a shot glass. He poured himself a shot, drank it, then poured himself another one but left it on the bar and put the bottle back on the shelf. "Before we make any moves," he said. "We need to figure out where we are. We need to get a little organized." He drank the second shot and put the glass in the glasswasher. "Is everyone okay with that?"

Eddie and Marilyn both nodded, and Eddie took a small taste of his beer.

"You might want to write some of this down, babe," he said. "Seeing it on paper might help put the pieces together."

Marilyn already had the pen in her hand and had written something at the top. To Eddie, she could look really young sometimes. Almost like a beautiful college girl, who didn't know she was beautiful yet. And that's how she looked now hunched over that pad.

Kim didn't have that same quality. It seemed that Kim always looked like a really put-together thirty-five-year-old, even back when she was twenty-five. But not Marilyn. Her hair was long and natural and was nearly touching the bar as she wrote. She was underlining something now. When Eddie looked over at the page, it had one line on it: _Eddie's fault._

"Let's start with the three phone calls," said Duff and looked at Eddie. When Eddie just looked back at him, Duff said, "Go!"

"Oh," said Eddie. "First call—_do what they say ... check the trunk ... no cops._" Marilyn was jotting this down. "That was actually two calls, but it was one right after the other," he said.

"Was the next call after we buried the bag?" said Duff.

"I think so," said Eddie. "That was the call where they said _prove it._" He took a sip of Guinness and then tapped Marilyn. "Wait," he said. "That wasn't a call. It was a text."

Marilyn nodded, wrote, and looked back at him. "Keep going."

"The next one was another FaceTime," he said. "And it was like the fifth reminder about no police but had no new information."

"Is that the one where you saw the red background?" asked Duff.

"Yeah," said Eddie. "And the last FaceTime was the one where Marilyn watched it with me."

Marilyn kept writing and said, "She told you to get cash, and she reminded us about no cops."

"And she had makeup and a ponytail," said Eddie. "Even though she didn't in the other ones."

"Whatever that means," she said and noted it.

"Now we need to just organize the people who could be involved," said Duff.

Eddie was quick on this one. "Al Young, Angie's family, probably not Carl."

Duff said, "Probably not any of these people."

"Why not?" said Marilyn.

"When Carl caught her trying to rip him off, he was probably pretty mad at her, but he doesn't need the money and doesn't seem like the kind of guy who would kill someone." He shook his head and added, "And I trust the guy. He seemed honest to me. I think he just enjoyed banging her."

"Okay," said Marilyn. "We can eliminate him for now, but those aren't great reasons."

Duff shrugged. "It's not him," he said. "And I don't think it would be the family either, do you?"

Marilyn said, "It doesn't seem likely. These are her brothers, right?"

"The two dudes are definitely brothers," said Eddie. "But who knows with Angie? They might just all work for the same people. Everything's a scam. They're taking orders from someone else, but there's something criminal about all of it."

"Well, if she's not their sister," she said, "then I think we have to keep them on the list. What if she tried to double-cross them in some way?" Then she looked over at Duff. "And why not Al Young?" she said. "Eddie owes the man money, and he's a famous bully, right?"

"He slaps people in public," said Duff.

"Huh?" said Marilyn.

"He's pretty mean," said Duff. "But I still don't see a guy in the Sheriff's Department doing something like this."

Eddie didn't want to write Al off. He'd seen the look in Al's eyes when he wanted his money, like he would have killed Eddie right there in the parking lot if he thought he'd be able to collect some other way. "He'd know how to do it," said Eddie.

"What do you mean?" said Duff.

Eddie wasn't sure how to explain it except to say, "He's law enforcement, but he's also kind of infamous for doing illegal stuff." He looked at Marilyn to see if she was writing this down. She wasn't. "For him to have gotten away with it all these years," he said. "It just makes me think he could do it."

Duff said, "Those Gypsies are ruthless, too."

Marilyn dropped the pen on the bar. "So now you're saying it could be the Gypsies or Al?" she said.

"I'm just trying to get the point across that we're dealing with some cold-blooded people," said Duff, and then the phone rang in his office. "I'm gonna get that," he said. "The distributors keep calling to ask if we need orders." He turned the corner into the office and yelled back, "We don't have any customers. What do I need to order?"

Eddie made eye contact with Marilyn. This was the first time he was alone with her since everything happened. He knew he should just shut up, but he couldn't help himself. "I still love her," he said.

She was quick. "Shut your mouth, Eddie." She had the pen in her hand, and she was holding it like a knife now.

Eddie took one step back and sat on a stool, his feet on the rung, ready to jump off and run if he had to.

"Did that girl know you were married?" she said.

"She did."

"Then screw her, too," she said. "I don't care if she's buried in some backyard somewhere."

Duff was back. "Okay," he said. "Let's take it easy." He was standing next to Marilyn now, his hand on her forearm. She put the pen down. "Apparently, a couple of bald gypsies just knocked on Carl's front door."

"That was Carl?" said Marilyn.

"How does he know they're Gypsies?" asked Eddie.

"He's looking out the window at them right now, and he recognizes them as two of the guys who are supposed to be Angie's brothers."

"Shit," said Eddie but couldn't think of anything else to say, trying to put the puzzle pieces together.

"They're walking around the property now," said Duff. "Carl says these are two guys who supposedly did some work for him over the past few months."

"Why did he call you?" said Marilyn.

"He doesn't know what to do," said Duff.

"Unlike us," she said. "He can call the cops."

"Agreed," said Duff. "But he thinks we can get something out of these guys—find out what happened to Angie."

Eddie was still trying to keep up. "But what if they're just looking for her?" he said. "They might not even know she's dead. They might think Carl did something to her. Carl *might* have done something to her."

"That's why I want to go up there," said Duff. "It's a two-minute drive. We could probably catch them before they leave."

Marilyn stood up. "What's Carl's angle?" she said.

"You can call bullshit," said Duff. "But I think the old guy's bored and wants to play. He doesn't like these guys."

"Let's go," said Marilyn.

"Maybe you and Eddie should wait here," said Duff.

Marilyn was already walking to the door. "Yeah, right," she said.

## 18

When they pulled up in front of Carl's home, Duff saw something moving in the alleyway between the houses. For a brief moment it looked to him like a baby Bactrian camel, meandering through the rocks and bushes on the side of Carl's house. However, once Duff focused in, it became clear that he was looking at a couple of bald guys in tan suits — the same kind of fitted, tapered look that Eddie had worn yesterday. The two guys were peeking in windows, and now the one with the struggling goatee was pulling on the doorknob.

Before Duff got out of the jeep, he looked up and saw Carl in the window, smiling and waving. This guy was loving it. He was shrugging and pointing and hamming it up while these criminals were poking around in his alley.

"Please stay in the car for now," said Duff, and both Eddie and Marilyn nodded.

By the time Duff had crossed the street, Carl had opened the front door and was standing on his stoop. He was wearing a pair of old school, grey sweats with Adidas and a green polo shirt. Duff was on the front walkway when the brothers turned the corner from the alley. The brothers and Duff were equidistant from Carl. They made a perfect triangle that kept getting smaller as they approached the old man at about the same pace.

The bald guy with the goatee was the first to speak. "Carl," he said. "We've been knocking on the door."

Carl said, "Sorry, boys. I was shaving." He rubbed his knuckles against his clean cheek to prove it.

The two bald guys looked over at Duff. They were all about six feet apart. Unintentional social distancing. No one was wearing a mask.

"You guys all together?" Carl asked with just the hint of a smirk, the man thinking because he was old, he could throw anything out there and people would just assume he was going senile. Duff thought Carl must have been using this tactic to his advantage since these people had inserted themselves into his life.

"We haven't met," said the goatee as he took a step forward but then stopped himself. "I'd shake your hand, but ..."

"Yeah," said Duff. "Michael Duffy. Nice to meet you."

"Derek," he said and pointed a thumb at the other bald guy, who could have been a twin. "This is my brother, Alex."

"How do you know Carl?" asked Duff.

"We've done some repair work for him," said Derek.

"Repair work?" said Duff, laughing a little bit. "You two win first prize—best dressed carpenters." He laughed again and looked at Carl. "These guys must have the shiniest hammers in the business."

Derek was smiling but not laughing. "We have an event to attend later," he said.

"I got you," said Duff. "Most of my friends are in the trades, but they don't clean up as nicely as you guys."

"Their sister, Angela, is the real reason we know each other," said Carl.

"Oh yeah?" said Duff.

"Yes," said Carl. "The two of us are in love."

Duff glanced at Derek and then Alex. "That's nice, Carl," said Duff. "Never too late to find love." Duff wasn't sure how Carl wanted to work this, but the man was doing a damn fine job playing an old-timer, flirting with dementia. Duff looked over at the brothers again and said with a wink, "You guys okay with your sister being in a May-December romance?"

Derek looked like he was trying to smile but that someone had put glue on his teeth, so all he could manage was a half-grin when he said, "I think there's some confusion." Alex had his hands in his pockets now and was nodding at Derek, who continued, "Angie's my wife. She has helped care for Carl over the past few months, and they've hit it off."

Duff reassured Derek with another wink and said, "That's very nice of her."

Carl grunted. "Must be an open relationship."

Derek ignored Carl and said to Duff, "What's *your* connection to Carl?"

"Oh," said Duff. "My dad and Carl were old buddies. Both worked in the criminal justice system."

Derek attempted another smile and said, "So you like to stop by to catch up, talk about old times?"

"I haven't been by in a while," said Duff. "But Carl's son called and asked if I'd look in on him." Duff took a step closer to Carl. "He lives in Ohio, runs a beach toy company, and doesn't get a chance to come out here as often as he'd like."

"I see," said Derek.

"Yeah," said Duff. "He's worried that Carl might not be making sensible decisions with regard to his estate."

"Do you not see me standing here?" said Carl. "Old people aren't deaf."

"Everybody needs a little help with big decisions," said Duff. "But your kids live in other parts of the country." Duff looked down at Carl standing beside him. He was still trying to get a read on what direction the man wanted the performance to go at this point. Duff was aware that he was tapping on Derek's exposed nerve but wasn't sure if the balds were going to flinch or not. "I think your kids would at least want you to keep them in the loop, say if you had a new girlfriend or something like that?"

"Don't screw with me, Duffy," said Carl. "I didn't know she was married." He looked like he was genuinely mad at this point or confused, breathing hard out of his nose, working on the Golden Globe nomination for best supporting actor in a drama—maybe just in a TV category, but still. "I feel bad about the whole thing now," he said, playing it as either senile or compassionate … or compassionately senile.

Derek broke in. "Where's Angie?" he said.

"How should I know?" said Carl. "Apparently, she's *your* wife." Derek looked over at his brother.

Alex tried to sound calm. "When's the last time you saw her, Carl?"

From his sweatpants, Carl pulled out a dog-eared pocket calendar and leafed through it like a movie star's personal assistant. He pointed at a page. "It looks like Thursday," he said and turned the little book around so that Derek and Alex could see the scribbled note.

"What about you?" said Derek, trying to stare down Duff.

Duff had tangled with more dangerous goons than these guys, but he was smart enough to avoid throwing rocks at the hornet's nest. "What *about* me?" said Duff.

"When's the last time you saw Angie?"

"I haven't had the pleasure," said Duff. "But I'm looking forward to meeting her. She's clearly brought some sunshine to Carl's life."

Duff briefly flashed to the memory of pulling that zipper over Angie's waxen face, the duct tape wrapped around her neck. Then he brought himself back to the moment. These guys were clearly looking for Angie. Especially Derek. They couldn't be part of the ransom plot because there was an obvious nexus between the murder and the kidnapping. The way Duff was looking at it, Derek was a victim now, just like Carl and Eddie and anyone else Angie was screwing.

"She brought more than sunshine," said Carl. "She brought me back from the dead. I'm Lazarus," he said, flexing his biceps like a carnival strong-man.

"Okay," said Derek, looking at Carl and holding his hands out in front of him as if he were fending something off. "We'll catch up with you another time." Then the two brothers strutted down the walkway toward the black Escalade parked just up from Duff's truck.

"Nice to meet you guys," said Duff.

"I wish I'd known they were married," said Carl in an old-man stage whisper, loud enough to cause Derek to pause before he stepped off the curb. The faltering was barely perceptible, but it was clear to Duff that Derek had heard the comment. Alex turned almost all the way around, but Derek palmed his brother's shoulder and the two kept moving toward their car.

## 19

Al hadn't used Walter in a couple years, but the man was reliable and knew how to keep his mouth shut. So, Al called and told him he had a job. Walter told him come on by whenever he wanted, so Al turned onto Divisadero Street and took it all the way past the car wash and Popeye's and 4505 BBQ until he saw Leon's Barber Shop.

Leon did a nice job, but the parking got so bad that Al started going to a dude named Marvin downtown, near the jail, where Al could easily park. But today he found a spot right out front. Maybe this was Al's lucky day. Walter lived in the apartment upstairs, an old Victorian, and when Al got out of the car, he looked up and saw Walter looking down at him from the window.

When Al's eyes moved back to the barber shop, the door was open, and Leon was looking right at him.

"Oh ... hey ... yeah," said Al. "Leon, how you doin'?"

Leon was holding his clippers, which he pointed at Al before saying, "Downtown man," and shaking his head. "Too good for the hood." Then he turned back to his customer and said to anyone within earshot, "You heard that? Too *good* for the *hood*. Should be a song."

Al had taken enough shit for one day, and he didn't have time to listen to Leon question his loyalty, so, without further comment, he walked to the side of the building. He found the stairs and, holding the railing, climbed up to Walter's place.

The door was open, so Al walked in and immediately smelled the weed. The place was a mess, Walter still acting like a teenager, almost fifty years old now. The coffee table had burn marks on it, and an old Navajo blanket covered a couch that, Al assumed, was covered in stains.

Walter was still standing over by the window, avoiding eye contact with Al.

"Walter," said Al. "What's up?"

He turned quickly and said, "*You* called me."

"Yeah," said Al. "I'm just asking how you doin'?"

"Good," he said. "Real good." Then he turned back to the window again, being short with Al for some reason.

Al was trying to figure out if Walter was feeling like Leon, like Al had somehow been disloyal the last two years for not calling on Walter. The truth was, Al had some close calls and was trying to stay clean until retirement. He just hadn't had any work for the man and didn't feel the need to explain himself to this small-timer anyhow. "We gonna do business?" said Al. "Or you got something else going on?"

"Let's do business," he said with the same neighborhood scowl he'd been wearing since he was a kid. "Have a seat." Then he pointed to the sagging couch.

Al didn't want to ruin his slacks and wasn't sure if he'd be able to get back up without help, so he sat on the arm, balancing himself before saying, "Brianna—"

But before he could get another word out, Walter cut in. "I didn't know it was you, Al."

Al was still trying to get comfortable. He could feel the arm of the couch starting to give way and his boxer briefs starting to ride up on him. The couch was making a groaning sound, as if it were in pain. "You didn't know *who* was me?" said Al.

Walter stared at him but said nothing.

"Walter," said Al. "What're you talkin' 'bout, man?"

"You said Brianna," he said.

"Yeah?"

"Yeah," he said.

"What about Brianna?" said Al and heard the couch whimper as he shifted his weight. "You need a new couch, brotha."

"It's not meant to be sat on like that," said Walter.

Al stood up, and Walter took a step back.

"You know about me and Brianna?" said Al.

"Know what?" said Walter.

"God damnit, Walter," said Al. "You tell me what's going on right now, or I'm gonna shoot you, and then I'm going downstairs, and I'm gonna shoot Leon, too."

"She paid me for the job," said Walter. "But I didn't know it was you until I started videotaping."

It took Al a moment, but then he felt the rage in the back of his throat, like bile, spreading into his chest and stomach. "Walter," said Al, but couldn't think of what to say next to this skinny-ass street hustler with his saggy pants. "Walter," he said again.

Walter puffed out his chest and started moving toward the kitchen. "She never told me it was you, Al."

"We're going to stop the bullshit right now," said Al. "I'm going to ask you some questions, and you're going to answer yes or no. If you say anything else, I'm going to choke you out." He sidestepped to cut off Walter's angle to the kitchen. "You hear that couch when I sat on it, Walter?"

Walter didn't say a word, trying to be polite now.

"I'm gonna put all my weight on you, Walter. You'll be squealing like that couch. You won't survive it, man."

"What do you want to know?"

"Yes or no questions, man," said Al. "That's what I'm throwing at you right now, and those are the answers I want to hear until further notice. You got it?"

Walter nodded.

"Did Brianna Guthrie pay you money to videotape me?"

"I didn't know it was you—"

Al was overweight, but he still had quick hands. He slapped Walter hard across the face before the man could finish his sentence, and then he used a soft voice to say, "Remember, Walter, you're doing yes or no answers for now."

Walter was holding his cheek and looked like he was trying to somehow blink away the sting. Al had seen Eddie Bilker try the same tactic the other day. Al liked the feel of it. He couldn't deny it. It was different from a punch. In some ways it probably hurt more in the short run. You wouldn't break a jaw or knock out a tooth with a slap, but, man, it caused some problems with the face. Walter was sniffling now, trying to control himself but not really making it.

"Did Brianna pay you money to tape me?"

Walter shook his head but said, "Yes."

Al liked this. He got the answer, but Walter was trying to qualify it. It felt like maybe Brianna paid Walter to videotape a person in a garage, but she didn't tell him it was Al. "Did you know it was going to be me when you went to that garage?"

Walter flashed a nervous smile, looking happy to set the record straight. "No!"

"Once you got in that garage and started rolling," said Al. "Did you recognize me then?"

Walter's smile faded. "She already paid me—"

Al slapped him again. This time he caught most of Walter's ear, and the weak-ass punk's knees buckled. After a moment, Walter regained balance, but his left eye didn't look right. It was trembling right there in its socket. The other eye was glassy, but it wasn't moving like the left eye. Al thought he might have done some serious damage this time, but he couldn't stop now.

"So, you eventually knew who you were taping, right?"

Walter was blinking again, maybe seeing stars. "Yes," he said and made a move to step back, but he lost his balance and ended up on his ass, looking up at Al.

"Okay," said Al. "I see how it is." Then he walked into what looked like a tiny dining room with a small table and two wooden chairs. "Come on over here and sit with me, Walter."

Walter used his hands to try to push himself up from his place on the hardwood floor, but his legs still weren't working right, so he turned over like he was going to do a push up, and he got himself up to his knees. He was close to the radiator, so he grabbed it with both hands and worked his way up. This was hard to watch. The man couldn't seem to find his sea legs as he staggered over to the table.

When he finally pulled out the chair and slumped into it, Al said, "You're gonna help me end this shit with Brianna one way or another."

"I didn't know it was gonna be you," said Walter, back to his old refrain, leaning on the table now with his head in his hands.

"That shit don't matter anymore," said Al. "We're working on a new job now, together."

"Al," said Walter with his head still down. "I'll help you with whatever you want." Then he raised his eyes to Al and said, "You can't slap me anymore, though. If you get mad at me, please just shoot me."

"You and I are gonna take a ride," he said.

"Just shoot me here," said Walter. "I won't even call the cops."

"That doesn't make any sense," said Al. "Do you ever listen to yourself?" Al stood up and walked around the table. He grabbed Walter by the elbow and helped him up. "You cost me a lot of money because of that video. Now you're gonna help me get it back." Walter was still wobbly, but Al straightened him out and said, "You know a bookie named Eddie Bilker?"

## 20

When they got inside Carl's house, Eddie felt like he needed a Guinness. Carl told them to have a seat, and then he went into the kitchen to get them all something to eat. Eddie was on edge. The brothers weren't particularly big guys, and Eddie had Duff and the old man, but these guys seemed like the kind of sick freaks who'd sneak into your house at night, cut off your balls, and make themselves sandwiches while you bled out. Then, afterward, they'd go visit their grandma. Eddie's mind was all over the place while Carl was out in the kitchen whistling the Tennessee Waltz and opening and closing cabinets.

Eddie was figuring on Velveeta and Ritz, but Carl came out with a full charcuterie board—olives, brie, different types of cured meats, dried fruits, and nuts—a nice looking spread.

"Wow," said Marilyn.

"I'll get us some beers," he said and disappeared into the kitchen again.

When he came back out, he was carrying a stainless-steel bucket filled with ice and Stella Artois. Eddie wasn't expecting Carl to have Guinness, but he was pleasantly surprised to see the Stella when Carl placed it on the coffee table next to the food. Carl was dressed like Eddie's dad, but, unlike Eddie's dad, this man was cut, his bicep flexed as he spun the opener around his finger.

"So, how'd I do?" said Carl.

"With the food?" said Duff.

"No," said Carl. "With the brothers. My act."

Duff smiled. "If you were trying to piss 'em off," he said. "You killed it. Bravo!"

"What about the aging dotard bit?" he said and started opening beers for everyone.

"That was pretty good as well," said Duff.

After Carl handed everyone an open beer, he said, "Okay, dig in."

Eddie had just taken a bite of a breadstick and was still chewing when he said, "So why'd you call us?"

Carl looked right at Eddie and said, "I didn't call *you*, son." Then he rolled up a thin slice of salami. "I called Mr. Duffy," he said and folded the meat into his mouth.

"Okay," said Eddie, thinking about Kim now and the last FaceTime: *Get Cash.* They hadn't heard anything from her in over an hour, but they also hadn't done anything to get the cash, and this guy wanted to sit around and eat cheese and crackers. "Why Duff?"

"To tell you the truth," he said. "When they started sniffing around today, I thought about handling them myself. I really did. I had some ideas." He closed his eyes and nodded like he was picturing himself *handling* these two clowns. He opened one eye and said, "Then I thought about it and remembered I'm an old man, and these guys are criminals." Both eyes were open when he continued, "I know criminals. Worked with them for years. I know what they're capable of."

"So, you called Duff?" said Eddie.

"I know he's ex-PD," said Carl. "You guys were here yesterday and seemed to be interested in Angie—" He interrupted himself. "Do you really think she's married to Derek? I honestly thought she was a sister. That's what she told me when they first came around."

Duff said, "I'd bet he's either married to her, or she's his girlfriend." He was holding the neck of the beer with one finger and smiling at Carl. "You were sure digging into him about your relationship with her," he said. "Did you tell us the truth about Angie last night?"

"Every word," said Carl and laughed.

Marilyn was looking at Duff and raising her eyebrows.

"Carl had an adult relationship with Angie," said Duff.

Marilyn gave Carl the thumbs up and said, "If these guys are such bad-asses, why didn't they go after you for boning the guy's wife?"

"I have two theories," he said and reached down to grab a couple of olives. He popped one in his mouth and chewed thoughtfully. Then he put the other one in and did the same thing.

"Well?" said Marilyn.

"What?" he said.

Eddie was wondering if the guy was still in character.

"What are the theories?" she said, and Eddie watched her eyes drift over to Duff, who was close to finishing off his beer.

"Oh," said Carl. "Either that my fling with her was part of Angie's job. That she was supposed to sleep with rich, old guys." He grabbed another olive. "Or, they think I'm senile and that I made up the whole thing in my mind. So, it's not bothering Derek if he thinks I imagined it, but if it's part of her job, he's one cold-blooded shark, doesn't mind a wrinkled old fart like me sticking it to the love of his life."

"I couldn't handle it if I knew my wife was out and about," said Duff.

"Yeah," said Marilyn. "'Cause you don't have a wife."

"True," said Duff. "Touché."

"Well, what do you think, Duff?" asked Eddie. "You believe Derek knew about Carl and Angie?"

Duff shrugged and reached for the cheese knife. "Do you think Derek knew about *you* and Angie?"

"I think these guys aren't sure about Carl," said Eddie and considered the possibility that the brothers might know about Angie and him. "I didn't see your senile old man bit," he said. "But I imagine you can do a pretty good job." Eddie had thought he understood Angie better than the old man. Eddie always recognized that she knew how to handle men, manipulate them. But Carl didn't seem to be bullshitting about the relationship, and he seemed to know she was after his money all along. Eddie was probably being used too, and he didn't know how to feel about it. He wasn't jealous. He had his own life. He was more disillusioned than anything else. If he'd been deceived by Angie, who else was messing with him? "Derek probably knew only some of what Angie was doing when she was on her own," he said. "She was freestyling. And I think she was pretty good at it, too. But if Derek's the jealous type, and now he suspects Carl, and Carl's putting a stop to their hustle, and Angie's missing…"

It was getting hard for Eddie to talk about Angie without slipping up to Carl about her current whereabouts. Carl didn't need to know. He was just a bit player in this whole drama. But Eddie was aware of the fact that he had just used the past tense when he was talking about Angie. Carl was a lawyer. He was looking for someone to slip up, and Eddie was concerned that Carl might start asking questions.

"I just don't know how this'll end," said Carl. "The jig is up. These guys aren't getting anything out of me." He had a handful of nuts now and held a fist up to his lips to release a few into his mouth. He was chewing when he said, "But they've invested in me." He swallowed and then said, "They probably don't want to go away empty-handed." He had some nut residue in the corners of his mouth. Aside from that, he seemed younger than his age, a tough old bastard, who wasn't afraid of anything, but he didn't seem to have a plan for the brothers.

"Hey, Carl," said Duff. "There's a chance we're going to need some cash right away."

When Duff paused, Carl broke in: "Jesus, is everyone trying to hustle me?"

Duff put the empty Stella next to the bucket and pulled out another. He opened it and said, "Carl, I know we've only just met, but my friends and I are in a world of trouble right now, and cash might be the only way to get us out of it."

Eddie didn't want Carl in on this. First off, it was embarrassing. Second, there was a murder involved, and it happened to be Carl's girlfriend. And Eddie's girlfriend. And Derek's wife. It just seemed like too much for the old guy. It was already too much for Eddie.

"With these Gypsies?" said Carl.

"We don't think so," said Marilyn. She had a handful of nuts and was rolling them around in her hand like she was playing craps. "But Duff's right. We're in some trouble."

"And you want me to give you cash?"

"Not yet," said Duff. "I want to try some other options."

"And I could try my dad," said Marilyn.

"Do we really want to get him involved," said Duff. "I don't know if he has any money anyway."

"But he has friends," said Marilyn.

"He does," said Duff. "But I don't know if I want to get those folks involved."

"Listen," said Carl. "I don't know what kind of trouble you're in. In fact, don't tell me. We'll all be better off. But if you kids are in a serious pickle ..."

When Carl let the words trail off, Marilyn said, "It's life or death."

"My goodness," said Carl. "How do good kids like you get yourself into whatever this is?"

Both Marilyn and Duff turned to look at Eddie but didn't say anything. Eddie said, "It's my fault." He didn't elaborate. He knew Carl didn't like him, and he didn't want to make it worse. Maybe Carl would respect him for being honest about it.

"But it affects all of you?" said Carl.

"It does," said Marilyn, who was trying to hold it together but looking more and more like she might lose it.

"Let's do this," said Carl. "You all do what you gotta do to get this cash. If you get stuck, you come see me, and I'll stake you. And next time, try not to let this dummy get you involved in stupid shit."

"Okay, Carl," said Duff.

"And I might ask you to put up The Boot as collateral," said Carl. "But probably not."

For some reason they were all standing now, and each of them put their beers on the table. Marilyn asked if Carl needed help cleaning up, and he waved her off. Carl seemed to understand the urgency now and was guiding them toward the door. There was a coat rack on one side of the door and a console table on the other side. On top of the table, there was what looked like a tackle box.

"You going fishing today?" said Eddie.

Carl looked at the box. "Just cleaning out the garage," he said and opened the front door.

# Part Two

## *Kimberly Bilker*

A common mistake that people make when trying to design something completely foolproof is to underestimate the ingenuity of complete fools.

—Douglas Adams

## 21

New York was getting ravaged by Covid, but San Francisco was still doing okay. Case rates and death rates were low, so Kim and her colleagues weren't getting swamped like their counterparts at the east coast hospitals. UCSF Mission Bay had increased staffing and cleared out space for a massive Covid-19 ward, but so far, the numbers were low. In fact, today, Kim's boss told her that she could take off early — there were too many nurses today, and Kim deserved a break.

She'd been transferred from UCSF Parnassus to UCSF Mission Bay just two days before but had to miss her normal day off in between. Other than being tired, the transition had been seamless. She'd worked with a few of the other nurses before, and the doctors were great. It felt like they'd all been working together for a long time. There was a strange kind of nervous energy on every floor as they were all watching what was happening in New York and New Jersey and wondering when more cases would pop up in California. They seemed ready, but Kim hadn't been at Mission Bay long enough to know what things might look like if the hospital were at capacity.

Kim hadn't even told Eddie about the transfer yet. They'd both been busy, and they hadn't eaten dinner together for almost a week. Tonight, she would tell him about the move from the middle of the city all the way out to the old China Basin, which had been a wasteland not so long ago, but was now a bustling neighborhood — home to the Chase Center and Oracle Park, new restaurants, and residential towers.

But for Kim, her favorite part of the neighborhood was that Mission Rock and The Ramp — old-time neighborhood mainstays — were a short walk from the hospital. When she was a kid, her dad used to frequent these two spots, both borderline dives back then, with splintered decks that sat above the bay and peered across the water at the Oakland Hills and Berkeley. Both restaurants had new management now and substantial upgrades, and Kim liked the vibe, so she decided to walk down to Mission Rock for a drink before she went home.

She didn't usually drink alone, but it was a warm afternoon, and she knew no one would bother her if she grabbed a little table on the deck.

She was wearing her scrubs and a black SF Giants fleece, not a particularly alluring outfit. Her hair was pulled back in a ponytail. Not a high, cute one. Hers was droopy and tired, just like she felt, and she was confident she'd be able to order one margarita and drink it by herself at her dad's old watering hole without interruption.

Once she got her drink, she sipped and let her mind wander back to the times her dad had taken her here as a little girl. When she was about seven or eight, she and her dad were sitting just across from where she was now. They were eating clam chowder together as they had many times before. But this time Willie Brown joined their table. He was mayor at the time, and everyone knew him. But he sat down at their table and asked her questions about school and dance class before her dad handed her two sourdough rolls out of the breadbasket and pointed down at a concrete slab below the deck. "Go down there and feed the seagulls for a while," he said. "I'll come get you in a few minutes."

The old slab was now the lower deck with high tables and umbrellas. Most of the tables were filled today because of the nice weather and the rumors that the city might shut down outdoor eating again if the Covid case-count rose above a certain level. Kim was looking down at the lower deck, trying to remember more about that day with Willie Brown, when she spotted Eddie being led by the hostess to a table overlooking the water. He wasn't wearing his sport coat, and the sleeves of his white oxford were rolled up. He looked like a lot of the other guys out today, but she could tell it was him from his walk. Good posture is important, but Eddie always seemed like he was overdoing it, looking to make himself taller than he was, pushing his chest out military style, always trying to impress. *Everyone's a potential client.*

It wasn't unusual for him to be going to lunch with a client, but today's client concerned Kim. The woman was wearing a form-fitting floral dress, just a little too short to be taken seriously. But that didn't seem to matter to the other men on the lower deck. As she walked by on high heels, every single one of them glanced in her direction, even a waiter, who was in the middle of taking an order from two older women wearing sunhats.

When Eddie and the client sat down, Eddie's back was to Kim. He chose the view of the water. The client was facing Kim. They were nearly a hundred feet away from each other, but Kim could tell that the woman was striking. She was built like a dancer and had the face of a movie star. Maybe the one who played the new Wonder Woman?

"Can I get you another one?" said a waiter who had materialized at her table.

She looked down and realized that she'd drained the first margarita. "I think I better," she said.

"So, one more?" said the waiter.

"Yes," said Kim, fake-smiling but keeping her eyes on the client.

Eddie was stretched out, chair pulled back and legs crossed at the ankles under the table. The client had her legs crossed at the knees, the hem of her dress rising up dangerously. The woman had a confident smile, and Kim let her mind think it was an intimate smile. She knew there was a difference, but she was conflating the two because this woman looked the way she looked.

The waiter was back. "This one's on the house," he said. "Thank you for your service." She took her eyes off the client for a moment, just in time to see the waiter glance down at her blue scrubs and nod in appreciation, obviously not knowing that the hospitals in the city were the same as they'd been two months before. Her life was in no more danger now than it had been in January.

But she smiled and raised her glass to the waiter before she glared back down at Eddie's midweek lunch date. It was hard not to look at the woman. She was practically shimmering in the sunlight, her tan leg bouncing, the backstrap on the shoe hanging off her heel and the shoe just barely clinging to her toes. It took a lot for Kim to not go down there. This woman was begging for Eddie to look at her legs, and from Kim's vantage point, she had no way of knowing where Eddie's eyes were.

If his eyes weren't on those legs, they might have been on the cleavage or the bare shoulders or the eyes made up like Cleopatra's. The woman's hair was up in a bun, and her cheekbones looked glamorous.

Kim took out her phone and tapped on the camera icon. She switched to front-facing mode and looked at herself. No make-up. Small pouches under eyes. And an indentation across her nose and cheeks left by the mask she had to wear for her entire shift. She was upset now and putting her phone back in her bag when she heard something that made her mood even worse.

Eddie's laugh.

It was almost like a cackle—high pitched enough to cut through the sounds of the seagulls, the water lapping up against the dock, the clinking of silverware, and the murmur of fifty conversations. Kim used to hear that laugh a lot when they were first dating. There was such unconscious joy to it. She used to think he laughed like that only with her. That he was so in love with her, he felt liberated to let himself enjoy each moment. To laugh like he was a little kid again.

But she hadn't heard that laugh in over a year. She sometimes felt they were doing fine, but Eddie didn't really seem to have fun around her anymore. It hadn't really occurred to her until just now, but as she looked down at him sitting across from this woman, Kim couldn't help thinking that he was getting bored with the marriage. He would chuckle at some TV show they might be watching together or a story that one of his friends would tell, but that unbridled giddiness seemed to have been retired.

Until now.

Kim took a sloppy swallow from her margarita and stood up. For a moment, she thought she'd go down and introduce herself, see how uncomfortable she could make Eddie. But then she watched him shifting his chair so that he'd be sitting closer to her—or was it to avoid looking into the sun?

Kim wanted to give him the benefit of the doubt, but then she zeroed in on his hand. The movements were subtle, but Kim knew what she was seeing; he was leaning in as if he needed to confide something, but his hand had dropped down off the table and was dangling near her thigh. It was only there for a moment before Kim watched him touch her. He used the back of his hand to graze her inner thigh way up near the hem of the dress, but it was clearly on purpose, and the woman didn't flinch.

Her reaction was only to pull a stray hair away from her eyes and smile.

Kim had seen enough.

## 22

Angie appreciated that Eddie wanted to take her to lunch, but she hoped he knew this was more of a business relationship than anything else. Sure, he'd taken her to a few hotel rooms in the months she'd known him, but lunch felt odd today. The man was treating her like some kind of girlfriend.

He knew she was married to Derek. She knew he was married to the nurse. She didn't need him getting lovey-dovey with her. She just wanted him to be able to handle the sale of Carl's house. Her great hope was that she'd be able to inherit that piece of choice real estate, sell it immediately, take the millions for herself, and quit Derek, Alex, Cristian and The Organization forever. They were keeping a close eye on her, and Derek was in love with her, but she had a plan that would keep the whole transaction a secret until she had the money in an account, and she was on a plane to Italy.

She didn't speak Italian, and she didn't know anyone there, but with millions of dollars, she believed she could make a good life in that country. She'd seen pictures of the Amalfi Coast and decided that she'd retire in that part of Italy—hopefully within the next four to six months.

She'd feel guilty about what she was doing to Carl—he was the only real man out of the bunch—but cancer had a hold of him, and there was nothing she could do to stop it from doing its dirty business. So, she would take her inheritance and go. She would have to mourn Carl from her new home in Sorrento.

After lunch, Eddie had to stop by his office and pick something up, and then he was going to drop her off at Carl's. She was waiting in the Porsche now, looking at the outside of Eddie's office. Taped to the window, there were pictures of all the houses that his agency was selling in San Francisco. Every house was worth at least a million dollars, and most of them were going for two million. And none of the houses in these pictures were as nice as Carl's. She knew she would be flush if everything fell into place the way it was supposed to. She could get a little place in Italy and have plenty left over to live her life away from Cristian and The Organization.

Eddie came out of the office holding some files that he threw in the back seat before he said, "Okay, off we go."

"Thank you," she said because she understood that he didn't like it when she went to Carl's. He knew she slept over sometimes and that she'd gotten herself into the will despite the fact that the old man had a son and a daughter. But he also knew that he was going to get a nice commission when the house sold. He'd told her that he could take care of the whole transaction without ever having to put a sign on the front lawn. "I can do this without even listing it," he'd said. "I would have several buyers ready for a house like that in this market." He seemed excited. The house was gorgeous.

He did *not* know, however, that she would be leaving the country.

"How much longer do you think the old guy has?" asked Eddie, pulling away from the curb faster than he should.

"Slow down," she said, "or *I'll* be dead before *he* is."

"It's a Porsche, babe," he said and shrugged as if the machine was built to be driven only on a racetrack — or by an asshole.

He was looking at her, so she tried to smile. "Yes," she said. "It proves what a successful real estate agent you are." She didn't know why she was busting his balls. He'd taken her to a nice lunch and was giving her a ride. Maybe she just didn't feel great about what she was doing to Carl. "I don't think he has much time," she said. "How long can you live with stage four cancer?"

"Who knows?" said Eddie. "For some people, if the therapy works, they can live for years."

"Well, Carl has used the word *terminal*," she said. "So, I don't think he has years. I think he has months."

"It'd be nice if he'd just get it over with," said Eddie.

"Really, Eddie?" she said. "This guy is going to take care of me, and you want to talk about him like that?"

Eddie was smiling and looking at the road. He seemed satisfied that he'd jabbed back after her comment about his career.

It was hard for Angie to believe that, for a minute not so long ago, she thought she'd be able to break up with Derek, leave The Organization, and live in the St. Francis Wood house with Eddie. Eddie was charming when they first met. He wore nice suits. He drove the

Porsche. But the longer she knew him, the clearer it became that he was a bit of a clown, not to be taken too seriously. Zero substance and mediocre in bed. Not as bad as Derek, but not good.

She looked back on her former self now and thought what a fool she was to think Cristian would let her leave anyway. She hadn't seen his brutality at that point. He was almost grandfatherly around her, but she'd heard the stories. Derek told her that Cristian had once cut off a man's thumb and preserved it in formaldehyde, the jar kept in a safe in his office. And when he wanted to let someone know he was serious during business meetings, he'd supposedly place the jar strategically in the middle of his desk.

Derek's brother Alex had too many beers one night and told Angie that when Cristian was a younger man, just getting started with The Organization, he put some guy in the hospital by pulling his hair. This was in the late 70's and the victim couldn't pay the vig on a loan. He had long hair like a lot of guys did back then, so Cristian used it against him. Cristian jerked the man to the ground and pulled him around the bar at the Club Vulpe so that anyone else there with an outstanding loan would learn the same lesson. By the time Cristian had gotten his message across, the other guy—head bleeding from the scalp—was unconscious and rushed to the hospital. The poor guy had head trauma and was never the same after that.

Cristian's boss at the time was angry with Cristian because, in his new condition, the guy almost certainly wouldn't be able to make good on his loan. But the boss still promoted Cristian for his unrestrained commitment to his job.

To Angie, Cristian's physical appearance didn't seem very intimidating, but his cold blue eyes and his infamous past seemed to work for him just fine. All his foot soldiers, including her, simply did what they were told. Angie couldn't tell if everyone practiced such loyalty to the man out of true devotion or simple fear. She knew she did what she was told mostly out of fear, but she did respect that the man had worked his way up from the bottom and made a fortune. She was committed to getting her own fortune and getting out with just one move. She was very attached to both of her thumbs, and her hair was extremely important to her as well, so she was being careful as she waited for Carl to die. She would keep proving her loyalty to Cristian and The Organization until the exact right time. She would make Derek think that she was at least trying to make their marriage legitimate though there were very few things she liked about the man. She would keep Eddie happy until the papers were signed. And she'd try to make Carl as comfortable as possible in his final days. She owed that to him.

"Where do you want me to drop you?" asked Eddie.

"Right out front," she said.

"Derek and Alex aren't doing a project?"

"No," she said. "They finished the water heater last week."

"I hope they're not putting any more garbage in that house," he said. "Remember, little things like a shitty water heater can have a major effect on the asking price."

"And your commission?" she said, still needling him a bit. Again, she didn't know why. It was a reflex right now, and she needed to stop before she blew the whole deal.

"Yeah," he shouted and snapped a look at her before slowing to a stop at 19th Ave. "It's like you're double-dipping here, Angie."

"Huh?" she said, giving him her best *I'm offended* look and putting her hand up to her throat.

"Are you serious?" he said, giving her a long stare now.

She knew what he was getting at, but she was going to make him say it out loud so that she could snap back at him for the accusation. She held all the cards here. She could simply tell him that she'd find a new realtor. His only leverage was that he could go to the police. Or to Carl. But she didn't think he'd do it. Eddie didn't have the balls, and he needed the money.

They were still staring at each other when the guy behind them blew his horn. Eddie put the car in gear and sped through the intersection. When they got to the stop sign at 17th Avenue, he turned to her and spoke in the kind of voice you might use with a third grader who didn't understand why you look both ways before you cross the street. *Idiots in Porsches ... that's why,* she thought as he spoke.

"Angie," he said. "You and Derek are getting paid every time him and Alex do a bogus job on that house. The window job alone will cost us tens of thousands on the sale. The material they used is cheap and looks terrible."

"Okay," she said. "So, we need some money now, and we're doing these jobs, but we're not double-dipping if it's going to cost us on the back end, right?"

She could tell he was grinding his teeth now. "Yeah," he said. "You're right. You're not double-dipping per say, but you guys are costing yourselves and me money by doing these half-ass jobs now instead of just waiting for this guy to die and getting a top price on the house. Jesus, is that so hard for you people to understand?"

*You people.*

They were in line with a couple of other cars at the stoplight on Portola now, pretty close to Carl's house. She knew she shouldn't be offended because she literally was one of *those people*. She was a rip-off artist. But at least she was good at it. Eddie wasn't good at anything. He sucked at selling houses. And now this golf tournament, which looked like it would be a cash cow for him, had broken his bank, and he had to meet with a crooked law enforcement officer to whom he owed a lot of money, which he didn't have.

She gave Eddie credit for at least not asking her to loan him the money to pay the man. Eddie was supposed to meet the sheriff guy this afternoon and work out a deal, but she had no faith that Eddie wouldn't step in shit again. He had a knack for it, and she didn't want to spend another second with him today. So, she opened the door and got out with the car still idling in traffic.

"What the—?" she heard him say as she slammed the door.

As she was walking to the sidewalk, she knew she looked good in the dress, so she gave him a little extra hip swivel. He honked at her. Without turning around, she raised her arm and extended her middle finger.

There were a couple of teenage boys with skateboards standing near the bus stop. They looked at her like she was the coolest thing they'd ever laid eyes on. She winked at them just as the light turned green, and, without breaking stride, she made her way across Portola on her way to St. Francis Wood.

## 23

Carl thought Angie would be over earlier, and he'd prepared a light lunch: chicken Caesar salad with homemade garlic croutons and a pitcher of sangria the way Angie liked it, with more fruit in there than anyone would need. But he did it for her, and when she wasn't there by one o'clock, he ate his salad, threw hers in the composting bin, and drank the whole pitcher of sangria while watching a World War II movie on television. He thought he'd seen all the best in this genre, but the one he watched this afternoon was top notch.

Either he was getting so old that he was forgetting movies he'd seen before, or there were so many movies out there that it had gotten harder to keep up with the good ones. This one didn't have a great plot, but it had impressive scenes and solid young actors. Nick Nolte was the only older actor. The rest were guys like Sean Penn and Clooney and Woody—a bunch of performers who went on to have big time careers. Carl thought parts of the film were better than *Patton* and *Saving Private Ryan*, and it pissed him off that he couldn't remember ever seeing anything about this particular picture when it came out. He considered himself a film buff, so he was starting to think he probably did see this movie when it came out and simply forgot about it. He figured this is how it happened. You started losing little pieces of memory. Why not a war movie from twenty years ago to make space for the bullshit he'd been watching on Netflix? How many books had he forgotten? How many trials? He should have been happy that he was able to enjoy the movie a second time, but he didn't like how he was feeling about it.

He was pissed that he'd become an old man. Pissed that he didn't have much time left, but happy that he'd be gone before he'd lost his memory completely. He didn't wish that on anyone.

A lot of this movie was ultra-violent, like that first scene from *Private Ryan.* Carl was in a contemplative mood, and when he was finished watching it, he forced himself to feel embarrassed about incessantly claiming that his court appearances were like *going to war.* He remembered repeating that mantra over the years to young, second chair associates preparing for big trials. He knew it was just a metaphor and that people used the expression all the time, but retirement and his wife's death and his cancer had become catalysts for self-examination. And as he sat in his TV room after finishing that pitcher of wine, he wasn't so proud of his life's work. Lawyers certainly weren't soldiers. He hadn't fought for any real causes. And he hoped his demise wouldn't involve the kind of ignominy that Woody Harrelson's character faced when he pulled the pin from a grenade while the grenade was still hooked to the back of his utility belt. The soldier literally blew off his own ass. Lousy way to go. Carl couldn't face that kind of death. The only thing worse than losing your ass would be having someone required to wipe it for you. And he knew that's what he was looking at some time in the next few months.

He recognized that he'd been very successful, but in his particular role in the justice system, success simply meant that he'd prevented a lot of guilty people from facing any real retribution. For his entire career, he'd known that the system—for it to work for all citizens—required vigorous legal defense against the power of the state. He also knew that most defendants were guilty of something, even if they hadn't committed the crime for which they were being tried. But, again, this system was obligated to provide a fair trial and equal justice under the law for everyone.

He knew all this. And he believed in it. However, the cancer put him on a short runway now, and he was allowing himself to climb out of his protective emotional bunker, barricaded by logic and argumentation but devoid of human feeling. That bunker was a prerequisite for defending the kinds of clients he'd represented for decades, especially after he'd built a name for himself in San Francisco. His criminal defense cases had transitioned beyond DUIs and petty theft. For the last twenty years before retirement, he'd represented corrupt municipal and state officials, the sons and daughters of wealthy businessmen, big tech cheaters, high ranking members of the church, and other varieties of the privileged class, who thought they were somehow insulated from punishment for their selfishness, carelessness, and plain old cruelty. And in a sense, they were right. Carl was at their disposal. He was their shield and sometimes their bazooka. He knew how to win. He understood how to keep those people out of jail, and they paid him handsomely to do it.

But he didn't feel so good about it now.

Looking back on it all, as one tends to do when he can see there are only a few pages left in his autobiography, none of it seemed very important. He knew it was significant that he developed a craft and cultivated it into something that made him and his wife and kids comfortable, but he also knew there were other, more admirable, undertakings that he could have attempted to achieve with the set of skills God had given him. He wished that he'd just once done something courageous with his life. He'd been bold. He'd taken chances. He'd even put his career on the line to help his clients. He would never consider himself a coward. But he never felt like he'd been courageous, either.

Only a few years back, he watched a Volvo in the fast lane lose control and flip upside down onto the shoulder of Highway 280. He happened to be in the same lane about fifty yards behind the Volvo when it happened. For whatever reason, he didn't panic when he saw the car lose control. He actually used his turn signal, pulled his car up in front of the overturned vehicle, and jogged back to the flipped car like he was going to tell them that their gas cap was open.

When he saw that the elderly couple had their seatbelts on and were hanging upside down, he knocked on the window and told the old man to unlock the doors, which he did, but neither door would open wide enough to get them out.

Carl was, however, able to open one of the back doors, so he climbed in, crawled over the tiny bits of broken glass sprayed across the ceiling, unfastened each of their seatbelts, and got them out of the car. They were bleeding but alert and thankful.

By the time he had both of them out and sitting on the ground next to the car, five or six other cars had pulled over, and people were standing around looking at him and the couple. Everyone else driving south on 280 was rubbernecking and causing a bit of a traffic jam.

Carl had a deposition in San Jose that morning, so when he saw that the couple was being cared for by a husband and wife who looked like they had medical training, Carl simply walked back to his car, got in, and drove to his meeting.

He wanted to think that he'd been brave, but he knew his actions didn't constitute any type of heroism. He was never really in any danger. The most he would credit himself with was that he hadn't been an asshole. He didn't just swerve around them and keep driving. He'd pulled over to make sure the people were okay. That was something.

He also gave himself credit for staying calm and felt that he could have used that talent in another line of work, but he was already looking at retirement at that time. After telling his kids about the adventure, he didn't really think about that day again until now, as he sat in his TV room, half tanked on sangria, reflecting on the war movie, and waiting for a beautiful woman to arrive.

When Angie eventually walked into the room, she was holding her shoes in her hand, and she had beads of perspiration on her forehead.

"What happened to you?" he asked and pointed at the leather recliner.

She sat down and dropped her shoes on the floor next to her. "Long story," she said, which was the way she handled most of his questions.

"You look thirsty," he said. She had her eyes closed so he was able to take a long look at her without being impolite. She looked great in her tight dress even though she was sitting like a little kid, slouched in the chair with her legs straight out in front of her, painted toes pointed toward the ceiling.

She opened her eyes and saw the sangria pitcher on the coffee table. "I could use one of those," she said.

"I'll make more," he said. "If you don't mind that I use the same fruit. I cut up everything I had in the kitchen for the first batch."

"That's fine with me," she said and closed her eyes again.

Carl went into the kitchen and opened a crappy bottle of red that his neighbor had given him for Christmas. It'd been sitting on the counter for months, and Angie wouldn't know the difference. He poured it in with the soggy fruit and also added his secret ingredient: Coca-Cola. The Basque do a version of sangria that tastes surprisingly similar to the Spanish form. No fruit though. Just red wine and coke over ice. They call it a Kalimotxo. Carl added only a little Coke to his version, but it made a big difference, and Angie loved it.

He garnished her drink with a lemon slice and brought the pitcher and the glass back to the TV room. Angie opened her eyes when she heard him and said, "Thank you."

Carl poured himself another one and sat down on the couch. "So, what's goin' on?" he said.

"I had to have lunch with a prospective client," she said.

"For your brothers?"

"Yeah," she said. "They have me go out to lunch with guys and give bids on jobs."

"Does it work?" he said.

"What do you think?" she said, crossing her legs and flashing a Hollywood smile.

"Yep," he said. "I bet you do pretty good."

"Except one time," she said, "with a client named Charlie." She was laughing now and put her drink down. "When I got to the restaurant, Charlie turned out to be a woman. She took one look at my dress, and the lunch was over."

"I do like that dress," he said.

"Oh, it wasn't this one."

"Yeah," he said. "But I get the idea."

"You're one of the few people who gets me, Carl."

Carl was trying to figure out if this was all part of the game. He knew she was trying to con him and already had with the bogus repair jobs her brothers had done, but the playbook couldn't have included her pulling back the curtain like this and discussing how she helped secure jobs for her brothers' semi-fake business.

Carl figured that her relationship with him was different, that she didn't see him as she saw her other targets. He'd floated the notion that he was going to leave her the house, but that was in a moment of passion he hadn't felt since he was a young man. Although he had no intention of leaving her anything, he knew that she had taken him seriously, so it was difficult to tell if she was still working him, or if she appreciated their relationship.

Either way, he was going to keep it going as long as he could. He felt a little guilty because she was trying so hard at this after he'd lied to her. But it had been only pillow talk. She wasn't so naïve that she could believe that he'd cut his own son and daughter out of the estate to give her the house. She just couldn't fully believe that.

But like clockwork, she showed up every Thursday—usually for lunch—and they'd eventually make it upstairs. And today, after they polished off the sangria, they were going to do just that.

## 24

Kimberly was doing her best to stay at least three cars behind the Porsche, but it was difficult because the streets were nearly empty. Some people were still going to work in offices, but most folks were working from home now, so the usual mid-afternoon traffic would be just a memory until there was a vaccine or a cure. Or maybe people would never go back to the office. Empty streets would normally be a good thing, but Kim didn't want to be seen and needed other cars as cover.

She was being careful even though her mind was racing.

There were moments during the early stages of the drive when Kim tried to rationalize what she'd seen at Mission Rock. Maybe Eddie was flirting with this woman in order to close a deal; maybe Kim's view from the upper deck presented an optical illusion, and Eddie hadn't really touched the woman's thigh; maybe the margaritas were too strong and that man in the white shirt wasn't Eddie at all. It could have been some other idiot with a ridiculous laugh and who walked with his chest pushed out in front of him like some city version of Foghorn Leghorn with a Porsche.

She let her brain play with these absurd ideas as they moved down 3rd Street through Dog Patch. But by the time they took a right onto Caesar Chavez, Kim had stopped lying to herself and committed to following Eddie and the woman wherever they were going. She went through a series of emotions that began with a strange kind of excitement that comes from tailing someone, literally chasing them through the city like in a movie. That excitement, however, transitioned briefly to a suffocating fear as she thought about what it might be like to be single again. What would happen to someone like her trying to date again? Would she be competing with girls like the one in the floral dress? If that was the case, she knew she wouldn't even try. She'd just be alone forever.

By the time they'd passed through Noe Valley and were turning onto Market, she was crying. Full on sobs. She used her sleeve to wipe at her face as they wound around Twin Peaks and eventually ended up moving west on Taraval Street. And when they passed Guerra's Market on Funston Avenue, she was screaming and pounding on the steering wheel. She didn't like the way the heels of her hands felt afterward, and she promised herself not to do that again.

Once they crossed 19th Avenue, she realized they must be headed to Eddie's office, and she wondered if Eddie was taking her there for sex. However, Eddie's office had glass walls, and there were several other people who worked there, so the odds of that happening on a weekday afternoon were slim. But she was right about his destination. He parked the car in front of his office, jumped out quickly, and looked like he was fiddling with his keys when Kim covered her face and looked away.

She drove past the office, took a U-turn about three blocks down, then headed back east until she pulled into an open spot in front of El Burrito Express. Even if Eddie spotted the red Jeep, which was unlikely, she could easily say she was picking up dinner. She'd just put the car in park when Eddie came back out of the office carrying something that he threw in the back seat.

In that moment, Kim was paralyzed when she realized that she was going to be seen. If he moved into his left lane, Eddie was going to drive right in front of her, and they would be face to face. For a split second, she considered ducking down behind the dashboard, but she abandoned the idea when Eddie pulled away from the curb and immediately skidded into a screeching illegal U-turn across two lanes of traffic so that he was headed back toward 19th, and she was safe from detection.

As she put the car back in drive to continue her pursuit, she was momentarily disappointed. If they'd just seen each other—had a moment of reckoning—that would be it. The two of them would be having a discussion later that night about why he was driving around with Wonder Woman in the middle of the day. And she would have to decide whether or not she would stay with this man, this buffoon, whom she'd picked out of the collection of available jerks in her dismal orbit and married him. She'd pledged to be faithful to her husband, who now seemed to have taken that pledge as a mere suggestion.

Kim had faced the challenge of feeling inadequate ever since her younger sister Marilyn hit puberty. Marilyn had been gangly and awkward until she turned about twelve, and then she transformed into an unwitting beauty. She never seemed to understand how pretty she was, and she never treated Kim poorly. Marilyn probably didn't understand her power because she'd known only awkwardness up to that point in her life. But her exquisiteness, even as a young girl, had been difficult for Kim.

It might have been easier if they were rivals, but they weren't. When Marilyn was in her late teens and Kim in her early twenties, Kim thought of them as best friends—confidants. They knew everything about one another, and, until she got married, Kim hadn't trusted anyone as much as she trusted her sister. In fact, now that she had no trust in Eddie, Marilyn was the only one left. And maybe Michael Duffy.

She was making herself feel like crying again or hitting the steering wheel, but she wasn't going to do it. She was just going to follow Eddie and confirm what she already knew was true. She wasn't sure how following the two of them was going to confirm anything, but the plan was to see how this all played out.

When they crossed over West Portal and were waiting at the light on Portola, Kim watched the girl get out of Eddie's car in the middle of traffic and slam the door behind her. Then, without turning around, she gave him the finger. If Kim didn't hate this woman, she would have thought the gesture was glorious. In fact, she *did* think the gesture was glorious. It wasn't crowded in the neighborhood, but there were people out and about, and this gal didn't care. She flipped him the bird right there in public and then strutted over to the sidewalk in that tight dress. She walked like a runway model even though they were on a pretty steep hill. Kimberly couldn't have walked like that in a pair of cross-trainers, but this woman was working those heels, and the teenagers on the sidewalk admired her as she walked past. They were elbowing each other and pointing surreptitious fingers at her as she sashayed into the crosswalk.

Now Kim had a decision to make. She didn't really have a reason to follow Eddie. He was probably just going back to work not selling houses. But she couldn't really follow this girl unless Kim parked her car, got out, and followed her on foot. But it was too late for that now, so when Eddie turned right onto Portola, Kim did the same. She thought she might catch him in some other secret bullshit.

He was driving south on Portola and took a right on Sloat, which seemed to be leading to their house, but he made a couple of funny maneuvers near Sunset Boulevard that had them twisted around and pulling into the parking lot at Lake Merced.

The lot was huge. Sometimes on Sundays, bus drivers went through training in this lot. So, there was plenty of room for Kim to go in the opposite direction as Eddie and find a spot near the trees where she could watch him. She saw him with another woman at lunch, and now she was watching him in the Lake Merced parking lot of all places.

Last week it was crowded here because of the golf tournament, but there was only a smattering of cars today, probably owned by joggers and fishermen. The fog was starting to roll in, and Eddie was standing in the middle of the lot hugging himself against the cold and checking his watch every ten seconds.

After about ten minutes, a sheriff's cruiser pulled into the lot and drove directly at Eddie. Eddie stopped hugging himself and stood now with his hands on his hips. There was a moment during which Kim believed that the sheriff was going to run over Eddie, but the car swerved at the last second and missed Eddie by inches. Kim yelped.

When the car had come within about five feet, Eddie had taken his hands off his hips and held them out in front of him as if he'd be able to somehow block the vehicle from hitting him. And when the car swerved, Eddie's knees buckled. The whole scene looked bizarre to Kim from where she was sitting in her car under the low hanging branches of a lakeside cypress. She was now seeing for the second time in one day a clandestine part of Eddie's life, and she almost wished she'd never seen any of it. Almost.

But now she was here, and she couldn't take her eyes off it.

The driver was a fat black guy. Not the flabby kind of fat though. This guy's massive round gut looked rock hard, his shirt buttons straining to stay fastened. As big as he was, he was wearing a light, tailored suit that almost looked chic. With his hands in his pockets, he waddled over to Eddie and stood in front of him with a nice, natural smile.

Kimberly was relieved. They must be friends. But the stunt this guy pulled with the car seemed too much. Eddie could have been severely injured by this joker, who was standing just a few feet from Eddie now, the two of them looking at each other eye to eye. But the sheriff was doing all the talking, and he kept the smile on his face for the entire conversation.

Eddie was nodding a lot and mixing in some shrugs. It looked like he tried to talk a couple of times but was cut off. Then, from out of nowhere, the sheriff's hand came out of his pocket quickly and struck Eddie in the face before Eddie could defend himself.

Kim felt the breath rush out of her. What on Earth was happening?

Eddie started to put his own hand up to his face, which had to be stinging in the cold afternoon air, but he stopped himself. Maybe he didn't want to give this guy the satisfaction. And now the sheriff was pointing at Eddie and talking again. He wasn't smiling anymore. He spoke for only a few seconds. Then he turned quickly, walked back to his car, and sped out of the lot with his light bar flashing.

## 25

Kim hadn't seen her dad in weeks.

Since her mom had died a few years ago, she and Marilyn had been good about calling and visiting, but Kim had been neglectful lately and was a little sheepish about showing up and looking for his help.

He lived in a small house in the Presidio—the beautiful piece of land at the northernmost tip of the city, which had been a military base for over two hundred years before it became a national park in the 90's. If it weren't federal land, the properties on the old base would be owned by some of the most affluent people in the world. Some of the houses had views of the Golden Gate Bridge and the Farallon Islands and Alcatraz, but this particular slice of federal real estate was not for sale.

The Presidio Trust managed the properties, and Kim's dad, Mr. Bill Tracy, happened to be on the board of the Presidio Trust and somehow cashed in on a political favor to secure his little home in the Fort Scott section. There were about fifteen other houses in his micro-neighborhood, formerly home to military officers but now inhabited mostly by families that had won a housing lottery, which provided below market-rate rent.

When Kim visited her dad, she felt like she was in another city, another state, maybe another country. The barracks near Fort Scott had rounded bell gables, red tile roofs, flat stucco walls, and the long arcades of a mission revival. Some were mansions that had been split into duplexes. None of it looked anything like any other neighborhoods in the city. That's probably why her dad liked it. He'd spent so many years in the dark offices and back rooms of downtown buildings that he must have appreciated the fresh air and trees that were all around him in his foggy, little oasis.

Kim walked up the narrow pathway and knocked on the door. She usually called first, but she didn't this time because she didn't really know if she was going to visit him or not when she left her house. She'd sat on the Eddie information for a few days now and was just driving around on Sunday morning. She skipped her bootcamp at the Presidio

YMCA, and she decided to drive up the hill and see what the old man was doing. Maybe ask for some advice.

When he answered the door, he was wearing an all-white Adidas tracksuit and a pair of indoor moccasins. His reading glasses were balanced at the end of his nose, and he was holding the Bay Area section of the Sunday paper.

"Well, hello stranger," he said and smiled, but Kim took it as a dig because she hadn't seen him in a while.

"Hi, Dad," she said and gave him a hug before walking past him and plopping down on the worn leather couch, the same one that had been in the living room of their childhood home, where Kimberly and Marilyn would climb on the armrest to see what their dad was reading. Everything else in his house looked more like his office though. Hanging on the wall behind her were dozens of campaign posters and other memorabilia from the decades of elections that he'd influenced one way or the other.

When Kim was little, she didn't know exactly what he did. When other kids would ask her, she told them what the great Bill Tracy called himself—a political consultant. In short, the man did stuff to get people elected and to keep them in office as long as he could so that he would stay on the payroll. And apparently, he was pretty good at it because every year he was either working with people who were trying to decide if they could win, who were preparing for a run, or who were actually in the midst of a campaign. That's what the man did.

He never really shared many of the details, but Kim had come to understand that her dad spent a lot of time eating lunch with people and talking about city politics or sitting in bars with people and talking about city politics. He always had stacks of legal pads with notes lying around, but Kim thought most of his work was the actual brainstorming with other guys like himself. He didn't do much polling, and he didn't work with the media. But Kim knew that her dad must have offered something else that was never really discussed in any detail.

"Coffee?" he said and shuffled off to the kitchen.

"Not for me," she said.

"I can put a little something in it," he said and leaned out the doorway to make eye contact.

"No thanks," she said. "It's Sunday, and you shouldn't put anything in yours either."

Her dad was a high-functioning alcoholic. In fact, she'd never actually seen the man drunk. But he was always drinking as if it were his job to hold tumblers with brown liquid.

"Sunday heats are the best," he said, his old mantra. For his work, the days of the week and even the times of day weren't really very important. He'd never been a nine to five guy. That's just not how it was for Kim growing up—she never knew when her dad would be around. So, for Bill, Sunday at 9:30 a.m. was as good a time as any to have a drink.

He came out of the kitchen holding his coffee mug and blowing over the rim. The room was dark except for the reading light that was illuminating his empty chair. The rest of the newspaper was scattered on the floor next to the chair. Big trees shaded the windows, so the room was perpetually dark, like she imagined the rooms in which he'd sat with other men discussing candidates and polls and endorsements.

"So, what's up?" he said as he lowered himself into the recliner and adjusted the lamp to brighten more of the room.

When she was driving around this morning, she really wasn't planning on telling anyone about Eddie, but now that she was here, she knew she needed to get it off her chest. "I'm pretty sure Eddie's cheating on me," she said and heard her own voice crack a bit at the end.

Her father nodded and slurped a bit of the coffee. Then he put the mug on the side table and rose from his chair. He walked into the kitchen and came back out with another mug and placed it on the coffee table in front of Kim. She could smell it—Bailey's and coffee—before she picked it up and took a sip. She loved Bailey's and coffee. To her, it tasted like a boozy milkshake. She knew that Bill Tracy put bourbon in his, so she appreciated that he kept a bottle of Bailey's Irish Cream around the house for her and Marilyn.

"How did you catch him?" he said.

"Saw him at a restaurant with a woman."

"What a dick," he said. "Right out in the open?"

"Mission Rock," she said. "I'm working down at Mission Bay now."

"Could there be any other explanation for it?" he said.

"She could be a client."

"But you don't think she looked like a client?"

"Not really," she said.

"Co-worker, maybe?

Kim shook her head.

"So, you just have a feeling," he said. "But you don't know for sure."

Kim nodded. "It didn't look good. They looked intimate."

"Yeah," said her dad. "But your mind can do funny things to you when you start to lose trust in someone."

"I thought about that," she said.

"I work in a dirty business," he said. "And when someone from the inner-circle does something even slightly suspicious, I can go nuts running around trying to check on him." He paused and shook his head, looking almost ashamed of himself. "I've dug into people's personal lives because of the suspicions I'd created in my own mind over things that had really been innocent."

"You mean you've done that more than once?" she said.

"Too many times to count," he said. "It's a character flaw." He took a long sip from his mug. "But it's served me well over the years. A little paranoia never hurts in my line of work in this tiny city."

"It's probably not a great quality for a marriage though," she said. "I should be able to trust my husband."

"But you don't," he said.

"Not anymore," she said and exhaled. She was considering whether or not it was even worth it to fight for a marriage in which she didn't trust her spouse. "When they left Mission Rock, I followed them."

He smiled. "Good for you," he said. "You find anything out?"

"While they were at a stoplight near St. Francis Wood," she said, "the woman got out of the car and slammed the door."

"Like they were having a fight?"

"Yeah," she said. "And then the girl gave him the finger."

"So probably not a client," he said. He was holding his mug with both hands now and leaning forward in his seat like he was listening to one of the old-time radio mysteries that he forced on the family when Kim and Marilyn were kids.

"No," she said. "To be honest, it looked like a lovers' quarrel."

"But you don't know that yet."

"No," she said but was becoming more and more certain the longer she talked about it. "And then he drove down and met a sheriff at Lake Merced."

"At the golf course?"

"No," she said. "In the big parking lot near the end of Sunset Boulevard." She pictured the scene in her mind now. It was all so odd.

"Are you sure he didn't see you."

"I parked about fifty yards away," she said.

"Did you get a good look at the sheriff?" he asked, eyebrows raised now.

"Fat black dude," she said.

"Tall?"

"Average height," she said. "But huge stomach. Nice suit, but huge stomach, almost like a pregnant woman's stomach."

"Huh," he said.

"What?"

"Keep going," he said. "What happened?"

"Well," she said. "They talked for a few minutes, and then the sheriff slapped Eddie across the face."

"That's Al Young," said her dad. "Why the hell is Eddie getting mixed up with Al?"

"Do you think Eddie's in trouble with the law?" asked Kim.

"Al Young isn't the law," he said. "The man's a grifter with a badge. I can't believe he hasn't retired yet."

"Do you think he's somehow connected to the girl?"

"Who? Al?" He rubbed the stubble on his chin and put his mug down on the side table. He looked at Kim for a long moment and then shook his head. "Who knows?"

Kim turned away and looked out the window where a little boy with long hair sticking out of a knit cap was pulling a wagon that kept banging into his heels. It didn't seem to upset him as he made his way down the little hill toward the baseball field.

The Bailey's had cooled the coffee so she was able to take a long swallow without burning her throat before she looked back at her dad.

"I guess I need to do a little more research or just ask Eddie what's going on."

Her dad reached down and started organizing the newspaper. Then he placed it on the coffee table and said, "I don't like that Eddie's involved with Al Young."

Kim didn't say anything. She didn't like it either. The fat man drove around in his sheriff's cruiser flashing his lights for no reason and slapping people in parking lots. For some reason, to Kim, this really frightened her. It was just so brazen.

"Kim?" he said. "You still with me?"

"Yeah," she said. "I don't like the way that man operates."

"Eddie or Al?"

"Well, both," she said. "But the sheriff really scared me."

"Good instincts," he said. "Do you mind if I put Uncle Leo on this?"

Uncle Leo was not really her uncle. Too young for that. He was a private investigator who worked for her dad. But Leo had quietly been part of the Tracy family for her entire childhood. He never stayed long, but he would stop by family dinners to say hello. He was at her graduation party. He was at her wedding. But Kim couldn't remember ever really having a conversation with the man.

"Does he still work for you?" she asked.

"Of course," he said. "And I'd like to put him on this if it's okay with you."

## 26

Carl's house was always hot. He liked it that way. But Angie couldn't take it tonight. Eddie had been a complete asshole this afternoon, and she'd planned to stay at Carl's, but she just wasn't feeling it. So, she told the old man that she had something early in the morning and had to get home. He smacked her on the ass when she rolled out of bed and told her he'd miss her. And she knew he meant it.

She and Derek lived in a duplex in the Richmond District. Alex lived in the other unit, where the two brothers spent their free time playing video games and yelling at each other.

Angie took an Uber from Carl's house in St. Francis Wood to her place on Balboa. While she was still in the car, she tied her hair back in a ponytail and reapplied some lip gloss so that she'd look presentable after being in bed with Carl.

She was still in the dress, even now after nine o'clock, and she was shivering as she jumped the stairs in twos all while still wearing her heels. She was looking in her purse for her keys when Derek opened the door. "Oh, thanks," she said as he stepped aside and allowed her to pass.

"I didn't expect you," he said to her back. "The last couple of times you stayed the night."

She walked quickly past the living room but noticed that Derek had porn going on the big screen TV. She just wanted to get out of the dress and the heels and get into some comfy loungewear to watch a movie before she went to sleep. She said over her shoulder, "Yeah, I was feeling sick, so I just left." She still had the image of the porn in her mind, so she added, "I think I might throw up. I'll sleep in the guest bedroom tonight."

She kicked her shoes into the corner and threw her dress and her bra on the bed. She was standing at her dresser when he came into the room. She knew she was married to the man, and, of course, they'd slept together, but she felt compelled to cover herself when he stepped into view.

She'd walked around Carl's house naked for weeks enjoying the freedom of it, but Derek was different for some reason. She pulled at her drawer with one hand and covered her breasts with the other. She grabbed a big t-shirt and turned her back to him while she put it on. Then she went back to the dresser to grab some sweats that she put on quickly. She didn't make eye contact with Derek until she was dressed. She walked over to the closet and slid her feet into a pair of slippers and then stood with her hands in the pockets of the sweats and faced her husband.

Derek had the same blank expression he had when he'd opened the door for her. He said, "Do you think leaving Carl's house was a good idea?"

For some reason, everything Derek said sounded like a threat. She said, "What do you mean?"

"I mean," he said, "we're trying to close this deal, right?"

She walked past him into the other bedroom and turned on the TV.

"Are you going to leave your stuff lying around?" he said.

"Oh, sorry," she said and walked back into the bedroom, where she picked up her shoes and placed them in the closet. Then she threw the dress and the bra in the hamper and walked past Derek into the other room. Derek stood in the hallway watching.

"Well?" he said.

"Did I leave something?"

He looked back in the bedroom. "No," he said. "I want you to tell me whether or not you think it was a good idea to leave the old man's house when we're trying to finish the deal."

"You know what's a deal-breaker, Derek?"

"Tell me."

"Blowing chunks on a man's Persian rug. People generally don't like that."

He smiled and nodded. "You don't feel well," he said and leaned against the doorframe, his arms folded over his chest.

"Yeah," she said. "I told you that." She was sitting on the edge of the guest bed with the remote control in her hand. She was not liking the vibe in the room.

"Yeah," he said. "You told me that."

She was pretending to flip through the stations, but he just kept standing there, staring at her. "What?" she said and put the remote on the bed next to her. She looked him in the eyes. "What do you want?"

"It'd be nice if you keep me in the loop when you make decisions like this."

"I haven't slept over every time," she said.

"But it had become a bit of a routine, so I'm sure that's what he wants. Don't break the routine again. Cristian feels like he's invested in this one and doesn't want to lose it."

"Cristian's invested?" she said. "I didn't know that Cristian spoons with Carl like I do. It's good to know we're both invested. I thought I was the one letting Carl feel my tits. Nice to know we're all invested."

Derek smiled. He wasn't an unattractive man. But he had what Angie thought of as a mean face. Cristian had one too. Something in the eyes, maybe the eyebrows. Maybe the vertical crease at the bridge of the nose. Mean. "Everything each of us does is for The Organization," he said. "You know that."

"I do," she said and decided that she had to tread lightly here. If anyone doubted her loyalty, she could kiss Italy goodbye. In fact, she could kiss this world goodbye. The Organization would be swift. "I'm committed," she said. "I just don't feel good, and I'm tired, Derek."

"That's the job though, right?" he said, stepping into the room.

"I know that," she said. "Sometimes a girl just needs a night off, you know?" He was standing next to her now, and out of the corner of her eye, she could see the glint of his belt buckle. She kept her eyes on the television. It was a show on MTV called *The Challenge,* in which guys and girls about her age lived together in a resort. They would do physical elimination rounds during the day and party at night. As she watched two girls wrestling in the sand, she couldn't help thinking that she'd eat all these girls for lunch and, with minimal effort, she'd take home the million-dollar prize money. It wasn't as much as Carl's house was going to bring in, but she'd feel better about it afterward, and she wouldn't have to spend one more night looking at Derek's mean eyes.

"So, you're not really sick?" he said.

"I don't feel good."

He had her by the wrist now and was pulling her off the bed. He jammed his other hand up under her t-shirt, and he was squeezing to the point of pain. "Stop," she said. "I don't feel good."

He let go of her wrist but now had his arm wrapped around her back and was pulling her into him. He put his mouth on her neck. His breath smelled like Cheetos, and she could feel his teeth. Between this stinky hickey and the violent mammogram, she was hoping she'd just pass out until it was over. She actually stopped fighting and just let her body go limp.

At that point, he tried to throw her on the bed, but he must have had trouble with the dead weight, and she bumped the corner of the mattress and ended up on the floor. She'd closed her eyes for most of Derek's seduction, but now she was sitting on the floor with her feet splayed out in front of her. Her t-shirt was twisted and hanging off one shoulder, and her sweats were pulled down to her thighs.

She pushed the hair out of her eyes and looked up at him. She wasn't scared. She was disgusted.

"You're supposed to be my wife," he said. She noticed that his cheeks were shiny with sweat, and he had spittle in one corner of his mouth.

She held up her hand to show him the ring. She considered showing him a different finger but didn't want to antagonize him anymore.

"I think it's time you start acting like a normal wife," he said. He was out of breath and almost gasping to get the words out.

When she'd let herself go limp, she was able to control her breathing, and she was quite calm when she said, "Normal wives don't get sent by their husbands to sleep with old men."

"That's going to end," he said, nodding now like he was trying to convince himself.

"Got it," she said. "Are you going to tell Cristian, or do you want me to?"

"I want you to speed up the process and get it over with."

"The man has stage four cancer," she said. "I think we can wait a few more months for a score this big. We don't want any suspicion. His children are probably going to contest the will."

"Expedite that job," he said and walked out of the room.

Angie closed her eyes, leaned back against the bed, and thought of the Amalfi Coast.

## 27

Leo Callaghan had worked with Bill Tracy since they were both young men. Bill had taken the standard path to his career. He'd gone to Santa Clara, majored in political science, worked as an intern for a city supervisor, eventually became chief of staff for a state assemblyman, and then became a consultant.

The only school Leo had attended after high school was a brief stint in the San Francisco Police Academy, where he was fired after two months for getting into a fist fight with one of the self-defense instructors. It was no solace to Leo that he'd won the fight. He was still out of a job and ended up working on the dock at Sunset Produce, way out in the Bayview, where Italian men would yell at him, "Stacka the bananas straight, you Irish culo!"

It was tough work, but it paid well, and the hours were ideal. He started at 6:00 a.m. and was done by two o'clock. This gave him plenty of time to focus on his real passion—sitting in dark bars with professional alcoholics, combing through the SF Chronicle and looking for some local news to complain about. It didn't matter if it was the teachers' union or the Department of Parking and Traffic or the new DA. These guys would do a few hours of analysis every day as they methodically got bombed. Leo was younger than all the other critics, and he knew he had to get up early the next day, so he kept his time there to a minimum and otherwise lived a fairly lonely existence.

And that was his routine for over a year until he started playing softball for a team called Bill's Ringers. Bill was, of course, Bill Tracy, and one of the Ringers was a guy with whom Leo had played ball in high school. Leo had been asked to show up just to fill a spot for one game, but he and the older Bill had struck up a conversation at the bar afterward, and Bill invited him to be on the team permanently.

And that's how they met.

Bill had already established a career and was working to get a politically moderate supervisor re-elected at the time, back when a moderate could still hold office in San Francisco. He knew Leo had afternoons off and asked him if he wanted some extra work. Leo said sure. He was starting to get sick of the Italian guys anyway and thought he might enjoy doing something in politics. And he liked Bill Tracy. He liked that the man was always working on something, not really a hustle but always something in that grey area between ethical and not so ethical.

So, he worked part-time for Bill for a while. Sometimes he'd be passing out flyers, and sometimes he'd be answering phones. But on rare occasions, Bill would say, "Can I trust you with something confidential?" And Leo would always say yes.

Most of these tasks had seemed innocuous to Leo. One time he sat outside North Beach Restaurant for an hour just so that he could tell Bill who got in which car with whom after some big wig dinner party. That was it. And when Leo delivered the news, Bill gave him a slap on the back and put cash in his hand.

Another time, Bill asked Leo to pose as a parking lot attendant at a garage for an apartment complex that didn't have a parking lot attendant. Once he got the keys to some lady's Jaguar, he was instructed to check her glove compartment for a parking ticket, and if it was there, he was to write down the name of the cop who'd written it. That was it. The ticket was there, so Leo took down the cop's name, waited for the lady to come back down to the garage, retrieved her car from the spot he'd chosen, handed her the keys, and accepted a modest tip.

Again, Leo gave him a slap on the back and a handful of cash.

Then about six months later, Bill asked Leo if he wanted a full-time job.

\*\*\*

And now here he was waiting for Bill Tracy's daughter, Kimberly, to come by his office because she was having a problem with her husband. Leo didn't mind. He thought of his work like good actors thought of their craft: no small parts, only small actors. For him, he almost always enjoyed the work whether he thought it was important or not. In fact, some of the jobs he did over the years that seemed menial turned out to be the deciding factor in a contested campaign. You never knew.

Leo's office was his apartment. Bill Tracy had introduced Leo to an old San Francisco politico who owned a nice Marina building with an in-law. Bill called it *the hole* when Leo first started living in the one-bedroom basement apartment. Bill said it was something to start with so that Leo could get out of his parents' house. And now it was almost twenty years later, and Leo was still taking advantage of the rent control. *The hole* worked just fine for him.

He used the small dining room as his office. He'd somehow acquired the desk of a former lieutenant governor, and he loved it. It was thick wood, chipped and dented in some places but still a beautiful piece. He sat in a comfortable leather swivel chair and had two four-drawer file cabinets against the wall behind him. The only other piece of furniture in the room was a comfortable parlor chair which faced his desk. The chair was there for Bill Tracy, but today, his daughter was sitting there and had just finished a long story about her husband and some woman. And somehow, that asshole Al Young seemed to be part of this.

"So, you don't have the woman's name?" he asked.

"I don't," she said. And she looked tired, an overworked nurse with an idiot for a husband. He felt sorry for her. Not a bad looking gal. Nothing compared to the younger one, Marilyn. That kid was a stunner. But Kim was an attractive woman, who just looked like she was on the verge of giving up.

"Are you and Eddie on the same phone plan?" he asked.

"The same plan?" she said, squinting like she was trying to put the question into focus.

"Yeah," he said. "Do you share the same iCloud?"

She shook her head. "I don't know, Leo. Eddie and I aren't great with tech stuff."

He reached out his hand, and she knew to take her phone out of her purse and give it to him. Some people were reluctant to hand over a phone. Kim was not. That was a good sign. She was going to be easy to work with. "Password?" he said.

She gave it to him without hesitation, and he was in and looking at settings.

"Good news," he said. "This could be easy."

"Oh, good," she said but looked a little scared about what he might find.

"But I need to keep the phone overnight," he said. "I have a lot of work to do."

"Oh," she said, not as enthusiastic.

"Do you have a reason you can tell Eddie that you don't have your phone?"

"Um," she said, and her eyes wandered up to the ceiling. "I guess I can just tell him I left it in my locker at the hospital."

"Well done," he said and placed the phone next to his little notebook. Her dad always worked with legal pads, but Leo liked little notebooks that he could fit in his jacket pocket or throw nonchalantly down a sewer if he had to.

She was quiet now and glanced once at her phone before saying, "What do you think you'll find?"

"We'll find out who the girl is and if the two of them have a thing," he said. "You'd be surprised what people say on texts."

"What about the sheriff?"

"That might be a little tougher," he said. "But I have other ways of finding out about that turd."

"Leo," she said. "What exactly do you do for my dad?"

"What did he tell you I do?"

"I think he once told me and Marilyn that you're a private investigator."

"That'll work," he said.

She smiled. And she actually was a truly lovely young woman when she smiled. "But really," she said.

In order to get an investigator's license in California, a person needs to work for another private investigator for three years. When Leo was younger, it might have been a good idea to get the experience and get certified, but once he'd been working for Bill for a while, it didn't really seem necessary. In fact, as the years went by, it ended up being better that he never got the license. He didn't have a license to carry a handgun, either.

"I'm a ghost," he said just to see how she'd react.

"What does that mean?"

126

"Try to google me," he said.

"You have my phone," she said.

"Not right now," he said. "I'm just trying to make a point that you won't find me."

"That's amazing," she said.

"Thank you."

"Can I ask a personal question?" she said.

"Fire away."

"Did my father want you to be …." She let the words trail off and looked up at the ceiling again, kind of cute. Like a little kid.

"What?" he said.

"Did my dad want you to be a ghost? Are you doing this for him?"

Bill never asked Leo to live his life this way, but it became almost mandatory after a while. No address. No driver's license or registered car. No registered guns. He had fake documents in case he needed them, but he hadn't so far. Not once in over twenty years. It would have been nice to have a credit card and a house and his savings in a bank, but that just wasn't in the cards for him now. He was a cash guy, like most people were just one generation before him. So, it was fine for him. He made it work.

"No," he said. "Your dad never asked me to live this way."

"But he likes that you do," she said.

"There are some good aspects to the life," he said but couldn't think of any offhand.

"I'll bet," she said, but he couldn't tell if she was being sarcastic or not.

"It has made my job much easier," he said.

"Private investigator," she said.

"We can go with that, sure."

"But you're really something else that I probably shouldn't know about." She was making statements like this, but they sounded like questions, and she'd raise her eyebrows when she was done. Looking very lovely with the sideways smile now.

"You ever heard of the term *rat-fucker*?" he said.

## 28

Al Young was sitting in his office at the Custody Operations Division. He was finishing off his second apple fritter of the morning and had just gotten to his coffee when he saw the text from Brianna Hines, a nice-looking piece of ass whom he'd helped out a few years back and continued to see intermittently during the subsequent years whenever Brianna wanted something. He'd first met her when she was working in County Jail #2 on 7th Street, the only jail that housed men *and* women. He was helping out with transport that day, bringing them a meth addict who'd killed two women in a hit and run at the end of Market. It was a high-profile case because the new DA had let this scumbag out on parole a week before, even though the dude was a three strikes felon with an incurable drug habit and a penchant for stealing cars and driving them into people.

When Al had walked into the lobby that day, he saw Brianna Hines leaning against a doorframe with her hip cocked like a gun.

She had long eyelashes, and he could tell she was curvy even in her boxy sheriff's uniform. "Get me out of here," she'd said to him earlier that day, and he thought she just meant at that particular moment, so he asked her to lunch. But she really wanted out of her current job and thought Al must have some pull in the department because he was in charge that day.

And she was right.

He knew people who knew people. He'd played the brown nose game for years and done some nasty favors for dudes who'd risen in the ranks. Around the department, folks understood that he was a man who could make things happen. Three months after their initial meeting, Al and Brianna were banging fairly regularly, and Al had found Brianna a cushy job as a bailiff for a seventy-five-year-old judge, who gave her expensive Christmas gifts.

But now, a few years later, she wanted more. Al was a division commander, and Brianna wanted a captain's position at the Projects and Planning Division. She'd only been in the department for six years, and he'd told her it was a longshot, but she thought he'd be able to pull enough strings to get her that spot. She should have known that it didn't work that way. The bailiff position was one thing, but captain was a big deal. He simply didn't have the kind of magic required to levitate someone to captain. Too many experienced sheriffs wanted that job, and Brianna simply didn't have the experience or the skills.

But he never fully explained that to her. He enjoyed the attention she'd been giving him during her ambitious stage, and there was a chance he led her to believe that she could land the job if the two of them remained *good friends*. But last week the announcement was made that Margie Watson would be the next captain. Margie had been in the department for seventeen years, and she'd been in Projects and Planning for five. She was white and had all the charm of a side zip tactical boot, but she was the right person for the job. She'd earned it.

Brianna didn't see it that way, and Al was sure she wanted to discuss the matter. He figured the affair was probably over, but he'd enjoyed it while it lasted. He thought back fondly to their last rendezvous just a couple of weeks before. They'd gotten it on in a parking lot, then again in an elevator, before hitting the trifecta in the janitor's closet of an office building.

Her text today was simple: *We gotta talk.*

He tried to smile at her when he walked into Wrecking Ball Coffee on Union and slid into the booth across from her. It was almost eleven o'clock, so the morning crowd was gone. There was one other couple though, so at least Brianna wouldn't be able to raise her voice.

She was wearing a blond wig these days. He didn't like that look on all sisters, but Brie could pull it off. She was a sexy woman. She must have had the day off today because she was wearing a tight-fitting skirt that looked like it was made out of jersey material, and she had a simple, white V-neck t-shirt. A gold chain with a locket was gently swinging just above the point of the V, as if it were peeking down at her cleavage with each pendulous movement. She already had a large cup of coffee that she was holding with both hands.

"Do you want something?" she asked.

"I'm good," he said, settling in, wondering what she'd throw for her first pitch. Knowing Brianna, he expected a fast ball, high and tight. That she'd get right to it, complain about Margie getting the captain's job, protest that he didn't help her enough with the written test, even though he'd given her most of the questions in advance. He could have lost his job for that. It had happened to some dudes in the fire department a few years back. People took that shit seriously.

So, he was ready for the high hard one, but she floated him a first-pitch curveball that put him back on his heels. "Do you know Rick Cardenas?" she asked.

Al knew Rick. He was an attorney who'd messed around in the city's criminal justice system for a long time. He was a slick dresser, one of the first guys to stop wearing a tie and socks. A lot of people thought he might be gay because he was a good-looking guy, still single in his forties, and liked the finer things a bit too much. Al thought the man was straight. Al had caught Rick's eyes lingering on tight slacked female defense attorneys sashaying in front of juries.

"I know Rick," he said, no idea where this might be going.

"I explained to him our situation," she said.

Al had no idea what situation she was talking about: that he'd helped her get the bailiff's job; that he'd tried to help her get the captain's job; or that they were screwing? He wanted to take a sip of coffee to buy himself some time to figure out how to play this, but he'd turned down the offer. His stomach was churning from the apple fritters. "Not sure why you'd involve anyone in our private matters," he said, and he heard the uncertainty in his own voice.

"Insurance," she said.

She was throwing more junk at him, trying to get him to swing at something out of the strike zone, but he was going to wait for the fastball. "Insurance for what?" he said and liked the sound of his voice, cooler now, more confident of his position.

She grinned at him and took a sip of her coffee. Her long, painted fingernails shimmered in the artificial light of the coffee shop. "Al," she said and laughed a bit. "You've made me some promises."

"I believe I promised to try to help you," he said.

"When a fierce woman like me lets a man like you balance that fat gut on her back, it's not so that you'll *try*, Al." She was shaking her head now. "You knew that."

"What else could I do," he said. "You wanted a job that was out of my range." He'd lost his confidence. As she continued to throw breaking balls, he couldn't get balanced, and he heard the cool run out of his voice again.

"But you didn't tell me it was out of your range, did you, Al?"

A couple of cops walked into the shop and nodded at Al. He nodded back and then turned his eyes to Brianna. "I said I'd try," he said and folded his hands in front of him on the table, preparing to be patient and not budge on this important aspect of their relationship.

"So, when your sweaty self was rubbing all over me, you thought I was allowing that because you were going to *try*?"

"We can do this all day," he said, feeling better now that she'd gone back to the same pitch twice in a row.

"And the slobbering all over my chest?" she said. "You thought *trying* was enough to let you desecrate this temple?" She sat up straight so that he could take it all in.

"I seem to remember you having a pretty good time," he said but was now considering the possibility that it was all an act.

"Shit," she said and let the word drag out a bit. She was smiling again. "You really do believe you're something."

"What does Rick Cardenas have to do with any of this?"

She raised her eyebrows and pursed her lips like she was in a high school musical about to break into song. "Rick gave me some good advice," she said. "He told me to take out an insurance policy on you, so I did." She closed her eyes for a moment before opening them wide. "I did it, Al."

Al felt that he was about to get screwed, but he still didn't know how. "I'm getting ready to leave," he said. "So, if you're going to make your play, you might as well get to it." He just wanted her to throw the fastball and get it over with even if it was right at his head.

"Oh, listen to himself?" she said and laughed again, enjoying this. "Well, here it is. I got video of you and me, and it's going to cost you fifty grand to get it back."

Al knew the hard stuff was coming, but he still felt unprepared. He let himself slip into a half-coma with his eyes glazed over. It must have been some kind of defense mechanism. And it was working. If he didn't do it, he might have slapped Brianna in public, but that would have added to his troubles.

"Rick says that's a fair number," she said. "But I'll let him work it out with you. And please don't try to mess with me, or I'll end you, Al. This video is ready to go out to the right people, get you fired faster than you can get your dick back in your pants."

## 29

Once Leo got possession of Kim's phone and the shared iCloud, it was easy to figure out what was going on. In short, Leo found out that Eddie was an asshole.

Leo felt like he was breaking Kim's trust by bringing the information to Bill first, but that was the deal. Bill wanted to control the process like he always did, and Leo did as he was told. He liked Kim a lot, thought she'd grown up real nice, but Bill Tracy was the maestro. Bill was going to compose the bridge and, Leo assumed, the coda, in the Eddie and Kimberly Bilker sonata.

A few minutes prior to four o'clock, Leo showed up at Bill's place in the Presidio just as requested. He knocked on the door, but there was no answer, so he walked around back. Bill had a small porch that looked northwest. There was a gap between two massive eucalyptus trees through which there was a decent view of the north tower of the Golden Gate Bridge. Bill was sitting in a rusted wrought iron patio chair looking up at the tower. There was a second chair and a small table, all rusted. A bottle of Jim Beam was on the table, and there were two glasses. The one closest to Bill Tracy contained about two fingers of bourbon.

"We meeting out here?" said Leo as he stepped up onto the porch.

Bill kept looking up at the tower. "I thought it'd be nice," he said.

Wisps of fog were blustering through the golden gate, but the back porch was somewhat fortified by the density of the trees and the angle in which it was built, so Leo sat down and poured himself a drink. This was how Bill liked to work. Leo would take his time with the booze, but Bill didn't know how. He simply wasn't wired that way. He'd be very sharp at the beginning of one of their strategizing sessions. About midway through, he'd be brilliant—creative—and by the end, he was either useless and angry or useless and happy. Either way, Leo knew the drill.

"So, what do you have?" said Bill, finally looking away from the bridge and meeting Leo's eyes.

"You never really liked Eddie much."

"No," he said. "Not much."

"Good instincts," said Leo. "I don't think he's much good for Kimberly."

"What do you got?" he said again.

"Well, there's a few things," he said and took a swallow of his drink. Despite the protection against the wind, it was still pretty cold, and Leo hoped the bourbon might take away some of the bite.

"I thought there might," said Bill. "Is he cheating on her?"

"He is," said Leo and watched Bill finish his drink and pour himself another. In the beginning, he used to refill Leo's every time he refreshed his own, but Leo told him he'd have to resign if he tried to keep up with Bill every time there was a bottle at a meeting, and there was almost always a bottle at the meetings. So, Bill filled only his own glass now.

"Is it serious?" he asked.

"Hard to tell," said Bill. "The gal's a real beauty, looks a little like Raquel Welch."

Bill exhaled out of his nose and said, "And Kim doesn't look like Raquel Welch."

"Kim's a good-looking gal," said Leo, not liking Bill's attitude toward his own daughter. "It's just that this woman looks like a movie star."

"And Kim has seen the woman?"

"She has."

"Ah, Leo," he said. "She must be devastated."

"She seemed okay when I met with her," he said. "But I think she might be worried about her age and being alone and her current joint finances ...." He made himself stop talking. It was starting to sound like he'd had a therapy session with Kim, and that's not how it went. But she was in a tough spot now.

"What do you know about this woman?" asked Bill. "If she looks like a movie star, what the hell is she doing with Eddie Bilker?"

"That's the thing," said Leo. "I think she might be trying to swindle the kid."

"Leo," said Bill. "Eddie doesn't have anything except that stupid car and the house. Why do you think she's trying to play him?"

"He might have fooled her into thinking he was loaded," said Leo.

"Anything else? Asked Bill

"I followed her."

"To where?"

"Club Vulpe."

Bill finished his drink and poured himself another one. Then he met Leo's eyes before breaking tradition and topping him off. Leo didn't object. He knew this was serious.

"So, you know who those people are?" asked Bill.

"I know who they are," he said.

Bill stood up and stretched his legs. He high stepped in place without putting down his drink. Then he took a sip and leaned forward to stretch his calves. He held the position like a man about to start a foot race, making sure to keep his back heel on the deck. Despite his nimble pose, he was still able to take a sip of his drink by pointing his chin upward. Then he switched legs and did the same thing. This time he waited until he'd straightened out before finishing off another bourbon.

"I've dealt with a lot of tough groups in this city," he said and then paused. "Chinatown syndicates, Mission District desperados, Irish developers … Geary Boulevard Russians." He stopped again, and Bill thought he might transition into some more drunk yoga or pour another drink, but he didn't. He looked out toward the bridge which was obscured by fog now. "These folks from the Vulpe," he said. "They're different."

"How do you mean?" said Leo, shivering a bit now, assuming it was from the cold and not Bill's drama about the gypsies.

Bill looked over at Leo and said, "Let's get inside. You look cold."

The inside of the house was warm. The heat was cranked up, and the front room was dimly lit. No matter what time of day, Bill's house always felt like a restaurant lounge. Bill was holding both the bottle and his glass now when he dropped into his chair. "What were you saying?" he said to Leo.

"You were talking about the Vulpe people," he said, putting his glass on the coffee table and sprawling onto the couch—starting to feel the bourbon now that he was inside.

"That's funny phrasing," he said. "You know what Vulpe means in Romanian?" He looked like he was excited to share some trivia.

"I do not," said Leo, feeling the warmth come into his cheeks.

"It means wolf," he said.

"Club Wolf?" said Leo. "Wolf club? Wolf people."

"It doesn't matter which way you say it," he said, leaning forward so his eyes looked polished now that his face was directly in the lamp light. "It's a misnomer no matter how you say it."

"What do you mean?"

"They're not wolf people, Leo."

Leo didn't say anything. He thought Bill might have transitioned into the next stage of intoxication during which he would vacillate between poetry and nonsense.

"Vulpe is a delusion of grandeur," he said.

Leo was trying to keep up. He didn't know whether Bill was going to start a stanza or just hurl some drunken baloney. When they were younger, and he'd get like this, a retired Irish mayor used to say that Bill was from County Gibbereen, holding forth in the language of his people—gibberish.

But Bill hadn't gotten to that point yet, so Leo was waiting for something more profound. "Why is it a delusion of grandeur, Bill?"

"Because these people aren't wolves," he said. "Wolves are proud animals, apex predators. The gypsies are coyotes. Coyotes are scavengers."

"Got it," said Leo.

"Coyotes prey on the weak," he howled from his chair, leaning back in the shadows now.

"Yeah," said Leo. "I've heard stories about 'em."

"Old people, lonely people, sick people," he said. "That's who they go for. It's in their playbook."

"So, what the hell do they want with Eddie?"

"I thought you were supposed to tell me," said Bill. "Unless they've added idiots to their playbook, it doesn't make sense to go after Eddie."

"Yeah," he said. "I'm still working on that."

Bill nodded, which meant that Leo was supposed to keep investigating. Then he leaned back and said, "My daughter described to me a sheriff that sounded a lot like Al Young." When he said the name, he made a face like he'd just coughed up some bile. "Is Eddie involved with Al Young?"

"He is," said Leo.

"How?"

"Bill," said Leo. "I'm pretty sure that Eddie's a two-bit bookie and that he owes Al a lot of money."

"Well, son of bitch," said Bill as he professionally swirled the last few sips in his glass. "I don't think we should be trying to help Kimberly salvage this marriage. I don't want this asswipe anywhere near my daughter."

Leo agreed. "So, what's next?"

"What's next?" Bill said after a moment, his eyes glossy again in the lamplight. "That's the question."

"That *is* the question."

"What's next?"

"Yep," said Leo. "What do we want to do with this information?"

"Just fix it," he said.

## 30

Angie was sitting in the back seat listening to Derek and Alex argue about how to approach Cristian in regard to the situation with Carl. She knew the best play was to wait it out, but in the meantime, she didn't mind watching these two clowns make fools of themselves in front of Cristian.

They were parked across the street from Vulpe. The windows of the SUV were closed, but she could smell exotic cooking wafting in from the middle eastern restaurant about two storefronts down. She couldn't tell if she was imagining it, but she thought she could also smell the hint of urine mixed in with the Persian spices as she watched a homeless guy pause in front of a thrift shop before pushing his shopping cart in the direction of the other smells.

She tuned out the brothers and gazed at the people waiting in line at the check cashing place. They were in the shadow of a palm tree, under which it looked like hundreds of people had used the tree bed as an enormous ashtray, cigarette butts overflowing onto the sidewalk.

She couldn't help wondering what got people to the point that they would pay the enormous fees to these places just to cash checks. What had they done in their lives that they couldn't just use banks like everyone else?

Angie had no illusions about who she was. In fact, she knew she probably had some things in common with the raggedy bunch standing in line to use the services of Tico's Money Mart. These people cashing their checks and applying for payday loans had probably lived lives more akin to hers than to the people with whom she identified—folks like Eddie and his wife, and Carl, and the people who have lunch at Mission Rock.

Deep down, she knew she wasn't really like the normals, who had direct deposit and got meals delivered from Blue Apron and planted succulent gardens in their backyards. When she got to Italy, she'd be like them, but until then, she was going to have to go along with this life and make The Organization believe she had no other aspirations.

"So, are we all on the same page?" she heard Derek say from the driver's seat. He was looking at her in the rearview mirror.

"Good to go," she said.

***

The three of them walked up to the bar and stood for a moment before Angie stepped toward the stools. Derek hissed at her and shook his head. So, the three of them stood in the middle of the bar and waited for Cristian.

"Why can't I sit," said Angie.

"Respect," said Alex, frowning at her and standing with his chest out as if he were waiting for the president or the Pope to walk in.

"Before I met you guys," she said, "I'd sit down and wait for Cristian. There was never an issue."

Derek said, "Well, now you've learned something."

"About what?" she said, leaning on Derek for a moment to fix the strap on her shoe.

"About respect," said Alex.

"Do you ever say anything else?" she said.

Alex ignored her and continued to stare at the hallway. His profile was an exact replica of his brother's.

"Today's meeting is serious," said Derek. "No wise-ass remarks. I don't want Cristian to have any reason to have doubts about our ability to serve The Organization."

Angie smiled. She knew Derek was talking to her because Alex was incapable of a wise-ass remark. "All business today," said Angie and winked at Alex.

"I'm serious," said Derek, who grabbed her elbow and squeezed hard.

She pulled her arm away and said, "Or what? You'll throw me on the floor?"

Derek took a step toward her but stopped quickly and turned his head toward the hallway, where Cristian was shuffling toward the bar in his baggy pants and loafers.

When he got close, he took a pair of glasses out of his shirt pocket and said, "Let me get a look at you all," as he secured the temple tips behind his ears. "You two with the nice suits and the haircuts, and you," he said and took a long look at Angie starting with her feet and moving slowly all the way up to her eyes.

He was probably around Carl's age, but when Carl looked at her like this, it didn't give her the creeps. When Carl did it, he was playful, like a ten-year-old boy with a Playboy Magazine. It was fun.

When Cristian did it, Angie felt like there were worms in her veins.

"Okay," he said. "I need to speak with you in my office." He put his hand gently on the small of her back and guided her toward the hallway from which he'd entered. Angie could hear Derek and Alex following before Cristian turned his head and said, "Not you two."

Angie didn't turn, and she tried to stay calm, but she also knew the scope of The Organization, and small jolts of anxiety knocked at her chest in time to the beating of her heart. Logic was telling her that there was no way anyone could know her plans, but the feeling of this man's hand on her back was affecting her whole biology.

\*\*\*

The office was as she'd expected. Beautiful pieces of ornate furniture and built-in bookcases behind him filled with old books, foreign-looking curios, and small wooden boxes with etchings on the lids.

Cristian didn't sit in his desk chair.

He adjusted the two guest chairs that had originally been facing his desk. Now they were turned toward each other with only a narrow lane between them. Cristian pointed to one of the chairs and allowed Angie to squeeze in. Then he took the other chair.

Angie was wearing a loose-fitting jumpsuit, and she could feel the cuffs of her pants touching Cristian's. She almost looked down. Her instinct was to push the chair back a bit to create some space, but she fought it off, smiling and keeping eye contact.

"Thank you for being here," he said. "Your work for us so far has been commendable."

"Thank you," she said, trying to make the smile look natural, unforced.

"The proceeds from the house in St. Francis Wood," he continued, "will allow us more flexibility with our other investments. In short, we will be able to grow our business."

Angie nodded.

"Your work with the owner, Carl … is it?

"Yes," she said.

"Astonishing."

"Thank you."

"The two boys out there. Which one are you married to, the shaved head or the greaser?"

"Shaved head," she said and felt her smile wilt for a split second before she revived it for Cristian, the man who'd orchestrated this union but didn't even seem to know who he'd forced her to live with.

"Yes," he said. "Derek. Of course."

She nodded but offered only a tight-lipped smile now. She didn't want to come off as phony. This guy was probably an expert at unmasking frauds.

"The boys out there are suggesting that we should accelerate the timeline on the house deal with your man, Carl," he said, no expression. "Do you have an opinion on this?"

"I do," she said and waited for Cristian's demeanor to give her something to work with. But it was as if he'd executed a hard shutdown, and she was looking at a blank screen. So, she didn't expand on her response right away.

"Please share," he said, still with nothing more than the gravelly voice and the cold probing eyes.

"I do as I'm told," she said, and she could hear just the hint of fear around the edges of her voice. She felt like she wanted to clear her throat but thought that might be a giveaway. She was also aware that she'd stopped smiling.

"I appreciate that," said Cristian. "But you know this man better than the brothers. You've been intimate with him?"

"Yes," she said without hesitation.

"Then, please," he said, "disclose your honest opinion on this very important matter. No harm will come to you for voicing your opinion. I consider you as an equal to the brothers." He gestured with his head in the general direction of the bar.

It felt like a trap to Angie. A loyalty test. But she didn't know whether Cristian was testing her loyalty to him or her loyalty to Derek. Too much hesitation was not going to help her cause, so she just said it. "Carl has a son and a daughter, and they both have kids of their own. They live out of state."

Cristian's lips were parted slightly, but his breathing was steady. His posture hadn't changed. And she knew she'd never get anything from his eyes.

So, she kept going. "But they're still very close to Carl. They talk on the phone a couple of times a week."

"Yes," he said.

"If Carl dies under suspicious circumstances," she said, "and the family sees my name in the will as the recipient of this incredibly valuable piece of property—their family home—people are going to be suspicious. There will be an investigation. I will be under the microscope, which means The Organization will be under the microscope." She thought she saw the light turn on behind his eyes, but she still wasn't sure if she was passing the test. "And I don't think it helps any of us if we have investigators sniffing around."

Cristian nodded once, his chin pausing at his chest before he looked back up and smiled. "You're right, my dear," he said and leaned forward. "Even if this man lives another six months with his stage four cancer, this house is worth the wait."

She tried smiling again and nodded back, hoping to look professional.

He laughed suddenly and gripped her knees with both hands, not violently. This felt more like a coach trying to motivate a player. "Are you willing to put in the work if this goes on for six more months?" he said.

"Of course," she said and liked the confidence in her voice. She knew it was authentic because she was, indeed, willing to put in the time with Carl. She needed that house. She needed Italy.

Cristian's grip loosened, and she felt his hands open and slide to the insides of her knees. She felt her stomach tighten, but she didn't want to flinch. This was important. Maybe another test. His hands slid up slightly to her inner thighs, and his eyes stayed with her.

She thought she could feel the pressure from his pinkies farther up now, and she knew his hands were pushing outward. There was a second when she felt her muscles instinctually contract against the pressure even though she knew that was the wrong move.

When she was a child, she was prone to temper tantrums. Her dad had no patience for that kind of behavior, but her mom had a soothing voice and was always able to calm Angie down. "Be spaghetti," her mom would say. And Angie would release all the tension in her body. She would loosen the muscles in her limbs and slow her breathing, and her problems would lift like steam from her body, and everything would be right.

*Be spaghetti,* she thought to herself and allowed her legs to butterfly. She even slouched a bit in the chair and closed her eyes. But then as quickly as it had started, it was over. Cristian tapped her knees lightly and said, "Okay, we'll go tell those boys the strategy to be employed with the St. Francis Wood property."

\*\*\*

When Angie and Cristian got back out to the bar, Derek and Alex were still standing about halfway between the barstools and the cocktail tables—almost the exact center of the lounge.

"Twenty chairs and fifteen stools in this bar," said Cristian, "and these two gentlemen choose to stand."

Angie laughed. "Maybe they don't want to wrinkle their suits."

## 31

It had been less than forty-eight hours, but Kim received an email from Leo this morning to let her know that he had the information from the cloud and that she should come by to get her phone back and see his report. Although some parts of the country were in a panic over the virus, UCSF was still slow and overstaffed, so Kim asked her supervisor if she could cut out early, and she drove over to The Marina to check in with Leo.

The apartment looked cleaner this time when Leo let her in. Nothing drastic, just a general tidiness. And Leo looked put together as well. He'd shaved, and his hair was combed and still damp from a shower. She thought she might have smelled the hint of cologne, but it could have just been the smell of the shampoo, still drifting out of the bathroom with the last of the steam.

As soon as she sat down, he handed her the phone and said, "Your guy's been involved in quite a bit of shenanigans." He was frowning and, with his index finger, tapping a file folder on his desk. "I don't know how much of it you're aware of."

"Start with the girl from the restaurant," she said and was a bit surprised with the assertiveness in her voice. She'd known Leo Callaghan since she was little, when he was in his early twenties, but she wasn't so familiar with him that she should be barking out commands. "Sorry," she said. "You can start wherever you want, Leo. I'm a little jumpy. This is sort of a lot for me."

"I know it, Kim," he said, taking off his reading glasses. "Just hang in there. I'll take you through the whole thing." They were sitting across the desk from each other. Leo had looked all business at first, holding the file in his hands and directing her to the chair. But now there was something more personal going on. She knew Leo loved her dad and maybe that love embraced the whole family. Maybe he worked to protect not only Bill Tracy but also Kim and Marilyn.

He was holding eye contact beyond the normal duration. Like he was trying to convey to her that she wasn't alone. Or that he wanted assurance that he wasn't alone, that the two of them were connected in this moment and that he could be trusted.

Then she realized that she also wasn't breaking eye contact. It wasn't uncomfortable. It was just strange to her in this setting, and she felt like she was acting as a willing contributor to the strangeness—not *staring* back, but holding his gaze, content with the intimacy of the moment. Finally, she said, "Okay. I'm ready."

Going along with what she'd requested, Leo started with the girl. Her name was Angelica or Angie. Kim learned that in addition to Eddie's cheating, his slut was actually a member of a crime syndicate. Leo didn't know whether or not Eddie was aware of her affiliations or if Eddie was, indeed, a prospective chump in one this woman's scams.

Kim couldn't imagine that a woman who looked like Angie would be interested in Eddie unless she was trying to get something out of him. But Eddie didn't have anything. Kim imagined Angie stealing his stupid car, and it gave her momentary pleasure.

Then Leo took her through Eddie's interactions with Al Young. Even though Al was a law enforcement officer, he was not averse to any of a variety of petty crimes and short-term money-grabs. And his most recent grab involved a massive bet on a golf tournament. Kim didn't even know that it was possible to bet on golf, but apparently it was, and the person with whom Al had made the wager was none other than Eddie Bilker.

But that wasn't the worst part. If Eddie had made a single stupid bet like this, she'd be angry with him, but she'd eventually forgive him if he promised to never bet again. But it wasn't just this bet with the sheriff. Leo informed Kim that her husband had been a neighborhood bookie for a couple of years.

"Are you sure?" asked Kim.

"I don't want to make up bad stuff about your man, Kim."

"So, you're sure he's a gambler?"

"I am," he said. "Talked to someone in the know yesterday. I have no doubts about what I'm reporting to you today."

Kim believed him and saw real compassion in his eyes. Heard it in his voice. She was breathing in from her nose and letting the air out slowly through her mouth. It felt like her whole body had a pulse. And it was hot in here. She was also experiencing a slight ringing, a tinnitus, that she'd only had once before, coincidentally, when Leo and her dad had taken her and Marilyn to the shooting range. She hadn't liked the shooting at all even though her dad told her that she needed to learn how to defend herself. And the ringing had lasted hours after they'd used up all the ammunition.

She didn't know why it was happening now. She thought she might be having a panic attack, but she was still able to control her breathing.

"Does he owe anyone else money?" she asked and was thankful that she could still control her voice.

"The good news is no," he said and turned the file folder so that it was facing her. "The bad news is that he owes Al a lot, and your husband has cleaned out your bank account."

She looked down at the bank statement but didn't say anything. The ringing was getting even louder. The number of large withdrawals over the past few weeks was devastating. Most of that money was hers. And the fact that he'd done this all behind her back made her sick.

She dropped the folder on the desk and stood up. Her legs weren't right, and the room felt like it was tilted. She saw a blurry Leo jump up from behind his desk, and she heard him say "Kimmy."

*** 

"How long was I out?" she said when she found herself on the couch looking up at Leo, who was handing her a glass of water.

"Just for a second or two," he said before taking her hand and folding it around the glass.

The ringing was gone, and she didn't feel as hot anymore. The water was room temperature, but it made her feel better. "He took everything we'd saved," she said. "It wasn't a fortune, but I worked my ass off for that money." She thought of all the overtime she'd done while he was driving around in his Porsche doing open houses on Sundays. "What a piece of shit I married," she said and looked over at Leo. He had to be ten years older than Kim, but he was in good shape, and he'd combed his hair for her. And his eyes were beautiful and compassionate.

He put his arm around her and said, "You're too good for him, Kim." Then he paused for a moment and said, "You're too good for all of us. We're a rotten bunch."

Kim leaned into him and began to weep. She felt comfortable with her face against his soft sweater. He was still facing forward. They were sitting side to side, and he pulled her into him. He said nothing. There was nothing more to say.

They stayed that way for a long time. Then without putting much thought into it, she shifted onto her knees. She felt the cushion give a bit, and she put her hands on his cheeks. He looked like he might have been crying, too. And she kissed him, long and soft. But there was an undercurrent of electricity. Something she hadn't felt in years and hadn't expected now.

Once they stopped, she sat back down and faced forward so that they looked like a couple in a movie theater. She tried to figure out if there was something genuine between her and her dad's right-hand man, or if the mere taboo of the kiss and her towering hatred of Eddie had been enough to provide the full-body fluttering she was experiencing now in the silence of Leo's room. There was one thing she was sure of: she would not be calling him Uncle Leo anymore.

But she did feel the need to talk. To have a conversation that had nothing to do with what had just happened. "Last time I was here, I asked about the work you and my dad do. At one point, you used the term *ratfuck*, but we got interrupted, and you never told me what it meant."

"And you're telling me you've never heard that word before?" he asked, still facing forward, looking across his room at his clean desk, only the Eddie file weighing down the blotter.

"I don't know that word," she said, and she didn't like the fact that a word so awful-sounding could be associated with her dad and Leo.

"Donald Segretti?" he said. "Watergate … *All the President's Men* …?"

Kim smiled at Leo and shook her head.

He smiled back and said, "I can't believe they don't teach any of that in school. It's the most interesting part of the history. It's real history." His expression turned more serious. "It's not the glossed over bullshit they put on the plaques under statues. It's what really happens behind the scenes, only these particular guys got caught."

"What guys?" she asked, genuinely interested now. Her whole life she'd lived in the audience with everyone else, and now Leo was showing her what he and her dad had been doing backstage.

"The word was first used back in the 70's when a bunch of punks at USC pulled some dirty shit to influence student body elections," he said.

"Did people really care about who the student body president was?"

"Yeah," he said. "It sounds stupid, but there was some prestige to it especially with Greek life, and these guys were kind of having fun with it."

"So ratfucking became famous because of some pranks pulled by college kids?" she said. "Can you use the word with an *ing* like that?"

"Yes," he said. "Nice usage." He was smiling again. "It didn't get exposed until later when the Republican Party got interested in these guys and actually consulted with them for Nixon's campaign."

"And the dirty tricks these college kids pulled could work at a national level?" she asked. "That seems ridiculous. What did they actually do?"

"They weren't college kids anymore," he said and closed his eyes for a moment. "Forgeries … fake news leaks … anything to cause confusion," he said. "And they were good at it. Masters of chaos."

"And that's what you and my dad do?"

"It's different now," he said. "It's easy to dig up dirt on people, catch 'em in lies or hypocrisy or saying something years ago that you can't say anymore. It's almost too easy."

Kim knew this kind of digging went on, but she never thought about the people with the shovels. Like most citizens, she just saw the dirt on the nightly news and was disgusted by all the "public servants" connected to the graft and bribery and sexual misconduct. They were mostly villains to Kim, but she wondered about her dad.

"So, who are the bad guys in all this?" she said and hoped that she sounded compassionate as she and Leo eyed each other, so close on the couch.

"Bill Tracy is a political consultant," he said, the light in his eyes seemingly dimmed by the statement.

"And what about you, Leo?"

"I told you," he said. "I'm a ghost."

# ~32~

The next day, Kim decided that she would ratfuck Eddie. Nothing big. But enough to let him know they were done.

He was headed to Tahoe for the weekend with a few friends. The casinos were still open but would be shutting down on Sunday night because of a spike in cases up there, so the idiot was going up one more time to see if he could hit the big one. This stupid, stupid man, who had lost all their money, was going gambling. It was hard for her not to stop him and expose him for the colossal moron that he was by telling him that she was aware of the fact that their savings had been drained. When he was talking about the trip, she was wondering whether or not he was really going with buddies, or if he and Angie had weekend plans.

But when she watched him get picked up, she saw in the truck a couple of guys from the bar, so now she knew what she wanted to do. She wanted to meet Angie. In fact, she wanted Angie to be a collaborator in the ratfucking. It wasn't a fully-baked plan yet, but she knew how she wanted things to end up. She just had to put together a few of the steps in between.

She wouldn't have any problem reaching the woman. Leo had given Kim all of his research. So, she decided she was going to call Angie and set up a meeting.

When Angie picked up the phone, she sounded exactly the way Kim imagined she'd sound. She didn't have an accent, but she didn't sound like someone from the neighborhood, either. It sounded like she was talking out of her nose. "Yes?" she said.

"Hi, Angie," said Kim, as if she were calling one of her girlfriends from work.

"Can I help you?"

"Yes," said Kim, strangely elated that she'd be able to deliver the following information: "This is Kim, Eddie's wife."

"I don't know any Eddies," she said, using the only strategy in the playbook for this situation.

"I found all the texts, Angie," said Kim. "Eddie's a piece of shit, but I don't have any beef with you. I just want to talk to you."

"Talk," said Angie.

"You know how some girls get furious with the sluts who sleep with their husbands?"

Angie didn't reply.

"Well, I'm not like that," said Kim. "I'm only mad at the jerk who took a vow to be faithful to me. You never did that, so, again, I have no animosity toward you."

"Okay," said Angie.

"Can I ask you to do me just one favor?" she said. There was really more than one favor, but this was the important one. "Can you not tell Eddie that I know yet?"

"Why?" said Angie.

"Here's the thing," said Kim. "I'm gonna leave him. Obviously, that's the best thing for both of us, but I want to do it my way, and I want to protect myself. He's already blown our savings, so there's no money left, but I just want to come out on the other side with some dignity."

"Why do I want to help you?" said Angie. "I don't know you."

"I totally get that," said Kim. "And I'm not going to pitch you some *women unite* slogan. But I do have something valuable that I'd like to sign over to you. I promise you it will be worth your while, and you can keep it or sell it. Whatever you want. You just can't tell Eddie that I know yet. Just for another few days. Can you do that?"

There was a long silence, and then Angie said, "Why don't you just tell me what you have for me?"

"No," said Kim. "I want you to come over and see it. And if you don't want it, you can call Eddie right there from my house and tell him that I know."

Again, a long silence. Kim wasn't even sure why she wasn't just telling Angie that she was going to give Angie the Porsche. In fact, she wasn't sure why she was giving Angie the Porsche in the first place. She wanted Eddie to suffer, and, for some reason, she thought it would be funny if his former lover—there was no way she was staying with him—was driving around in his car. Kim could picture Eddie putting gas in a used Mazda and then seeing Angie driving by in the Porsche. Maybe she's wearing a brightly colored scarf that's blowing out the window, and that's what catches his eye.

The scene began to fade, and the silence had gone on for too long, so Kim was just going to tell her about the Porsche, but Angie broke the silence.

"I can come by the house in the morning," she said. "Eddie won't be home, right?"

"No," she said. "He's not due back until the afternoon."

"Okay," said Angie.

"We live at—"

"I know where you live," said Angie and then hung up.

Kim felt weird. She couldn't give away the car. She and Eddie were basically out of assets. They needed the car. She was realizing now that she was acting impulsively, and she wasn't an impulsive person, so she wasn't very good at it. She had friends who made thoughtless decisions all the time and ended up fine, but she wasn't one of those girls. She was organized. She was a planner. Maybe she just wanted to meet this woman face-to-face and see if she knew where all the money went. There was a chance that Angie could shed some light on what was going on with Eddie and the sheriff, and she figured she was going to take a crack at it.

The problem was that this woman had some kind of connection to organized crime, and now Kim had invited her over to the house. Kim wasn't just scared. She was terrified. She wondered whether Angie might love Eddie and want to come over to dispose of Kim and get on with her life.

She wished she had a gun, and she considered calling Leo to see if she could borrow one of his, but he would come over and make her stop the whole meeting. He would tell her to leave it alone for a day until he could figure out what to do. But she wanted to try her hand at ratfucking even though she had no idea what she was doing.

She did have one option in terms of self-defense. Michael Duffy had a gun at his house. Marilyn had once shown Kim where he kept his off-duty gun. Kim and Marilyn were both afraid of it. But she could picture the spot in her mind. It was in their bedroom in some kind of holster that clipped onto the underside of his nightstand.

Kim knew Michael and Marilyn were eating dinner over at her dad's house tonight. She'd declined the offer. Didn't really want to see anyone. Maybe Leo. Oh, not Leo either. They'd had their fun this afternoon.

But Kim did have a key to Marilyn's house. She was going to drive down and get that gun. She knew how bad she was at being impulsive, but she'd already made the mistake of inviting a crime princess over to her house, so Kim was going to make sure she had protection. She wasn't even going to load it. She just wanted to maybe wave it at Angie if Angie started to act like a tough girl.

And what was she going to tell Angie she had for her? That was the promise. That Kim had something valuable to give this woman. She guessed she could offer her a glass of chardonnay.

Kim had been in Marilyn's house many times, but there were always other people and lots of distractions. This evening was different. She was alone, not just in this house, but in life. She, of course, had Marilyn and her dad, but her dreams of a life with Eddie and kids and growing old together were gone.

The quiet of the house seemed to stimulate these thoughts. The Great Highway had sparse traffic, so the uniform repetition of the waves crashing on the beach across the street were the only sounds. She had planned to run in, grab the gun, and get out, but the house was peaceful.

Marilyn and Michael didn't have nice stuff, but everything was clean. Kim walked around the living room, running her hand along tables, and mantles, and chairs. There didn't seem to be any sharp edges in Marilyn's house. Everything seemed to have been rubbed smooth, like the wind had swept in off the Pacific and softened everything into the texture of sea glass or driftwood or old bones.

The walls were covered in paintings and prints and photos of palm trees, tiki huts, and surfers. Marilyn and Michael admitted that neither of them was very good at the sport, but they both loved it. They enjoyed the weird camaraderie with folks from all walks of life. One time on an unseasonably warm day, Kim had watched from the window as a guy in a business suit and another guy in a UPS uniform stripped down next to their cars and then squeezed into their wetsuits. Right there on the sidewalk in front of the house. When Kim called Marilyn to see the show, it turned out that Marilyn knew both of these guys. Regulars.

Kim decided she was going to ask Marilyn for a lesson.

Then she walked back into the bedroom, got down on her knees on Michael's side of the bed, and reached under the nightstand.

## 33

Angie was going to play this cool.

Eddie had promised her that he already had a buyer and that they'd be able to sell the house without listing it. She needed that to happen immediately after ownership had been transferred to her. There was going to be a very small window of time during which she had the deed and could keep that information from Cristian. Once he knew she owned the house, it was over. She could kiss Italy goodbye.

But Eddie was her ticket to getting this done, and he stood to get a nice commission if he could sell it quickly and covertly. If Cristian found out that ownership had been transferred to her, he would use The Organization's realtor, who would oversee everything. At that point, her take on the deal would shrink to about five percent.

She simply wasn't willing to let that happen. But if Eddie's wife — this Kimberly — gummed up the gears, it could be ruined for everyone. So, Angie would attempt to charm her. She knew it wouldn't be nearly as easy as it was with men because Kimberly wasn't going to be interested in her tits. So, she was going to have to be friendly and understanding. Perhaps a shoulder to cry on. That wasn't really in her nature, but she could play that role if she had to.

The Uber driver dropped her in front of the house, and Angie admired the flower boxes under the windows and a colorful bougainvillea that climbed a trellis up the stucco between the front steps and garage door. She planned to have a garden at her villa. Depending on the amount of profit she would make on the sale of Carl's house, she probably wouldn't have to work, so she'd need something to keep her busy. A garden seemed nice to her. Peaceful.

Before Angie got to the top step, the woman was opening the door. "Come in," she said and stood to the side as Angie walked past her and then waited to see which room Kim would choose to begin the match, for which Angie didn't know the rules yet.

Angie had seen Kim once before. Kim had been walking out of a Walgreens on Parnassus Street, and Eddie pushed Angie's head down as they drove past her near the hospital. Angie had only gotten a quick glimpse of her in scrubs walking out of the store and scowling at the traffic. She looked different today. A pleasant looking woman in jeans, a sweater, and flip-flops.

She pointed to the living room, so Angie went in and sat on the loveseat.

Kim sat in a chair and looked at Angie with expectant eyes, as if Angie was supposed to start the conversation. Angie tried to say with her face, *Well, here we are,* but she wasn't sure how she was coming off. She didn't want to look cocky. She didn't want Kim to think that Angie felt she was superior because she'd stolen the woman's husband. Finally, she said, "I'm so sorry," but didn't know where to go from there.

Kim nodded. "For breaking up my marriage?" she said, no attitude, like a teacher trying to cajole an obvious answer out of one of the slower kids.

But Angie remembered the earlier conversation, how Kim didn't blame her. That Eddie was the one who broke a vow. "Well," said Angie. "I guess I'm sorry that it's come to this."

Angie thought she saw the hint of a smile at the corner of Kim's lips. "Like it was just bad luck?" said Kim. "Like we're all just victims of circumstance?"

Angie wasn't sure how to play this now. Kim didn't seem unhinged, but she did seem very content with this extremely uncomfortable situation. Angie wondered if that was a specific type of unhinged. Maybe Kim was actually enjoying this exchange.

Angie was tough. She'd been in uncomfortable situations before. She'd been in dangerous situations. Just the other night, she'd thought Cristian was going to rape her, but that didn't break her. A couple nights before, Derek assaulted her in her own home. Again, she'd walked away unscathed.

But this moment with Eddie's wife didn't feel right. The woman wasn't trying to intimidate her. Kim was simply trying to make Angie feel bad, and it was working. They were sitting in this little living room with a wedding picture on the consul table and gold candlestick holders on the mantle, and Angie did feel the pang of guilt for playing a role in the demise of this union.

"Look," she said. "I know you mostly hold Eddie responsible for this because he took a vow, and you don't really know me. But I do feel bad that two people who were together don't seem like they are anymore, and I had something to do with it. I feel bad about that." Angie wasn't much of a talker unless she was scamming someone, so this was new territory for her. She was unsettled by it, but she decided to keep going because Kim was nodding and listening. Kim seemed to care about what Angie was saying. "And you seem like a good person," said Angie, "who doesn't really deserve to have someone cheat on her. You're a nurse, right?"

"I am," said Kim, and her voice sounded labored, a closing up of the throat.

"So, you help people ...," said Angie but didn't know where she was going with it and decided to stop.

"And you're a criminal?"

She didn't say it like she was trying to challenge Kim. She sounded inquisitive. She looked like a lady who just wanted some answers. "Not really," said Angie. "I don't break the law. But I have a way of getting people to give me things." She thought that was a fair description of her occupation, and she felt herself nodding afterward, as if she were trying to convince herself. She also wondered where Kim had acquired this information if she hadn't talked to Eddie yet. She couldn't have guessed it.

"So why Eddie?" said Kim. "We don't have anything. What are you trying to trick him into giving you?"

This surprised Angie. She was finally starting to see things through Kim's eyes. Kim thought Angie was not only sleeping with her husband but also trying to con him. "It's not that at all," she said and leaned forward on the loveseat. "I met Eddie at his office. I needed a real estate agent."

"And you went to Eddie?"

"I got a burrito across the street and just walked in," she said. "Eddie's desk is the one closest to the door."

"And that's how all this started..."

"Yeah," said Angie, trying to figure out if this information was making things better or worse. "I just needed someone to help me sell my house."

"Did he sell it yet?"

"It's not really my house yet," she said. "But it will be mine soon, and Eddie already has a buyer. Easy deal. Big commission for you guys." Angie tried a little optimistic bounce at the end of the sentence like she'd heard high school kids do at the mall, consoling a friend over some small emotional injury.

"Use someone else," said Kim, no more hint of a smile playing at the corners of her mouth, as serious as a loaded gun now.

And Angie could feel her own heart rate shift into a new rhythm. "But I kinda need Eddie on this," she said. "We already have it all set up."

"Your relationship with my husband is over," said Kim, standing. Not raising her voice, but the tone was confident.

"I don't think you understand," said Angie. "This deal is not going to happen if we don't handle it the way that Eddie and I have it set up." Kim was shaking her head the whole time Angie was talking. "You'll lose out on tens of thousands of dollars in commission."

"You think I give a shit about money right now?" said Kim.

"Well, I'd give a shit if I were you," said Angie. "If you're going to leave him, at least get some money out of it."

Kim's eyes were open wide now, and the half-smile was back. "I'll show you how little I care about money," she said. "Come with me." She led Angie down to the two-car garage. The Porsche was parked next to a red Jeep. Kim walked over and sat on the Porsche. "I want you to walk away from Eddie, and I'll give you this car," she said. "Right now. You can drive away in it."

Kim was starting to look and sound a little crazy. Angie needed to handle this just right. Kim seemed like she was leaning over the edge of something. Fearless. Angie was holding her purse in front of her with both hands, trying to look meek to avoid any kind of physical altercation. But she knew her face and her voice betrayed her when she said, "I don't want that car."

This seemed to hurt Kim's feelings. "Who are *you*? You're a thief," she said. "But you don't want something for free? You'd prefer to *steal* a car?"

Angie wanted to explain about Carl and the house and Cristian and Italy. She wanted Kim to understand that this whole deal had layers and that Eddie was a part of it. "You don't understand —" she started.

"The hell I don't," said Kim. "*You* don't understand. You seem to want to have your cake and eat it too."

Angie had never understood that expression. Why would someone want to have a cake if she wasn't going to eat it? "If this real estate deal isn't handled exactly right, I'm going to lose the house, and Eddie's going to lose the commission. It's extremely important that Eddie and I execute this plan exactly as we've assembled it. It could happen within the next few weeks. I'll stay away from Eddie except when the papers need to be signed and filed. That's it. I'm done with him except for closing the deal." Angie could feel herself talking with her hands and the blood rushing to her cheeks, but she felt that she was otherwise calm and reasonable. She just needed Kim to be reasonable as well.

Angie had seen people in The Organization take on the same stance as Kim, and it was never beneficial to anyone. These were people who would prefer to punish someone for his or her sin than to accept some form of reparation for the offense. Angie always thought these men were short-sighted — immediate satisfaction rather than deferred gratification. Machismo over pragmatism. They'd later claim they needed to send a message, but, in the end, they always missed out on any kind of benefit for the damage that had been done to them. Except, of course, watching some kind of immediate harm administered to the original instigator. It was heart-over-head nonsense. And Angie just wanted Kim to use her brain here and let things play out so that she could get some or all of Eddie's substantial commission.

But Kim was standing her ground. "I don't give a shit about your house," she said. "In fact, it would make me happy if you both got screwed on the whole deal."

Angie could see this was going nowhere. She reached into her purse to get her phone. It was time to call Uber and get the hell out of here.

"Freeze," she heard Kim say, but she kept digging. "Don't make another move," said Kim.

Angie was still feeling around for her phone when she raised her eyes just in time to see the gun, hear the pop, and feel something snap at her neck. Her ears were ringing, and in her mind, she was trying to say, "What the hell?" but it came out as a gurgled mess. She reached up to where she felt the burning. It was wet. She tried to focus, but Kim was just a blur of moving colors coming at her. "What the hell?" she tried again, but this time it sounded like someone very old trying to clear her throat.

The last thing she heard through the ringing was Kim crying, "You were going for a gun!"

It didn't hurt anymore. She closed her eyes. She saw a still postcard shot of a rocky beach with deep blue water. The bluest water she'd ever seen. And then the still shot started to move, the water lapping up against the shore. The scene opened up to jagged cliffs surrounding the beach, a small bar, perched on the rocks, built into the topography of the cliff overlooking the cove. There was a waiter serving a fancy drink to a woman at one of the small tables. The sound of the water was soothing. The sea was deep blue with glimmers of light, brilliant as they reflected off the tips of the small waves. The blue was dazzling.

## 34

All Kimberly wanted was to feel that she had some control over her life. When Angie got to the house, Kim wanted to put on a performance to show her strength, her power. She knew Angie was involved to some degree in criminal activity, and that was kind of scary, but this was a domestic matter. Angie had intruded into Kim's marriage, and Kim deserved to be in control for a few minutes while she got some answers from Angie and demanded that Angie separate herself from Eddie immediately so that Kim could analyze her marriage without distraction.

And, to Kim, this woman was a distraction. She was beautiful in a way that other women could appreciate. Some beautiful women—usually blondes—could have bitchy faces. Angie did not. She had soft features and almond shaped eyes and tanned skin. She appeared almost shy as she walked past Kim and sat down in the living room.

From the beginning, the conversation never felt right. Angie apologized but didn't look like she meant it. Early on in the conversation, she'd said, "I'm sorry it's come to this." Kim wasn't even sure what that meant. Come to what? And as the conversation continued, it became obvious to Kim that Angie wanted only one thing: to preserve some kind of professional relationship with Eddie. There was a real estate deal from which she apparently stood to collect a substantial amount of money. This meant that Eddie would earn a nice commission. But Kim didn't understand why Angie couldn't just get another agent. Either way, Kim liked the power she was feeling. And she didn't even need Duff's gun to feel that she was somehow in command, that she had some authority over this crime princess. Kim even stood up during the conversation so that she'd be looking down on Angie.

For a moment during the discussion, Angie looked like she was almost desperate. She kept trying to bring up money and how Kim was going to be missing out on a jackpot. But Kim didn't care at this point. She was already planning on starting over. Unlike Eddie, she had a good job with steady pay, and she was still young enough to start a new life on her own. She would appreciate it if Eddie would pay her back for stealing from their savings, but that wasn't her main concern at the moment. She just wanted to have control over someone else, and she liked the way her assertiveness was affecting Angie. The more she called Angie a criminal and a thief, the stronger Kim felt.

She'd changed her mind several times in regard to Eddie's stupid car, but she was so insulted that Angie thought she could somehow influence Kim with money, that Kim made the flash decision to give Angie the damn car. That's how much she cared about money at this point.

But when they got down to the garage, Angie wasn't reacting the way Kim wanted her to. Angie didn't seem as desperate anymore. She was standing there holding her oversized Gucci bag up to her chest, and it was clear that she didn't want anything to do with the car. She also suggested that she was going to continue on with Eddie despite Kim's mandate. Angie was actually scowling at Kim now, a sudden confidence that scared Kim and reminded her of Angie's background, her family.

But Kim didn't care. The hell with it. "I don't give a shit about your house," she said. "In fact, it would make me happy if you both got screwed on the whole deal."

Angie had been looking toward the garage door, away from Kim and the car. But when Angie heard the statement about scratching the real estate deal, her head snapped up, and her eyes met Kim's for a split second before Angie reached into her purse.

While they held onto each other's eyes for that brief moment, Kim was seeing the ruthless criminal that Angie was. Kim saw it in the woman's cold squint, a wolf's predatory glare.

Kim bounced off the car like she was sitting on a spring, and she reached onto the shelf between the snow chains and a box of old paperbacks. She grabbed Duff's gun from where she'd stashed it this morning. The smooth handle was near the edge of the metal shelving. She really only wanted it for show. But she wasn't really thinking now. She was reacting. She was certain that Angie was going for her own firearm. Through some innate skill, Kim's hand folded around the gun, and her finger instinctively hooked the trigger. This all happened in a second or two. "Freeze," she yelled and pointed the gun in Angie's direction, still just trying to intimidate. But Angie continued to rifle through her purse for her own gun. "Don't make another move," Kim cried, but Angie kept digging.

And when Angie finally looked up, her hand coming out of the bag now, Michael Duffy's gun went off. Kim was certain she hadn't pulled the trigger. She just wanted Angie to see the gun so that Angie would stop going for her own. Kim might have shaken the gun a bit for emphasis, which, in retrospect, seemed like a stupid thing to do. Shaking the gun would surely throw off any semblance of aim she might have needed, but that's when she felt the kick and heard the firecracker pop. All of her senses were merging into one in this single moment, and it was difficult to discern the timing. There was even a smell now. And it took only a second before Kim saw the blood and could hear Angie gurgling.

Kim's nurse instincts kicked into gear, but she almost immediately knew it was too late. The bullet must have hit the carotid artery, and Angie would have only a few seconds to live. Kim went back to the shelf and found a roll of duct tape next to Eddie's toolbox. She got down on her knees and wrapped it around Angie's neck to try to slow the blood. It was futile, but her instincts wouldn't allow her to just watch another human being die like this.

Once Kim had wrapped the duct tape around Angie's neck, she reached down to get a pulse, but, of course, there was none. CPR was not an option. Her only thought now was that she was going to prison. She'd shot her husband's mistress with a stolen gun. For a moment, she pondered how a jury would see her. She began rehearsing lines she could use to explain how she'd tried to save Angie's life once the gun had accidentally gone off. She only wanted to scare this woman who had broken the sanctity of her marriage. She just wanted to wave the gun around to intimidate a person who had refused to stop seeing her husband even after she'd been caught. And, finally, if she didn't shoot Angie, Angie was going to shoot her.

Kim scrambled on her knees through the blood over to where Angie had dropped the purse. She knew she was going to find a weapon. For some reason, in her mind, Kim imagined that the gun would be one of those little ones that you'd sometimes see a femme fatale carry in the movies. A sexy gun. A pocket pistol that an old west saloon whore would hide in her garter. But she tore through the Gucci bag and didn't immediately find any weapons except a pepper spray keychain. Kim wondered if that was enough to justify a shooting.

There was hardly any makeup—just some lip gloss and eyeshadow tangled up with a set of earbud cables. There was a silk scarf and a pair of leather gloves. Tic Tacs. An Italian dictionary. Her wallet. The same pair of cat-eye sunglasses that Kim had seen her wear on the deck at Mission Rock just a couple days ago when Angie was so alive, turning heads in that dress. There was a flower-print facemask and a small bottle of hand sanitizer.

Kim wanted there to be something dangerous in that bag. Something that proved she was a threatening street thug, capable of horrible acts of violence. But Kim couldn't find anything. She just kept pulling out items and dropping them in the smeared blood beneath her. Another pair of gloves. A folded-up printout from Trip Advisor for some place called Camogli. Dental floss. A small stack of business cards secured by a rubber band. All the cards appeared to be from elderly care facilities.

There was a story in that purse, but not the one Kim wanted to find. She was hoping for brass knuckles and a pager and vials of cocaine. A lock-picking device. Forged checks. Burner phones. And the gun that she was reaching for. Where was the gun?

The duct tape had stopped the bleeding, but Kim had crawled across the concrete floor, so she was covered in blood. When she'd first started out as a medical professional, she was an emergency room nurse at SF General, so she'd seen plenty of gunshot victims, but none of them were beautiful. And none of them had bags filled with many of the same things that Kim had in her bag—Kim had that same facemask. This blood was different, and Kim's hands were covered in it.

Since she'd first seen Eddie with Angie, Kim had chewed at her cuticles so intensely that almost all her fingers had tiny cuts near her nails. Angie's blood was now mixed in with her own. For some reason, this made Kim wonder how many times Eddie had had sex with Angie and her on the same day. Blood sisters.

She got up slowly. Suddenly tired. She wiped her hands on her jeans and looked around at the gruesome scene. She'd always been one to analyze her emotions while she was having them, but she couldn't do it. This was unique. No comparisons. She felt like she didn't even have to breathe, and she didn't for a long time. Her body didn't seem to need air. When she eventually exhaled, it was a gentle release, as if everything had slowed down, and oxygen wasn't important anymore.

She walked to the garage door and peered out the mail slot to see if anyone had heard the gunshot and come over to check on her. Nobody. They must all be doing what Kim did when she heard a loud noise: *It must have been a car backfiring or a firecracker*.

She looked back at Angie whose eyes were open. Angie didn't look surprised. She looked disappointed. Like she thought Kim was better than this. Like maybe she had something important to do today and was annoyed that she wouldn't be able to do it. Kim knew she had to call the police and take care of this, and she wanted the cops to be there before Eddie came home.

But she didn't call the police.

She called Leo.

## 35

Leo didn't realize how lonely he'd been until Kim kissed him last night, and the pleasure center in his brain lit up after being dormant for so long. Once Kim pulled the lever and activated Leo's long abandoned facility, the dopamine and serotonin sparks made him almost dizzy with confusion and excitement and a new sense of purpose.

Her scent still lingered in his apartment the next day. He was pondering the warmth of her touch on his face, and then her name popped up on his cell. He nearly dropped the phone as he scrambled to accept the call. Then he took a deep breath and laughed a little bit at himself before he answered.

"I really need you right now," she said.

"Tell me where you are," he said.

*** 

When he got to her house, and she opened the door, he could tell that she'd been crying. She was wearing a bathrobe, but he assumed she hadn't taken a shower yet because she was a mess. Her eyes were red, and her cheeks were puffy. Her hair was all over the place. And her hands looked like they'd been rubbed raw.

"What's going on, Kim?" he said and looked over her shoulder to see if anyone else was in the house. "Are you alone?"

She looked like she was trying to smile, but it came off looking like someone who might be getting ready to throw up. "That's an existential question I'm not prepared to answer at this time," she said, her eyes glazed over like a sleepwalker's.

Leo stepped into the house and scanned the rooms in his direct sightline. "Kim, tell me what's happening." he said.

Kim didn't say anything. She stepped to him in her bare feet and her robe, and she embraced him. He imagined that he could feel her heart beating against his abdomen. Then she stepped back, took his hand, and led him to a staircase that he assumed went to the garage. Part of him was hoping there was a room down there and this was Kim's attempt at some kind of seduction. He wished she'd cleaned herself up a bit, but he also would have told her that she didn't need to play any games. He was ready and willing.

But as soon as they got to the bottom of the stairs, and it opened up into a two-car garage, Kim sat on the bottom step, and Leo turned the corner to see what looked like something from a waxworks Chamber of Horrors. Leo sucked in a short breath but otherwise didn't move. It was the girl, Angie. And from what he was seeing, he presumed that Kimberly had killed her, maybe in a moment of passion. And Leo was the one who'd provided her with the information about Angie, so he immediately felt that he was an accomplice.

Angie's face looked almost normal. Her eyes were open. So, Leo knew that Kim hadn't beaten her. There were no facial cuts or early bruising, so it didn't appear to be some kind of physical altercation that had gone haywire. But there was blood everywhere. For a moment, Leo thought Angie was wearing a scarf, but on second glance, he realized it was duct tape around her neck. Kim must have slit her throat and then changed her mind.

"Where's the knife?" he said.

Kim didn't answer.

"I need the knife," said Leo, looking back at her now.

Kim shook her head. "There's no knife."

"All this blood had to come from somewhere," said Leo. "Judging from the duct tape, I think it's a good bet that her throat's been cut." Leo figured that Kim was still in shock about what she'd done, but the sooner she snapped out of it, the sooner they could decide on a strategy.

"I shot her," said Kim.

It was hard for Leo to imagine Kim owning a gun and even harder to imagine her firing it at another human being. She was a nurse, for Christ's sake. "C'mon, Kim," he said and faced her now.

"I did," she said.

"You have a gun?" he said.

"No," she said and covered her face with her hands.

"You took Angie's gun from her and shot her with it?" he asked, trying to put some pieces together for her and maybe setting up some kind of self-defense scenario that could keep her out of jail.

"It's Michael Duffy's gun," she said.

"Marilyn's Michael?" he said. "Duff?"

Kim nodded.

"Did Duff shoot Angie?" he said. "Kim, you gotta help me out here. I can't do anything for you until I know how Angie ended up like this."

"I did it," she said. "Don't you see, Leo? I shot her in the neck. I hit the carotid artery, and she bled out."

"Why did Duff give you his gun? I thought he was a smart kid."

"I stole it from him," she said. "I committed two awful crimes in two days."

He wanted to console her, but they didn't have time. "Where is it?" he said.

"What?"

"The gun," he said. "Go get it."

She left the garage, and Leo sat down on the steps to think this out. He looked around the garage for supplies. He was surprised at himself. He knew the best thing to do right now was to tell Kim they had to call the police. Although there were awful consequences to confessing, Kim wouldn't have to go through the mental anguish of trying to cover this up. Leo was trained to handle cover-ups. He'd been involved in them for most of his professional life. Granted, none of them involved dead women with duct tape around their necks, but he felt he was conditioned to shut down emotions and handle problems. It's what he did.

There was a Costco-sized stock of paper towels on a shelf next to rolls of toilet paper. There was also an extremely large piece of luggage leaning up against the wall in the corner next to a set of golf clubs and a stand-up paddleboard.

When he heard Kim at the top of the stairs, he turned around to see her. She was holding the gun, and tears were streaming down her face. She handed Leo the gun and said, "Maybe we should just call the cops."

"Before we do anything," he said. "Maybe you can just give me the short version of what happened."

"I'm so stupid," she said and sniffed and huffed for a moment to try to control her breathing.

"Kim," he said. "We need to try to shut down the emotions for about an hour or so. Do you think you can do that?"

"I can try," she said.

"Good," he said. "Tell me what happened."

After Kim had taken Leo through the deranged story of trying to give away Eddie's car and then thinking Angie had a gun, the account ended with Kim not even really fully believing that she'd pulled the trigger. She said that she'd shaken the gun at Kim to scare her, and the thing just went off. Then it was too late, and the duct tape stopped the bleeding, but Angie'd already lost too much blood.

"How did all that stuff end up in the blood?" he asked. "Did it fall out of her purse when she fell?"

"I was looking through her purse to find her gun," she said.

"But she didn't have one?"

Kim shook her head and started crying again. Leo needed to give her a task. "Kim," he said. I need you to get some dishwashing liquid, a plastic bucket, garbage bags, and some hydrogen peroxide if you have it."

"There's a bucket right there," she said and pointed to a plastic tub against the wall near the front tire of her Jeep. "I'll go get the other stuff. Should I get bleach?"

"No," said Leo. "I don't want it to smell in here. When Eddie comes home, he's going to ask why it smells like bleach. The hydrogen peroxide is odorless and will work just as well."

The two of them had never come to any agreement that they were going to forgo the call to the police and hide this body, but it seemed like that was the path they were on. He was tempted to call Bill and run this by him, but Kim was a grown woman, and she'd called Leo, not her dad, so Leo was going to take care of this himself.

He grabbed two rolls of paper towels and the long piece of luggage. There was probably a throw rug in the house in which they could roll her up, but the bag was right here. The logo said CaddyDaddy. Leo figured it must be for transporting golf clubs. Angie was small, and he thought she'd probably fit.

He dabbed at the blood with the paper towels. He didn't want to rub it in any more than it already had been from Kim crawling around in it. When she came back down the stairs with the cleaning supplies, she seemed surprised that Leo had already gotten to work.

"What time is Eddie supposed to be home?" he asked.

She put the supplies on the floor and checked her watch. "I think we have about an hour and a half."

He looked at his own watch and said, "Okay. No problem. I think we need to get Angie in this bag first. Get her out of the way and then get the blood cleaned up. We have plenty of time to make the garage look like it did before Eddie left, and then we can get Angie out to my car."

"Or we could do something else," she said. Her voice sounded the way a voice would sound when someone was smiling, but Kim's face was blank.

"What do you have in mind?" he said.

"Since it looks like we're doing this," she said. "I'd still like to ratfuck Eddie if you don't mind."

## 36

Leo didn't want to mess around with this. He wanted to get the garage cleaned up and get Angie in the ground somewhere out of the area, either up north near Bodega Bay or down south near Santa Cruz. He knew places in both spots with soft earth for digging, and where you could lose a body forever.

But Kimberly had something else in mind.

Leo was using the paper towels to dab at the puddled-up blood before he was going to use the detergent and eventually the hydrogen peroxide for the stubborn stains. Kim held open one of the garbage bags into which Leo was throwing the used paper towels.

"I want to put the body in Eddie's car," she said.

Leo was on his third roll of paper towels now. "No," he said. "We're going to pull your Jeep out of the garage. Then we'll back my car in there and put the body bag in the trunk. None of your neighbors will see anything."

"Leo," she said. "I don't want you dealing with this shit show anymore."

"I'm already in this, Kim. There's no reason to complicate it now."

"Leo," she said. "I need to do this my way." She dropped the almost-filled garbage bag at her feet. A few soiled paper towels spilled out. "Eddie and I are going to take responsibility for what happened here. It's the only way I'll be able to move forward with my life afterward."

"We're not telling Eddie," said Leo as he stood up to grab the hydrogen peroxide. He was pretty sure he'd be able to get the rest of this clean. He looked at Kim before he bent down to grab the bottle. He was trying to figure out if she'd lost her mind. Her face still wasn't giving anything away.

She turned away and walked over to Eddie's Porsche. She reached into the open driver's side window and popped the trunk. Then she stepped to the CaddyDaddy with Angie's body already contorted into the limited confines. Leo watched her push down on Angie's knee as she attempted to zip the bag from foot to head. The zipper got momentarily stuck when part of Angie's blouse was caught in the teeth as Kim rushed to close the bag. She ripped out the fabric and immediately went back to zipping, pushing parts of Angie deeper into the bag as she pulled the zipper shut in two-inch increments. She had to adjust Angie's head slightly when she got to the top. The last foot came together easily though a few wisps of Angie's hair escaped Kim's last violent jerk and fanned out over the side of the bag.

When she had the zipper fully secured, she looked up at Leo. She was sweating. Then she walked over to Angie's purse with all its bloody contents, picked it up, and jammed it into a long side-pocket in the CaddyDaddy.

The bag had small wheels like any piece of respectable luggage, so she wheeled it over to the open trunk and then balanced it against the quarter panel. She looked back at Leo but didn't say anything. She looked like she was waiting for him to help her, but he wasn't going to do it.

"Can we stop this now?" he said.

"This is my mess," she said. "I'm not letting you dispose of this body, but I'd appreciate some help getting it into Eddie's trunk before he gets home."

"And then what?"

"And then you were never here."

"Okay," he said. "I get that. You're trying to protect me. But what's your plan with Eddie?" He walked over to her now, and he still had no intention of letting her ruin her life. She didn't know how to do this, and if she made even a small mistake, she could end up in jail or dead. Angie's family did not play. "If you tell Eddie, that's one more person who knows and one more person who could slip up. I'm actually more concerned with Angie's family than I am with the cops. The cops don't tend to waste too many resources investigating the disappearance of criminals. They just assume The Organization dealt out its own form of justice, and then the cops let it go after a cursory glance. Shit, Angie's people might not even call the police." He considered this for a moment. "The family might just go after any suspects they can dig up themselves, and you don't want to be a suspect."

Kim was doing a lot of nodding as Leo's diatribe dragged on, and when he finally stopped, she said, "Can you help me get this into the trunk?"

"Jesus, Kim," he said. "Are you not hearing me? This isn't a game."

Kim leaned back against the car. She actually looked as if a sense of calm were washing over her. "Eddie got me into this," she said, breathing easier now. She used one of the paper towels to dab at the sweat on her forehead. "Now he's gonna help me get out."

"Don't you have some concerns about him turning you in?" he said. Eddie was a weasel. Leo could see the man betraying Kim without hesitation if he thought it would save his own ass.

"I don't think so," said Kim. "He'll be feeling some guilt about the fact that he was cheating on me. I'll let him know that Angie came over here and attacked me, that this whole thing was self-defense."

"Okay," said Leo. "But if it was self-defense, then why didn't you just call the police? And what about the gun? How are you going to explain that you had Michael Duffy's gun? And what's the explanation for Angie coming over here in the first place? Are you going to pretend that you never saw them at the restaurant and that I never did any research on Eddie?"

"I'll tell him that she just showed up at the house and started making threats, that I didn't know who she was until she explained that she was Eddie's lover and that she wanted me out of the picture."

"Did she seem like that kind of person?" asked Leo. "Did she seem like she was in love with Eddie?"

"She was in love with a real estate deal that, for some reason, she needed Eddie to broker for her."

"It was probably some kind of illegal shit," said Leo. "I'm surprised I didn't find anything about it in the phone records."

"She said she didn't even own the property yet."

Leo knew how these people worked. "She's probably inheriting it, and she's just waiting for some old fart to die before she can collect."

"That's evil," she said and pushed herself off the car. She walked away from Leo, back toward the garbage bag. There was a wet spot on the floor where the hydrogen peroxide had foamed up over the blood and then magically lifted it from the cement before Leo had wiped it clean. Kim walked over and stood on the spot. "She was a nasty person."

"These people prey on the vulnerable," said Leo, trying to make Kim feel a little better about what she'd done. "They're low-risk con artists. They manipulate. They create emotional attachments with people who have something they want."

"That sounds like most people," said Kim.

"Yeah, he said. "Maybe it does. But Angie and her crew aren't like most people."

"What's the difference?" she asked.

Leo had to think about it. There was a difference. He knew that. But Kim had a point. Everybody seemed to be trying to get over on everybody else. "Here's the difference," he said, finally. "I think most people feel guilty about it afterward."

"And people like Angie don't?"

"People like Angie feel guilty if they *don't* take advantage of an easy target," he said. "They feel like they've let down The Organization."

"That's pretty dark," she said.

"You think?"

"I can't believe people live like that," she said.

"They do," he said. "And those are the people who're going to be looking for you if you don't let me take care of this for you."

Kimberly nodded at Leo but didn't say anything for a long time. "Here's how I want you to help me, Leo," she said. "I need to get the bag up into Eddie's trunk before he gets home, and then I need you to get the fuck out of here before anyone sees you."

## 37

Kim was surprised that Leo refused to help her get the body into Eddie's trunk. "You're gonna blow this," he'd said and walked out without looking back.

But it turned out, she didn't really need his help. She simply squatted down and wrapped her arms around the CaddyDaddy which was still leaning against the car. It felt like a strangely affectionate embrace, the kind of hug you'd have with an old friend before she went on a long trip. Then she moved the bag from the quarter panel to the trunk by using a series of short, quick lifts and almost bouncing the bag to the back of the car. Finally, she felt like one of those Scottish pole tossers as she was able to get her fingers under the bag and then tipped the heavy end into the trunk and pushed it all the way to the back.

The whole bag was too long to fit, so she turned it to a diagonal and pushed hard. This time, one side of the back seat tilted inward to provide some extra room. Kim didn't know the car had this feature, but it worked. The bag was at a diagonal, and the top was peeking into the back seat, but that was okay. She got into the back and pushed the seatback up as far as she could. There was still a small crack, but she didn't think Eddie would notice.

Then she took one more walk around the garage to see if she'd missed anything. Everything was clean, and the wet spot was nearly dry. She picked up the garbage bag and then put it down after a few steps to tie the top. When she reached down to grab it again, she saw Duff's gun resting on top of an igloo cooler next to the metal shelving.

She put the plastic bag in the back of her Jeep. Then she grabbed the gun and put it in her glove compartment.

She went back upstairs to return the cleaning supplies and took a quick look around to make sure everything looked normal. When she got to the bathroom, she took an oxycodone left over from Eddie's shoulder surgery.

Finally, she went into the bedroom and packed an overnight bag.

When she returned to the garage, she got into the back seat of the Jeep and pushed the seat all the way back so that she was lying down flat on her back, her face just inches from the garbage bag filled with bloody paper towels.

She closed her eyes and waited. She couldn't help thinking of Angie lying down a few feet away in Eddie's car.

Eventually, a sense of calm washed over her as she measured her breathing and imagined a plan that she knew not to set in stone. She understood that plans were important: *failing to plan is planning to fail.* But she also knew what happened when people relied too much on their plans: *Man plans, and God laughs … the best laid plans of mice and men …* all that stuff she'd learned in high school. It was all real. Her marriage was evidence of it.

Angie probably had a plan.

Kim had a pretty good idea of where she wanted this to go, but she knew enough to stay nimble. This was going to be organized freestyle — until it wasn't. Then she'd really have to wing it. Just as she was shifting to get comfortable, she felt the vibrations of her phone and checked to see a brief text from Leo: *Remember to get what's on the cooler.* Kim wondered if Leo liked to freestyle. At least it appeared he still cared.

\*\*\*

When Eddie finally got home, he came in through the garage like he always did after a trip. From her hiding place in the back of the Jeep, Kim heard him drop his duffle bag on the washing machine. Apparently, Kim was supposed to continue cleaning his clothes despite the fact that he was cheating on her.

Then she heard him walk up the stairs. He'd texted this morning to tell her that he needed to go into the office today, so he must have been going up to their room to change out of his stinky Tahoe clothes. But she couldn't be sure. She didn't know what to believe anymore. Maybe he had several girls on the side. She was tempted to raise her head and peek out, but she was able to control her breathing again and let the feeling of serenity pump out from her chest to her arms and legs and ultimately into her fingers and toes. She didn't know if the feeling was occurring because of the intense emotions that she'd experienced over the past few hours, or if the oxycodone was kicking in quickly because she took them on an empty stomach. Either way, she knew she wouldn't panic. She could actually fall asleep right now as she waited.

And maybe she did and woke up when she heard Eddie's car door close and the engine start up. Now she was wide awake. She wondered if he would see his back seat pushed forward or feel the drag from the extra weight in the trunk. She just wanted him to get that car outside, and then she could start.

Kim squinted at the Jeep's ceiling as she listened to the garage door open and then close as Eddie pulled the car out onto Country Club Drive.

She checked her phone to see how much battery she had left. 52%. Plenty for now. She got out of the jeep, walked to the passenger side, and took the gun out of the glove box. Then she walked around and sat on the back bumper. She went into her cellphone and googled *how do I take bullets out of gun.*

It sent her to a YouTube video that showed her how to press the mag release and remove the magazine from the handle of the gun. The guy on the video told her that it would be different if the gun were a revolver, but Duff's gun didn't look like a revolver. So, she found the mag release, pulled it, and, like magic, the magazine dropped out of the handle. Then she followed the YouTube guy's instructions—he said this was the most important one—and racked the slide at which point the round popped out and landed on the floor between her feet.

She placed the gun, the magazine, and the round on the bumper next to her and put her phone on front camera mode. Then she held the phone up close to her face and tried it from several different angles, all of which captured her face in a variety of light and shadow. She found one that she liked. She held the phone over her chest and looked down at it. It was six inches from her face.

Then she started to groan. She kept it low so that the neighbors wouldn't hear, but she had to get herself in the right mindset—actor's studio time. She imagined her high school drama coach: *Focus on the emotion, not the result.* She used to be good at this. If she could conjure the right moment from her past, she'd be able to summon the tears. Even in college, she'd done it once to a professor when she hadn't finished her term paper. The tears came almost on cue, and he'd granted her an extension. But she had to think of something horrible or she wouldn't be able to do it.

She looked back over her shoulder at the garbage bag and then tried to imagine what it would be like to be inside of that golf luggage in the trunk of the Porsche. Nothing. She put the gun in her hand, careful to keep her finger outside the trigger guard even though it was empty now. And she tried to remember what it looked like when Angie put her hand up to her neck to stop the blood. But Kim couldn't remember any of it. It was as if her brain was trying to protect her from the horror of the carnage that took place less than two hours ago. She closed her eyes and tried to picture it, but she couldn't even remember what Angie's face looked like anymore. She thought she might be having a nervous breakdown. She was tempted to open the back of the Jeep and look in the bag of bloody rags just to remind herself of the horrific scene in which she'd participated. She needed something to help stir some emotions.

But she couldn't do it.

Instead, her mind reflexively travelled back to Mission Rock, and now her brain was a movie camera. She closed her eyes, and it was like watching a film starring Eddie and Angie as they walked out onto that deck. The director was using a high angle shot to make the subjects look vulnerable, powerless. It was exactly the way she'd seen it from the upper deck, but the colors were different, muted. Angie was even more beautiful than Kim had remembered. But now her walk wasn't the strut that Kim had originally seen. In fact, Angie seemed a touch bashful as the men ogled her from behind their sunglasses. When she sat down, she made sure to secure the hem of her dress so that her thighs would be covered. A few strands of hair concealed her eyes.

And before Kim could analyze any of this, the tears were streaming down her cheeks. She grabbed her phone and FaceTimed Eddie, but the asshole didn't pick up.

The third time she called, she had to work a lot harder to get the tears going, but she was able to get there, and he finally answered the call. She held the phone up close to her face and screamed, "Just do what they say."

After his weak response, she said, "Check the trunk!" and hung up.

He called back almost immediately. She held the gun up to her head with one hand and held the phone with her other. She gave him just a glimpse of the gun. Her face took up the rest of the screen. "The trunk!" she shouted again. And then, "And no cops, Eddie,"

She imagined him seeing the sticky note and was a little embarrassed at her attempt to disguise her writing by using her left hand and also a little ashamed at her campy note: *Bury Me.*

# Part Three

*Everyone Else*

He may talk like an idiot, and look like an idiot, but don't let that fool you: he really is an idiot.

-Groucho Marx

## 38

"Plug that in," said Duff and pointed at the charger on the small desk by the front window that overlooked the beach.

"What?" said Eddie.

"Your phone," said Duff. "We need to keep it charged. If we miss a call from Kim because your phone is dead …." He let the sentence fade and looked over at Marilyn, who was sitting on the couch with her eyes closed. She was holding a pillow up to her chest. She would sometimes assume this posture after a hard day and actually fall asleep sitting up with all the lights on.

But today was different. Marilyn had always had a mouth that, in its relaxed state, was a low-key smile, like she'd just thought of something mildly amusing that one of her kindergarteners had said in class. But as she sat on the same couch today that could induce those early afternoon naps in a different life, the corners of her mouth were turned down. She actually looked like she was in some physical pain, waiting for an emergency room doctor to give her something.

"You okay, hon?" said Duff, trying to be delicate. He knew she was reaching a breaking point.

"Michael," she said, her eyes still closed. "What are we going to say about the money the next time these people call?"

"We tell 'em we got it," he said. At the very least, he knew that Carl had promised to stake them if they couldn't come up with anything on their own.

"Yeah," she said. "We can do that." She opened her eyes now and looked at Duff. "But like how much do we say we have? They never gave a specific amount."

Duff looked over at Eddie, who was leaning up against the desk and picking at something on his sleeve. "Eddie," said Duff. "What about your parents? Could we ask them for some cash?" Out of the corner of his eye, Duff could tell that Marilyn was looking at Eddie now, probably staring a red dot scope at his forehead.

Eddie dropped whatever he'd picked off his sleeve, and Duff watched it float to the floor. "My parents are on a fixed income, Duff," he said. "They just have the house."

Duff listened to Marilyn's sigh and knew it would get a reaction out of Eddie.

"Do you want me to lie and say that my parents are rich?" he said. "That wouldn't get us any money, Marilyn."

"No," said Marilyn. "I'd like you to have never been born."

"Okay," said Duff. "When they call, we'll just tell them that all we could come up with is twenty thousand. I think that's all we can borrow from Carl, and the people who have Kim can't really expect us to get much more in cash on such short notice. They have to know Eddie has limited resources."

Marilyn nodded, the corners of her mouth still weighed down by the events of the last two days. "Let's say they accept it. That all they need is $20,000, which doesn't seem worth all the trouble to me. But then what?"

Duff sat down next to her and put his hand on her back. "It's been more than the money," he said. "We disposed of a body for them." He was still trying to work out whether or not the body was part of the payout, or if it was a mistake that somehow occurred during or prior to the kidnapping and then needed cleaning up. Killing a woman and kidnapping another to get some quick cash seemed insane to him.

"Remember Denise Huskins a couple of years ago?" said Eddie. "That's what I've been thinking about."

"I remember the name," said Duff, but he couldn't place her.

"She's the pretty blond gal from Vallejo who got kidnapped," said Eddie. "But the cops and the media said it was a hoax. Until they caught the kidnapper."

"I do remember that one," said Duff. "The kidnapper was ex-military. Crazy. But he didn't like that the woman was being called a liar after what he'd put her through, so he confessed."

"Yeah," said Eddie. "That's the guy. The point is, he brought her all the way down to southern California and tied her up for a few days. Went to a lot of trouble. But he only asked the boyfriend for $8,500. I looked it up last night."

"Yeah," said Duff. "That was nuts. I think the woman, Denise Huskins, ended up suing the cops and the newspapers. $8,500. You'd think there'd be an easier way to get that amount."

"My point," said Eddie, "is that crazy people or people who have been down and out or come from other parts of the country might think twenty grand is plenty."

Marilyn sat up straight, and Duff pulled his hand away from her spine, which had gone rigid. "Even if they'll take twenty thousand, how do we make an exchange? How do we give them the money and get Kim back?"

Eddie was silent, and Duff hadn't gotten that far in his projections yet. "I think that's up to the kidnappers," he said. "They kind of hold all the cards right now." As soon as he said it, he regretted it. He knew he should be trying to reassure Marilyn right now, not tell her that the criminals had all the power. Even though they clearly did.

"Okay," said Marilyn, visibly trying to keep it together. "What do we need to do to get a hold of some of the cards?" She was looking at Duff now as if Eddie weren't even in the room. "Tell me what to do to get my sister back."

Duff was looking at the TV even though it wasn't on. He wanted to avoid looking into Marilyn's eyes. He knew his own eyes would betray him. The fact of the matter was that these assholes had been stringing them along for two days, and there was nothing he could do to gain any control. He felt like he should have brought in the police a lot earlier, despite Kim's desperate pleas to keep them out of it. He felt like he should be closer to bringing Kim home by this point, but he didn't feel like he'd made any progress, mostly because the kidnappers had been unclear about the next steps. They'd only demanded money. But Marilyn was right. Even if they were able to get the money and hand it over, then what?

"I think there're a few ways of making the exchange," he said, finally. "But we'll need to hear what they're thinking before we ask for any modifications."

Eddie chimed in, "And we don't even know when they're going to call."

Marilyn stood up and walked in front of the little fireplace. "So, what are these ways of making the exchange?" she said, sounding calm, like she was just curious.

Duff was quiet for a moment.

"Do they teach you that in the academy?" she said.

"They do not," he said. "All my knowledge on this subject comes from TV and the movies. And maybe a few novels."

"So, you really don't know much more than me?" she said.

Duff nodded. "In *Get Shorty*, there was an exchange where they did something with bus station lockers, but there wasn't really a hostage, and there were plenty of complications. I can't remember what happens, but I don't think we want to deal with lockers."

"That doesn't really help then," said Marilyn.

"I know," he said. "I'm just thinking out loud. *Fargo* is a ransom movie, too, but it's more complicated than our situation. The main guy, the red-headed guy, paid criminals to kidnap his wife, and I think they were all going to split the money afterward somehow."

"Doesn't that end with someone getting put in a woodchipper?" she said.

"That was the criminals turning on each other," said Duff.

Eddie was walking around the room now scratching his chin. "*Key Largo* had hostages," he said.

"Eddie," said Duff. "Are you like eighty years old?"

Eddie appeared insulted. "Bogie and Bacall," he said and threw his hands up as if to say that Duff and Marilyn should know the reference.

"Is there a ransom exchange?" ask Duff.

"I can't remember," said Eddie. "Sorry for bringing it up."

Marilyn was looking desperate again. "Can you please go stand by your phone, Eddie?"

Eddie obeyed and said nothing more.

"I think this is how it probably has to go," said Duff and knew that neither Marilyn nor Eddie would want to hear the reality of the situation.

"Go ahead," said Marilyn.

"They're probably going to ask for a dead drop," he said and figured neither of them would know the term. He wasn't even sure why he knew it.

"What's that?" said Eddie, never shy about revealing his ignorance on a myriad of topics.

Duff took a deep breath. "It's like a prearranged secret spot, where we'll hide the money, and then leave, with the agreement that no law enforcement will be involved." He paused to see if there were any questions, and he thought about whether or not he would bring his gun.

"Do you think we should involve law enforcement?" asked Marilyn.

"Let's see what they want," he said. "If they give us the dead drop option, they probably won't give us Kim right away. They'll wait for us to leave, and they'll make sure no one is watching. And when they secure the money, they'll let Kim go free." He didn't know much about this stuff, but he did know this was the most common practice. He was pretty sure it happened a lot in Mexico. Without any data to support it, he added, "Almost every time, the kidnappers let the person live, especially if they're pros."

Eddie said, "That would make sense. If they kept kidnapping people and then killing them, no one would ever pay a ransom, right?"

"Exactly," said Duff, surprised that Eddie was using some common sense.

"What if they're *not* pros?" said Marilyn. "These people seem like they might not be very good at this."

"I don't know," said Duff. "They're definitely not bad at it. They somehow got Eddie's girlfriend into the trunk of his car and got us to bury her. That seems pretty professional to me."

Eddie was leaning against the desk, looking at his phone. Then he looked right at Duff. "How the hell did they *do* that?"

## 39

Walter was still dizzy when he was following Al Young down the stairs and around the corner to the front of the barber shop. His legs felt like jelly. Leon was sitting on the stoop smoking a cigarette, but Al ignored him and unlocked his car remotely.

"Get in the back," Al said to Walter, who reached for the handle but stopped short when he heard Leon's voice.

"Say, Albert?" said the old man without taking the cigarette out of his mouth, his lips curled in like a toothless vagrant.

Walter wondered if Leon was still pissed that Al found a new barber. Most dudes liked Leon. His clientele was crowded with lifetime neighborhood folks, but Al had stopped coming to Leon about the same time that Al had stopped using Walter for jobs. And Leon liked to talk shit about how Al thought he was better than the rest of the neighborhood folks.

"Yeah?" said Al, looking over the roof of his car at old, broken-down Leon. Al looked angry just to be giving Leon the time of day.

Leon took a long drag from his cigarette and then flicked it into the storm drain. "You ever wish you had longer arms?" he said, big smile snaking across his face.

"Say what?" said Al, his thick hands resting on the roof.

Walter wondered about Leon's question. He couldn't help thinking that if Al had longer arms, he could slap Leon's face from over the top of the car.

"I asked about your arms," said Leon. "You ever wish they was longer?"

"The hell you gettin' at, Leon?" said Al.

"Just thinking thoughts," said Leon, still smiling, but showing his rotten, yellow teeth now and scratching at the white whiskers on his chin. "I'm tryin' to figure out how a man like you takes a leak. Because they ain't no way—if all you got is regular-sized arms—you could reach all the way around that belly to get at your zipper." Then he let out a throaty laugh. "Not possible," he said and laughed again.

Walter felt his stomach tighten. For some reason he thought Al was going to take this out on Walter just because he was closer than Leon.

But all Al said was, "Go back and cut some hair, old man." Then he opened his door and said, "What are you waiting for, Walter?"

Walter shook his head and said, "Oh," and then looked once more at Leon.

Al had already gotten in and shut the door, so Leon yelled, "How he gonna reach that zipper with regular arms?" The laugh now a breathy half-cough. Then he looked at Walter and said, "He bringin' you along to do his zipper for him, Walter?"

When Walter got into his car, Al was looking at his phone. "This dude lives all the way out near the zoo."

"Who?" said Walter.

Al looked over his shoulder and said, "The bookie." He had a look like he was staring at a mental patient. "The dude that owes me money. Eddie Bilker."

"Yeah," said Walter. "I remember." And he did, but he felt almost stoned after getting his head slapped like that. He was certain he had a concussion, and he had a nasty headache near his temple, feeling like his brain might have knocked up against the back of his eyeballs.

"Well," said Al. "We're going to that man's house, and you're going to go into his house and get me the money I need to pay off Brianna so I don't lose my pension over that video you made. You dig?"

Walter had done this kind of thing for Al in the past, but he was always paid for it. He assumed today would be pro bono. The video was a mistake. Walter knew that now. And he wasn't confident Al would forgive him even if he was able to get something from this guy, Eddie.

"How do you want me to do it?" asked Walter. "Is the man waiting for me?"

Al looked at him in the rearview mirror but didn't say anything.

"I just don't know what you want me to do," said Walter.

Al didn't even look back this time.

"I don't have my piece," said Walter, thinking this mission was starting to feel like it might be dangerous.

Al pulled the car over into a bus stop. He turned as far as he could, but his stomach was pressed hard against the steering wheel. "Let me simplify this for you," he said over his shoulder. "If the man's home, you force the son of a bitch to lead you to the money. He's gotta have some. He runs a cash operation. If he's not home, you need to find the money on your own." He gave Walter a tired look, like he was bored having to explain this to him. "Dude owes me a lot of money."

Walter knew he had to play this carefully with Al, who would not be patient with stupid questions. So, Walter had to find the right questions and ask only those. "Do you have a gun for me to use in case he's home?" he asked but worried this was the wrong question. He was trying to come off as professional, but he sounded like a bitch. He was glad Al didn't have the mobility to take a swing at him.

Al didn't answer immediately. He turned away from Walter and, using the fingernail on his pinky, picked something out of his teeth. "I got a gun for you, Walter," he said and took a peek in the rearview mirror.

*\*\**

It wasn't hard to break in. In fact, Walter didn't even consider this a break-in because the back door was unlocked. He contemplated telling Al that he had to pick the lock so that Al might consider giving him something for the effort, but the thought disappeared as he soft-shoed through the kitchen and listened for any movement in the house.

He gripped the gun and was ready to shoot, but he wasn't against running either if the situation called for it. Al had parked around the corner next to a high hedge. He said that he would keep the engine running.

After a quick check of all the rooms, including the two bathrooms—Walter had once been surprised by a dude in a bathroom some time ago in an apartment in the Mission—he decided that Eddie Bilker was not home. Although it would have been easier to find the money if the man were there to guide him to it, Walter was relieved. He didn't like conflict, and, with his concussion, he didn't know how well his reflexes would be if there was some kind of confrontation.

But the problem now was that he had to either find the money—if there was any—or go back to the car and tell Al that he'd come up empty. Walter actually felt a chill when he considered the fact that he might have to face Al with a big bag of nothing.

Walter was in the system, so Al had given him a pair of medical gloves to wear, but a lot of these places had cameras now, so there was a chance he'd be caught on video. One of the significant advantages of the pandemic was that a lot of people were wearing masks, so he kept his on, and no one walking down the street would recognize him or suspect him. Except that he was black, and this neighborhood was not.

He thought about how getting caught on video might be ironic. He'd always had trouble with the exact meaning of the word *irony*, but he wondered if it would apply to a situation in which he got caught on camera trying to get money for Al, who had to make a payoff because *he'd* been caught on camera.

All this was drifting through his still foggy brain as he checked drawers and looked under mattresses and in the backs of closets. He was in a hurry, but he didn't disturb the house. He never understood why burglars would tear a place apart when they were looking for stuff. He liked to get in, get the goods, and get out while keeping the place looking like he was never there.

His theory was that if the homeowners didn't figure out right away that they'd been robbed, it would be hard for anyone to investigate the crime. Hard to report a crime if you don't know when it happened. But all these amateurs just loved to pull the drawers out of the dressers, leave cabinet doors open and throw sofa cushions across the room. And they liked to break shit. Walter didn't understand that. If you were already going to be stealing from these folks who didn't do anything to you, why would you also need to break their shit on the way out?

Walter knew a good fence, who could move goods almost immediately, but Eddie Bilker didn't seem like the type to have anything valuable enough to compensate Al for the money he was due. And Al definitely wanted cash to pay off Brianna. Unless she'd be interested in something else. Knowing Brianna, Walter had an idea that if he could find some diamonds, this chick sheriff might go for it. She was flashy. But she also might say just give her the money, and she'd get her own diamonds. Either way, he was looking for money or jewelry at this point. Electronics wouldn't bring in nearly enough cash for what Al needed.

And then Walter found a wooden box on the floor in the closet under some extra pillows. The box held some official papers that Walter laid back on the floor. But it also had a padded shipping envelope containing rings and necklaces, all tangled up but looking pricey. There were two diamond rings in there at the bottom, old-fashioned, maybe heirlooms. He still didn't know if this would be enough, but he placed the documents back in the box and put the pillows back over the top and stepped out of the closet.

He pushed the envelope down the front of his pants and zipped up his jacket. At least he had something to bring back to Al, who wouldn't like it, but it was something. The man needed cash, but Walter had been in the house for almost forty minutes and couldn't find a stash anywhere except the jewelry. He would take a quick look in the garage and then go back out to face the music.

When Walter pulled the Porsche up next to Al, he motioned for Al to roll down his window.

"What's this?" said Al. "Where's the money?"

"No golden fleece," said Walter and immediately regretted it.

"What the hell are you talking about?" said Al.

"Jason and the Argonauts," said Walter. "It doesn't matter. I searched the whole place. Unless they have some kind of secret vault under the house, there's no stash."

Al's eyes had a moment of clarity. "You got a fence for that car?"

"A good one," said Walter.

"How much can we get for it?"

"I looked it up on my phone," said Walter. "Brand new, the base for this model is ninety-five grand."

"Jesus."

"Yeah," said Walter. "And this one has only about eight thousand miles on it."

"So, what does that mean?"

"I'm not sure," said Walter. "My man, Khalil, does only luxury cars. Lots of money in it if you know what you're doing."

"Can you take a guess?" asked Al.

"The thief," said Walter, "usually gets between forty and fifty percent."

Al smiled. "So, this might work?" he said, pulling his bottom lip up over his top lip and nodding. "You said this model's worth ninety-five?"

"That's brand *new*," said Walter, not wanting this guy to get his hopes up.

"Yeah," said Al. "But you also said that was the price on the base model. Does that look like the base model to you?"

Walter had never been in a car this nice. Even the steering wheel felt like something he wanted to take home with him. "Probably not," he said, but he really had no idea. Maybe the base model in a car like this had a nice steering wheel. And the seat was warming up for him now. Maybe the base model had that too. Either way, when he did the math in his head, he knew they'd be able to get around forty for this transaction, and, hopefully, Al would leave him alone.

"But there was nothing else in there?" said Al. "Not even a little cash?"

Walter felt the envelope digging into his abdomen as he leaned toward the window. "Nothing," he said.

## 40

Leo was watching Kimberly from across the room. She was wearing a pair of his grey sweatpants. She'd rolled the waistband a few times and pulled the string tight. She was also wearing his cashmere V-neck with nothing on underneath. She looked cozy and uncomfortable at the same time. She and Leo had been arguing for almost an hour.

"But my sister is involved now," she said.

"It doesn't matter," he said. "We're in damage control."

"I don't care," she said.

"So, you want to just tell them everything?"

"I think I have to."

"No," he said and felt his ears getting hot. "It would be the worst thing you could do."

"I thought you said my whole plan was the worst thing," she said.

Her arms were folded across her chest, and she looked like a petulant little girl. She was perplexed, and Leo was learning that when she got confused, she argued. Like it was her way of figuring things out. She didn't seem to mind if she was wrong as long as she could think through an argument by forcing someone else to reason with her. Leo had hoped this one would be quick, but it was dragging on.

"That was then," he said, working hard to get her to understand. "It was a really bad plan. Maybe one of the worst I've ever seen. But now we're working on the next one, and you're about to make another foolish mistake unless you let me help you."

"I can't let my sister worry about me anymore," she said. "I had no idea Eddie would go to her and Duff, and now all I can think of is Marilyn being worried sick when she doesn't really have to be."

Leo took a deep breath. "Kim," he said. "Marilyn has plenty to worry about. It's not for the reasons she thinks, but if you tell her everything that's gone down, she's going to be worried about the fact that you killed someone." He raised his eyebrows, a technique that had worked with her father on occasion if the man had already had a few. "So, either way, your sister would be feeling awful right now, but the murder part will never go away. If she knows about it, it'll hang over you two always."

"But at least she'd know the truth."

"If you let Eddie and Marilyn and Michael Duffy know what really happened, I think it might put all of them in danger." He was stretching this a bit, but she needed to hear it if he was going to get her to give up on her hysterical proposal. This was not a time for emotions. "We'll make this easy," he said. "We'll immediately accept whatever amount of money Eddie comes up with. You're owed that. And then we'll have *you* show up a few hours later. It'll be quick, so Marilyn will only have to worry for a few more hours rather than worrying for the rest of her life."

"If we're going to do it your way, why wouldn't we just make the exchange all at once? They hand over the money, and then the kidnappers hand over me."

"Kim," said Leo. "That won't work." He moved close to her and took her face in his hands. "You're not really kidnapped. There's no one to accept the payout and hand you over. Get it?" He wanted to shake her a bit. She was a smart person, and he needed her to snap out of this now.

"Of course," she said, looking a little embarrassed.

"Good," he said and kissed her on the forehead.

"So, we tell them to drop the money somewhere, and then we can wait as long as we want to pick it up. We don't ever have to get it if we think it's too dangerous. But after it's been dropped off, I just go home … like the bad guys grabbed the money and set me free, right?"

"That's how we do it," he said. "And I guess you're right. There's not a rush to pick up the money. Once they see you, they'll assume your bad guys got it, and we can grab it whenever we want, as long as we pick a good drop spot where no one else can find the cash."

"Yeah, but I'd still really like to tell Marilyn what's going on, so we can avoid all the spy shit."

"Kim," he said. "We've been over this. If Marilyn and Duff know what you did, they become accessories after the fact if the police ever get involved. And we don't want that, right?"

"No," she said and shook her head side-to-side very slowly as if she wasn't quite sure about her answer still.

"We'll do one more FaceTime with Eddie, and that should be it," he said. He took her hand and gave it a squeeze. He didn't want to move on until she'd acknowledged that this was the only way to proceed.

"Eddie buried a dead body. All three of them know about the dead body. None of them reported a dead body. And they're delivering money to kidnappers," she said. "They know they were involved in some bad stuff, but, in a way, they were forced to do it in order to save me. Is that even a crime?"

"Yes and no," he said. "You're not supposed to bury a dead body on your own, especially one that was clearly murdered. But you, or rather the bad guys, put Eddie in an impossible situation—bury the body or have his wife get murdered." Leo considered that this particular aspect of Kim's plan was somewhat ingenious. "I guess Eddie could consider telling the police after they get you back. That would probably reduce any charges they might bring against him because he was coerced into the crime and then confessed once you were safe."

"Well, maybe that's what we can do then," she said. "I'm pretty sure I don't want the asshole to go to jail."

"No," said Leo. "We don't want anyone going to jail." He pulled a chair in front of Kim and sat down so that they were looking at each other eye to eye. "We want this to go as smoothly as possible. As long as they come up with some money—any amount—we'll accept the offer and set up the drop."

She was keeping eye contact and nodding now, hopefully coming around to the idea of getting this done today and sleeping in her own bed tonight, and probably telling Eddie to sleep on the couch. "Where do we tell them to drop it?" she said.

"We need a place where they won't be seen by anyone," he said. He had a few places in mind. He remembered when Kim and Marilyn's guinea pig died, and Bill asked him to get rid of it. For some reason, he couldn't just wrap it up and throw it in a garbage can, so he found a spot deep in Golden Gate Park and dug a small grave. He didn't want to have to lie to the kids about where their beloved pet was laid to rest, so he found a nice spot near a pond. He was a little embarrassed as he thought back on it and felt strange to be alone with Kim, who was now a grown woman wearing his sweater with nothing on underneath.

"If they could get out in the bay," she said, "and tie it to a buoy or something, that could work."

"That's actually a really good idea," he said. "It would solve the witness problem." He actually knew a guy with a boat, but he didn't know if Eddie had any access. And they needed this to happen quickly. They had to do it tonight.

"So, you want to do this as a water drop?" she said. She actually looked excited that her idea was being considered. She was sitting forward on the couch with her elbows on her knees. Leo couldn't stop peeking into the V-neck.

"Does Eddie have access to a boat?" he asked.

She shook her head. "But maybe Duff and Marilyn do."

"It can't be *maybe*," he said. "Or else it might take another day for them to be able to find a boat and figure out a way to get the money to the drop spot. We need to make it easy because they're probably spending all their time right now trying to get the cash."

She nodded and closed her eyes for a moment. "How about when I get home?" she said.

"What do you mean?"

"Like what's my story going to be?"

"This is *your* plan," he said. "What was your story going to be when you started all this?"

"I never got that far."

He was falling in love with her even though she was frustrating the hell out of him right now. Maybe this was a test. If he could fall in love with someone who did something as stupid as Kim had done, perhaps it was true love.

He let out a long breath and met her eyes. She was squinting at him as if she were trying to predict what he was going to say. "You need to say that you were blindfolded the entire time except for the few minutes when you did the FaceTime calls."

"Should I say I was sexually assaulted?"

"What? No. Why would you do that?"

She looked like she was about to smile, but she pulled her lips back tight against her teeth and said, "I just thought since you keep looking down my shirt, that the kidnappers probably wouldn't be able to resist."

"Jesus," he said. "First of all, that's my sweater, and secondly, why did you take your bra off?"

"You said I should get comfortable," she said, smiling now.

Leo could feel himself heating up and wasn't sure what to make of it. "You do look comfortable," he said and folded his hands in his lap.

"Come on over here and sit next to me," she said.

"I don't think I better," he said. "At least not until we get this all figured out."

"Your loss," she said and leaned forward again.

## 41

When the phone started to buzz, Eddie tried to hand it off to Duff.

"What are you doing?" said Duff and pushed the phone back to Eddie. "*You* need to talk to these people."

"Sorry," said Eddie, shaking his head and going flush. He took a deep breath and then activated the FaceTime call.

Marilyn was standing right next to Eddie but probably couldn't be seen by Kim. Duff stood in front of Eddie, so he was seeing only Marilyn's and Eddie's faces.

Her voice was clear and calm when she came on. "Listen carefully," she began, and the room went quiet. Marilyn sniffed quickly before Kim was back to talking. "Here's what they want you to do."

Eddie and Marilyn were both nodding. Duff grabbed a pen and an envelope out of the desk drawer. He was poised to take notes if things got complicated.

"First," said Kim, "let me assure you that I haven't been harmed, and the people holding me have no intention of hurting me if you do what they say."

Duff was nodding at Eddie, trying to reassure him. It made sense. There would be no reason for them to harm Kim unless she could identify them. So, Duff was hoping the kidnappers kept their masks on while she was there. It would just be an extra task for them to kill her and get rid of the body. He thought back to the digging marathon that he and Eddie had completed just a couple of days ago and couldn't imagine anyone having any interest in that kind of work.

When Eddie didn't reply, Kim said, "I believe these people, Eddie, so there's no reason to bring the police into this. Just drop the money where we tell you. Can you do that?"

Eddie nodded confidently at his phone, but Marilyn stood by with tears running down her cheeks. Maybe she was seeing something in Kim's eyes that didn't look right to her, but Duff liked the sound of Kim's voice. He felt like Kim trusted that these people would keep their word. If she were scared that they were lying and intended to harm her, he would have heard it in her voice. But he didn't. She sounded good, ready to get this over with and come home.

"They want me to ask you how much money I'm worth," said Kim.

Eddie looked like someone suddenly awakened from a night terror, not completely sure what was real and what wasn't, but determined to soldier through it until he could tell the difference. "How much you're worth?" he said and then left his mouth open like there was more to come, but that was all he had at the moment.

"They wanted me to ask you that, Eddie," she said, still sounding confident to Duff.

Eddie only closed his mouth so that he could swallow, his Adam's apple bobbing as he looked over the top of the phone at Duff.

Duff started to pantomime something but stopped himself and scribbled on the envelope: *Can't put a dollar value on human life.*

Eddie got the message and said, "You can't put a dollar value on a person's life."

Duff was good with that answer. He also knew Eddie's reply required a follow-up, but Duff didn't really have time to play Cyrano with the kidnappers waiting for a response. So, Duff took a step toward Eddie and nodded at him so hard that Duff felt the tension in his neck when Eddie looked back at the camera.

Eddie said, "I love you, Kim, but all we could come up with on the short notice is $20,000. If I could sell the house right now and get the money to these people, I would. But it takes time."

Duff wished he could see Kim's face to get some kind of read on this. Instead, he looked to Marilyn, who had wiped the tears from her face and was staring intently at the phone. They all waited. Duff wondered if Kim was off-camera consulting with her captors, discerning whether Carl's loan of twenty grand would be enough.

"Separate the money into ten stacks of twenty hundred dollar bills and put them in a sealed freezer bag. Then put the freezer bag into a plastic shopping bag—something that isn't see-through. Do you got it, Eddie?"

For a moment, Eddie looked startled again, as if he weren't the person responsible for responding to the question. Like he was watching a YouTube video on his phone about people with whom he had no relationship. "Yes," he shouted finally. "What's next?"

"Do you know where the casting pools are?" she asked.

Eddie began to shake his head, but Duff jumped up and gave the thumbs up. He'd been there a few times—huge concrete pools, where people practiced fly casting. He'd never seen anyone casting before, but Marilyn had explained to him their purpose years ago. The pools were right next to the Polo Fields in Golden Gate Park.

"Yes," Eddie said to the phone and then looked back up at Duff to make sure he'd said the right thing.

Kim said, "Take the bag of money to the casting pools tonight. It'll be dark. If you park behind the lodge and walk up the path, you'll be facing the three pools. Are you with me?"

Eddie looked over the phone at Duff again. Duff nodded, and Eddie said, "Yes."

"Okay," she said, still in control. "There are paths on either side of the center pool that can get you to the far side. Take the one on the right and walk all the way across so that you're looking back at the lodge. Can you picture it?"

Eddie opened his mouth again but said nothing. Marilyn was nodding and nudged him. When he looked at her, she whispered *yes*. She knew the area. So, Eddie looked back at the camera and said, "Yes."

"If you look at the concrete sidewalk, right on the edge by the water," she said, "you'll see numbers painted on pavement. Walk to number 105."

Duff wrote this down on the envelope and then showed it to Eddie and Marilyn as if they'd forgotten what Kim had just said two seconds before. He was realizing that he was probably as nervous about this as Eddie.

"Once you see 105," she said, "Turn around and walk ten paces. You'll cross over the pavement and into the dirt. Stop there and dig a shallow hole. Stick the bag in it."

She paused for a moment, and Eddie said, "That's it?" His voice was shaky, and his face had red blotches on it now. The man looked like he had hives. "It seems like that might be tough to find in the dark."

"Pick up a bunch of pinecones," she said, "Put a little stack over the spot. These people will find it. Are you going to do it tonight?"

"We'll do it as soon as it gets dark," he said.

"Well, that's it, unless you have questions."

"How do we make sure that you'll be released?" asked Eddie.

"They're going to release me, Eddie," she said. "Tell my sister it's going to be fine."

## 42

Derek hadn't treated Angie well. He understood that. But he also knew that he'd tried in the beginning. Cristian had set the whole thing up, and Derek shouldn't have expected anything beyond a working relationship, but he did.

He wasn't sure if he'd been in love with her, but he liked being with her. When she drank wine, she was like some character in a movie. But they hadn't gotten drunk together in months. And the last time *he* was drunk, she wasn't, and she'd ended up on the floor looking up at him like he was some kind of monster. He would have preferred that she'd looked at him with fear. But that wasn't it. It was disgust. And at that moment, he'd known it was over. But he never expected that she'd just take off like this. She'd left all her clothes. Everything.

And now she'd been gone for days.

So, Derek and Alex were looking through her things, trying to find something that might lead them to her. But she didn't have much. It was her policy. No extras. Everything in one suitcase. Except shoes. She had lots of shoes.

"Jesus," said Alex. "I've never seen so many." He picked up a red one with a spiked heal. "Jesus," he said again.

"How about up there?" said Derek, pointing at the shelf above the dresses, all hanging in different lengths over the shoe racks.

Alex reached up and pushed some boxes around. "More shoes," he said. But then he pulled one down. "This one's lighter," he said and shook the box with both hands. "Maybe it's socks." He laughed after, but Derek just extended his hand, and Alex surrendered the box.

Derek walked over and sat on the bed. With the box on his lap, he pulled off the top and tossed it aside. "What's she got in here?" he said to himself and started placing items on the comforter. She had two new covid masks. A very old looking ring with an inscription in Romanian, which neither Derek nor Alex ever learned to read.

Angie also had a gold watch in there. Some gold coins. A two-dollar bill. A photograph of her and her deceased twin brother from when they were nine or ten. There were other photographs of people Derek had never seen. A fancy looking pen. Some credit cards with names of people Derek didn't know. A little pin of the Italian flag. An old driver's license from when Angie was a teenager. He could tell she had braces in the picture but was trying to smile without showing her teeth. There were a couple of business cards and a phone bill for her cell service. And finally, Derek unfolded a small piece of notebook paper with a series of codes written on it. He assumed they were passwords, but he didn't know for what. Maybe for everything for which she needed passwords. She was always forgetting them. Most of these followed the same pattern, but they would end with different numbers or an exclamation point, which Derek assumed coincided with password renewals.

He looked at everything laid out on the comforter and sighed.

Alex said, "Not much, huh?"

"No," said Derek. "She liked it that way. She wanted to be untraceable."

"What are the business cards?" said Alex.

There were only a few. Derek picked them up and started to shuffle through the deck. Old folks' homes. He flipped them one by one onto the bed until he got to last one. A realtor. *Eddie Bilker*. "Why would she have a realtor's business card?" he asked and held the card up for Alex to see.

Alex shrugged and picked up one of the other cards on the bed. "Does she have deals going with people in all these homes?"

"I know of only two current relationships," said Derek.

"Relationships," said Alex. He threw the card back on the bed and moved back to the closet where he shook a few more boxes on the high shelf. "Shoes," he said.

Derek was still looking at the realtor's card. He flipped it over and saw a hand-written phone number. "Cristian has his own realtor," he said.

Alex sat down on the bed and picked up the small Italy pin. He held it between two fingers and squinted at it. Then he pulled the back off and tested the sharpness of the pin. "And?" he said.

"Why would Angie need this guy's card if we already have a realtor?"

Alex returned the back to the Italy pin and dropped it on the bed. He picked up Angie's old driver's license. He stared hard at it and said, "Who are you?" He held the ID up for Derek to see and shook his head.

"She's a con artist, Alex," said Derek, who closed his eyes and watched a rapid-fire slide show of Angie race through his mind. He was angry with her and surprised that all the images were sexual. They were mental snapshots of Angie in different poses and in different stages of dressing. He opened his eyes for a moment and then closed them again. This time, the image was Angie walking off to Cristian's office at the club. If he loved her, he should have insisted on being in there with her. But he didn't do that. He did what Cristian told him to do.

"I *know* she's a con artist," said Alex. "She works with us."

"That's not what I'm saying," said Derek. "I think she might have been conning us—The Organization."

Alex sat up. "You think?"

"I don't know," said Derek, trying to mine his memories for a clue. "Do you think she could've been planning on selling Carl's house on her own after he dies?"

"On her own?" said Alex. "And keep the money?"

"Yes," said Derek. "She'd walk away with millions of dollars."

Alex picked up the driver's license and stared at it again. "Would it be worth it for her to have to be looking over her shoulder for the rest of her life, waiting for Cristian to find her and drag her around the neighborhood by her hair?"

"Totally not worth it," said Derek. He walked back over to the closet and put his hand in the pockets of the four coats she had hanging with the dresses. Nothing. One dry cleaning receipt. That was it. "But that doesn't mean she wouldn't try it."

"Has anyone ever tried to betray Cristian before as far as you know?" asked Alex.

"I can't even imagine it," said Derek. That's why he didn't follow Angie back to Cristian's office that night. He couldn't even imagine it. The man could have killed her back there, but Derek didn't even consider trying to protect his wife. It seemed strange to him now that the thought never entered his mind. He couldn't understand why it was bothering him now. And he couldn't understand why he'd let her go back there on her own. He finally settled on loyalty. Cowardice bounced into his mind for a moment, as did thoughtlessness and greed. But loyalty was the notion that stuck, and he forced himself to get comfortable with that.

Alex was looking through Angie's end table drawers now. He pulled out all three and placed them on the bed. They were nearly empty. One drawer had a sleep mask. A file folder with their marriage certificate. A nail clipping kit. And a couple of magazines. The second drawer had a figurine of an angel. Ear plugs. Dice. A mass of tangled cords. And a Swiss Army Knife. The last drawer contained a few airplane bottles of brandy and an old cell phone so small it looked like a toy. Alex was dumping everything on the bed now. A brochure for a resort in Italy. A couple of Elmore Leonard paperbacks. A retainer in its plastic case.

"Does any of this mean anything to you?" said Alex.

Derek shook his head. "I don't know where to look," he said. "If she's planning on trying to take that house for herself, she'd have been better off sticking to the plan and working with Carl to get the deal done in secret instead of disappearing like this."

"That would be tough," said Alex. "We've been watching that particular play very closely."

"Agreed," said Derek. "I don't know how she can do it without us catching her. And then she'll have to deal with Cristian."

"Maybe she was planning on it but chickened out before Carl had a chance to die," said Alex. "But figured we might have been on to her, so she ran."

"What if she didn't run?"

"You mean, you think someone took her?"

"Or maybe she's living with the old man, somewhere in that big house."

"That would take a set of balls I'm not sure Angie has," said Alex. "And just live there until he died? Then simply start living there on her own? In that big ass house?"

Derek took a moment to think about Angie washing dishes in that big kitchen or doing laundry down in the mud room. He couldn't create a clear image of her doing those things. "I don't think she'd live there,

Alex. I think she wanted to sell it and skip town, hence the realtor's card."

"Yeah, yeah," said Alex. "I'm getting mixed up. Forgot about the realtor. That had to be the plan."

"So, who do you want to go see first?" said Derek. "The old man or the realtor?"

Alex looked confused. He shrugged and started putting items back in the drawer.

"I think I want to take one more run at Carl without that younger dude there."

"The dude who was checking in on him?" said Alex.

"Yeah," said Derek. "There was something I didn't like about that guy."

"The way he was being Mr. Nice Guy but also kind of intimidating?"

Derek thought about that. Alex was right. That guy was posturing without looking like he was posturing. There was something professional about him. The confidence. Maybe it was arrogance. Like the old man had hired security but didn't want anyone to know. Derek took another moment to ponder why Carl would need private security. "Let's go over there right now," said Derek. "I think Carl might know more than he's leading on."

"I think he's losing his mind, Derek."

"I'm not so sure about that," said Derek and thought about whether or not Carl would be as bold without his muscle there. See if he'll talk about sex with Angie when it's just the two of them, looking at each other eye-to-eye.

## 43

Carl wondered if he should change out of his robe and put on some clothes before Duffy came back for the loan. He wondered if he should even be giving Duffy the money. $20,000 was all he had in the safe, and he barely knew this kid. But there was something about him and the girlfriend, Marilyn. A compelling couple. Good people in a bad spot. Most likely caused by the other idiot.

He decided to compromise. He'd loan them the money, but he wasn't going to change out of the robe.

He was in the den when he heard the doorbell. He tightened the belt on his robe, which was weighed down by the envelopes in his big pockets, each holding ten thousand dollars in hundred-dollar bills. Now that he was walking to answer the door, he felt stupid in the robe, like he was trying to be cooler than he was. Hugh Heffner. But it was too late now. And how could they judge him?

He felt himself smiling as he opened the door because he did like these kids, and he was excited to be a part of their caper. But he'd only opened the door a crack before it came crashing into him. He saw the bald heads just before he fell back into the console table and felt the tackle box dig into his back. He was able to find his balance by putting both hands behind him and grabbing hold of the table, which he heard crash into the wainscoting.

"Hi, Carl," said the one in charge, Derek. "We had a few more things to talk to you about that we didn't get into yesterday."

"Well, that's an odd way of coming into a house," said Carl, trying to decide if he should keep up with the senile old man bit.

"Sorry about that, old-timer," said the other one, Alex. "We wanted to make sure we had your attention for this."

"Well, you got it," said Carl, straightening up now and tightening the belt on his robe again. He felt the weight of the envelopes, and he had to be intentional about keeping his hands out his pockets. He felt the urge to reach in and clutch the envelopes, but he knew he'd be drawing attention to them. So, he put his hands on his hips. A ridiculous pose, but he had no idea what to do with his hands. He considered a boxer's stance, but decided that might be provocative, so he stuck with the hands-on-the-hips thing.

"Good, good," said Derek. "We just want to make sure there's nothing else you can tell us about Angie. I know you said you two are tight, so we're hoping you might be able to remember something she might have said about where she was headed. We haven't seen her in a few days, and we're really just worried about her safety."

"And yours, too," said Alex.

"What?" said Carl.

"What can you tell us about Angie's whereabouts?" said Derek.

"You guys know I have problems with my memory," he said and already knew that he'd blown his cover. He didn't have time to get into character, and his voice didn't sound nearly as confused as it had the last time he'd done this routine. His initial instinct was to needle Derek more about not knowing where his own wife was, but he fought it off and said, "I'd tell you if I knew anything. I'm worried about her, too."

Both brothers were quiet now, just looking at Carl, waiting for more, but he honestly had nothing more to give them. He actually felt comfortable for a moment because he wouldn't have to tell any lies. How could he get caught bluffing if he had no information?

"Do you take medication, Carl?" said Derek. He was smiling now and took a look over at his brother.

"Rarely," he said. "I was on a bunch of stuff for the cancer, but I stopped taking it a few weeks ago." He didn't know where they were going with this, but he added, "They tell me I'll want the pain meds once my body starts to break down."

"Hmm," said Derek. "Because you seemed so out of it yesterday. Like you were a different person. Older."

"Like you were drugged up," said Alex.

"Or putting on an act," said Derek.

"To what end?" said Carl.

"That's what we're here to find out," said Derek. "Why would an old man pretend to have dementia if his brain was still working fine?"

"I'm an old man," said Carl. "I have good days, and I have bad days."

Alex was leaning up against the door, and Derek was walking around a bit, looking at furniture and paintings.

"What you playing at, old man?" said Derek, turning his head from an oil painting of the Golden Gate Bridge and staring directly at Carl.

"I'm telling you the truth," said Carl, trying to remember whether or not he'd fastened the latch on the tackle box directly behind him. "I have no idea where Angie could be."

"That might be true," said Derek. "But you haven't been straight with her, have you?"

Carl felt a wave of nausea. "I'm very fond of Angie," said Carl. "I wouldn't do anything to hurt her."

"Who said anything about hurting her?" said Alex, who stepped away from the door and presented a more dangerous posture.

Carl was quick. "I meant her feelings," he said. "I'm very fond of Angie."

"Is she in your will?" said Derek.

Carl had a feeling this was it. They had him. He didn't know what they planned to do, but if they'd been expecting to inherit the house, they were going to be pretty pissed. He didn't say anything, but he scratched at his forehead and peeked behind to see the secured latch on the tackle box. Alex was about five feet away, and Derek was at least ten, but he was pacing. Sometimes he was as far as fifteen feet and sometimes as close as three or four. Carl knew he could get into the box pretty quickly, but he wanted to wait for the perfect moment. He wondered if there was a way to open it quickly without causing alarm. "The will?" he said, reaching a hand back and touching the old metal box.

Derek laughed. "He's senile again, Alex."

"He has good days and bad days."

"What do you guys want from me?" said Carl, angling his body so that neither brother could see his hands behind his back. And when Derek laughed loudly again, Carl flipped the latch. It was happening. This was why he'd brought it up here in the first place, but that was all just make-believe two days ago. And now it was actually happening.

"I know you're old and losing your mind," said Derek. "But I'd like you to answer the question."

"What was the question again?" said Carl.

"This is such bullshit," said Alex and took a step toward Carl.

"Okay ... okay," said Carl and put his hands out like a traffic cop trying to hold off oncoming cars, hoping to encourage Alex to move to his spot near the door.

Alex miraculously stepped back and said, "Answer the question, grandpa."

When Carl saw that Alex was on his heels, Carl turned around, opened the tackle box, and grabbled for his gun, which he had resting on top. He had already decided that he would shoot Alex first and hope that Derek was pacing in the wrong direction, which would give Carl time to turn and shoot Derek immediately after.

Before Carl could even get his hand out of the box, Derek had come up behind him, grabbed the lid, and closed it down hard on Carl's hand. Carl felt himself drop the gun inside the box, and then he watched Derek pull up the lid and bring it crashing down on Carl's hand two more times. Carl was surprised he wasn't quick enough to pull his hand out. It was as if his brain was sending the wrong messages to his hand.

Derek looked him directly in the eye and brought the heavy metal lid down hard one more time. Then he lifted the lid and pulled Carl's hand out. He pushed him to the floor. Carl was dizzy with pain, but he could see Derek pull the gun out and point it at Carl's head.

Carl let his head roll back to the floor, but he kept his eyes open and looked up to see Alex's face. The man's mouth was wide open, like you might see from someone who'd just witnessed a car accident or a man's hand getting jacked up in a tackle box.

"Grab his foot," said Derek, as he slid the gun underneath his belt and reached down to take hold of Carl's ankle. Carl saw that one of his slippers was missing, but he could feel the second one half-way on the other foot.

Alex pulled it off and threw it across the room. "What are we doing with him?" said Alex.

"This piece of shit," said Derek, dropping the old man's foot, "told Angie she was in his will so that he could keep bangin' her." He was talking to Alex, but his eyes were on Carl. "But she's not in the will, so this job is over."

"I gave you boys plenty of work," said Carl and was surprised how old he sounded. His hand and wrist were throbbing.

"Grab his foot," said Derek.

"Where we bringing him?" said Alex.

"Up to his safe," said Derek, his hand wrapped around the ankle like a shackle. "We're gonna take whatever he's got in there. He'll give us the combination or he's gonna lose his testicles."

"You can have whatever I got," he said. There was no reason for him to endure any more pain. "I'll walk up there with you." He felt the urge to check his pockets, but his right hand didn't seem to work anymore, and his left hand was too close to Derek, who hadn't taken his eyes off Carl for several minutes now.

"I prefer dragging you up there," said Derek. "You're light."

The brothers slid Carl across the hardwood toward the uncarpeted stairs. Carl held his head up as much as he could, but he felt each step jabbing into his back and neck as the blood rushed to his brain. Eventually, he couldn't hold his head up anymore, and he felt it banging against the last few stairs before he was sliding on hardwood again.

The brothers' voices sounded muffled now, and Carl couldn't tell the difference between them anymore. When he looked up through blurred vision, he heard one of them say, "The safe is in the closet in the bedroom." Carl fantasized that the brothers had found the safe when they'd been doing jobs in the house, but in his heart, he knew that Angie had told them.

As he slid into the bedroom, he saw the closet door open, and he saw the safe open as well. He'd never closed it after filling the two envelopes. The belt on his robe was loose, and the rest of the robe was tangled around his neck like a cape for the worst superhero ever.

He heard the brothers laughing. "It's open," one of them said. They'd dropped his feet, and he was lying flat on his back now with his eyes closed. When they saw no money in there, he didn't want to watch Derek shoot him with his own gun. He only hoped the envelopes had stayed in his pockets. Duff and Marilyn needed that money.

"Old man," said Derek. "Why is this safe open?"

Carl kept his eyes closed and tried to speak but nothing came out. It gave him a moment to come up with something. He cleared his throat. "It's always open," he whispered.

"This guy …," said Alex. "Why have a safe if you're gonna keep it open?"

Carl opened his eyes and looked at the ceiling. "I only lock it when I have something valuable in it."

"You don't have anything valuable?" said Derek.

"It's all in a safe deposit box at the bank," said Carl, his voice coming back to him now.

Derek walked over and kicked the door to the safe. "You're a real piece of work, Carl."

Carl wanted to check the pockets to see if the envelopes were still in there. "How could I keep anything valuable in this house with you two guys hanging around all the time?" Once he said it, he regretted it, but there was no turning back now. "I actually considered hiding the silverware."

Derek moved into Carl's line of vision and stared down at him. Carl didn't blink. He knew this was probably it for him. Then Derek stepped on his mangled hand. It sent a shockwave through his whole body, and he tried to scream, but it came out like someone gagging. He felt Derek's foot twisting now, like someone putting out a cigarette. There was a moment when he thought he might faint, but he retained consciousness.

Carl's ears were buzzing, but he heard Derek say, "I'll do a sweep of the house." Carl had tears in his eyes, but he opened them to see the blurred image of Derek handing the gun to Alex. "Maybe there's something here we should take. Cristian is not going to be happy."

"Should I kill him?" said Alex.

"Go ahead," said Derek. "I'll check the garage. Maybe he's got a baseball card collection down there."

Once Derek was out of the room, Carl wanted to get Alex talking. He had a stupid idea he wanted to try, but he'd also come to terms with the situation, and he was at peace. He hadn't been looking forward to the deterioration of mind and body that was coming down the pike.

"I'm dying," said Carl.

"Yep," said Alex. "I just don't want to get any of your brains on my suit."

"Yeah," said Carl. "What I mean is that I'm comfortable with that, and I do feel badly about how I treated Angie. I want to make this easier for you guys, and I don't want to suffer anymore. I'm ready."

"That's good to know," said Alex. "Maybe I'll show up to the funeral."

Carl was happy to be dealing with Alex. "I think I can make it easier on *you guys*," he said. "We can make this look like a suicide. It would make sense with my diagnosis and all. And it would keep the cops away from you and your brother. There's plenty of evidence that you all have been around the last few months. You'll certainly be persons of interest in this."

"What makes you want to help the people who are going to kill you?"

"You're young," said Carl. "So, you don't know what it's like to be staring down death up close like I've been doing for a while now."

"Nope," said Alex. "That's a different perspective, I guess."

"I want to meet my maker with a clean conscience," said Carl. "I want my last act to be one of selflessness."

"So, just out of curiosity, what's the plan," said Alex.

"We make it look like I shot myself in the head."

"That sounds good to me," said Alex. "As long as you're dead, we'll be happy."

"Okay," said Carl. "Do you mind if we get it over quickly, so I don't have to think about it too much?" He sat up but kept his eyes on Alex.

"Again," said Alex. "Sounds good to me." He walked over and put the gun up to Carl's head.

For a moment, Carl thought he might have overplayed his hand.

But then Alex said, "Okay, how do we do it?"

Carl didn't like the feel of the gun pressing against his temple, but he stayed calm. "Obviously you want my fingerprints on the gun," said Carl.

"So, you need to hold the gun," said Alex.

Carl nodded but said nothing.

Alex went to the dresser and pulled a t-shirt out of the drawer and wiped down the gun. Then he stood behind Carl and actually grabbed Carl's bad hand and placed it on the handle of the gun while Alex, with his other hand wrapped in the t-shirt, held the barrel up to Carl's head. The pain from the manipulation of Carl's hand blasted all the way up his arm, but he didn't flinch. He waited. Then Alex took Carl's finger and wrapped it around the trigger.

"This might burn your hand a bit," said Carl.

It was for only a fraction of a second, but Carl felt Alex loosen his grip. Carl had been waiting for this reaction. He jerked the gun away from his own head and fired wildly behind him.

Alex released the gun. When Carl turned his head to look behind him, he saw Alex slapping at his own face with both hands like a monkey or one of the three stooges. He wondered if this was Alex's primitive way of expressing anger. Carl leaned on his elbow and pointed the gun, ready to fire again, but then he saw the blood running down Alex's face from a small hole above his eyebrow before he toppled forward and lay face down on the floor.

Carl felt the approaching vibrations of Derek's footsteps coming down the hallway. Carl's hearing was a mess from the gunshot going off so close to his head, but he was fairly sure he heard Derek say, just before he entered the room, "Alex, what the—?"

Carl was leaning on his elbow and had the gun pointed at the doorway. As soon as he saw Derek's shoulder and arm, he fired. There was a brief moment when Derek's eyes met Carl's before Derek ducked away and the bullet splintered the doorframe.

Carl tried to listen for footsteps on the stairs or the front door opening, but his ears were still ringing. He lifted himself back up into a sitting position—his robe still twisted around his neck— and leaned up against the wall. He kept the gun aimed at the doorway, but the gun was heavy in his injured hand, so he pulled his knee up. He rested his wrist on his knee to keep the gun in a ready position. He eventually added his left hand, and he sat there with both hands holding the gun for many minutes.

## 44

Al thought it might be worth it to check in on Brianna, maybe see if she was interested in the car rather than the cash he would have to net from dealing the car to Walter's people. He was interested in skipping a step and ending this shit. The thought of him getting fired and losing his pension was keeping him up at night. To him, it was worth it to at least ask Brianna if the car would suffice. Walter's guy would have to get it painted and use his contact at the DMV to create some documents, but that's what the man did. It was his business. It would be secure. And once Brianna saw the car, she might end the extortion.

They dropped off Al's car, and now Al was driving the Porsche up to Brianna's condo in Diamond Heights near the Police Academy. Walter was sitting in the passenger seat playing with the radio, checking through the former owner's programmed stations, two of which were playing Huey Lewis and the News. Walter was trying to find any station that didn't play white music.

"You think Brianna will go for it?" asked Al.

"I would," said Walter. "It's worth a lot more than the cash you owe her."

"Yeah," said Al. "But do you think she'll go for it?"

"I hope so," said Walter. "I want this whole thing to be over. Y'know, I had no idea it was you when she paid me to videotape—."

"Shut up, Walter," said Al. "Once you saw it was me, you had free will to put that camera back in the case and drive out." Al was getting pissed all over again. "But you chose to screw me, Walter. You had a choice."

Walter didn't say anything. He left the radio on an old school station playing Wilson Picket and slumped into the leather seat.

Al still needed Walter, so he said, "But we partners now."

Walter nodded but kept his eyes focused on the road as they drove past the Diamond Heights Safeway up the hill toward Brianna's.

"She might want to take a test drive," said Al. "So, you have to get in the back. And you need to help convince her that it's safe to take the car."

"I'll just tell her the truth," said Walter. "Untraceable. These cats are moving a couple of luxury cars a day. They got a whole operation going. Dudes are experts in the field. Rich as all hell because they so good at this."

Al nodded and pulled up in front of her house. Walter switched seats. Al had texted her earlier. She was home. She thought he was bringing the money, so he and Walter were going to have to be convincing. Otherwise, he'd be forced to tell her that she'd have to wait to see the cash. And she might be all out of patience by now. Al wondered what her fancy-cocktail-drinking attorney would advise and whether or not she'd listen to him.

She came out of her place looking good, wearing a tracksuit with some kind of sparkles on it. She leaned into his window and said, "If you can afford this car, Al, I assume you got my money." Then she leaned farther into the car and saw Walter in the back seat. She hesitated before saying, "Oh, hey Walter."

Walter tilted his head. "What's up, Brianna," he said.

Al didn't have time to play, so he got right to it. "I figured out it was Walter who made the porno movie starring me and you, Brianna."

Brianna nodded and said into the dark of the back seat, "And you're still alive, Walter?"

"Walter and I are partners now," said Al. "He helped me secure this luxury automobile."

"Where's my money?" said Brianna.

"Check this out," said Al. "I'm providing some options."

"I'm about to send out that video, Al Young."

"Do you want to hear the options," he said.

Brianna nodded and looked at her fingernails.

"You like this car?" he said.

She nodded without looking up from her nails.

"It's yours instead of the money, if you want to do it that way," said Al.

"You think I want a stolen car?" said Brianna.

Walter spoke up from the back. "I got a guy who'll paint it and process it for you," he said. "He'll get you all the paperwork, and you'll be the owner of a Porsche."

"Do I get to pick the color?" she said. "I like this blue, but if we gotta change the color, I'd like to be able to pick."

"So, you want the car?" said Al. "We have a deal?"

"Do I get to pick the new color?"

Al turned around to see what Walter knew about this. Walter nodded.

"You pick the color," said Al.

"Then, yeah," she said. "I can see myself in this car."

Walter said, "Can we trade your old car to pay for the paint and papers?"

She paused and looked up at the sky. "My Jetta?" she said. "Yeah, that'll work."

She looked good when she smiled. "How about a test drive?" said Al.

"Right now?"

Al opened the door and climbed out. "Get in," he said and smiled like they were still a thing.

Brianna said she wanted to open it up on the freeway, see how it felt. So, they took O'Shaughnessy down past Glen Park Station, hung a left on Alemany Boulevard, and merged onto Highway 101. Al watched her face light up when she moved into the fast lane.

Once Brianna got it humming, she asked, "So why the car instead of the money?"

Al sighed. "The bookie never got me my cash," he said.

"So, he still owes you the money?" she said.

"Well, we took the car," said Al. "I'm considering that payment."

"But he doesn't know it was you," she said. "And he's going to collect insurance on it. So, he still owes you the money."

Al thought about that. Damn, she was looking sexy behind the wheel talking about getting more money from Eddie Bilker. And she was right. Al smiled at her and said, "Should we drive over there right now and see if old Eddie found some money yet?"

"Can I keep driving?" she said.

Al put his hand on her thigh.

"You don't want to start that up again," she said, and Al moved his hand up higher.

***

When they pulled right up in front of Eddie's house, Walter said, "You gonna let the man see you sitting in his car?"

"What's he gonna do?" said Al, enjoying the leverage now that the Brianna problem was solved and wanting to let her see him as the hard guy again. "Call the cops and tell them I took his car because he owes me thirty grand on account of the golf?"

Walter looked confused. "He can't report you 'cause he'd be reporting himself too?"

"That's the situation, Walter," said Al. "Not bad, right?"

Al watched Walter in the rearview mirror, this two-bit hustler trying to figure out if he was in some kind of pickle or not.

Al used the control to adjust his seat. Brianna was running her hands over the steering wheel like it was a new pet. She smiled at him. He'd done good. He didn't want to get back into any kind of relationship with this crazy-ass bitch, but, damn, she looked good in her sparkly outfit. "Hey, Walter," he said, friendly, like he was talking to the minister after church. "Why don't you take a walk around the block? Let me and Brianna have a moment of privacy to finalize the business arrangement."

Walter looked out the window, and so did Brianna and Al. The fog was rolling in off the Pacific, and the streetlights were a dim, blurry orange, strobing in the mist. "It looks cold out there, Al."

Al was still talking nice, looking into the mirror again. "You know what's cold, my brother?"

Al caught Walter's eyes in the mirror before Walter shook his head and looked away.

"I'll tell you what's cold," said Al. "Taking money to set up an old partner. That's cold, frigid shit." Al tried to catch the man in the mirror, but Walter was still squinting out at that fog.

"What about Briann—?"

"Get out the car, Walter."

Brianna opened the door, and Walter climbed out. Al heard him swearing under his breath, but Al and Brianna wouldn't need much time. The only obstacle was going to be this little car, but they'd figure out a way to make it work.

## 45

Duff didn't like any of this. He didn't like driving around with bags and a shovel. He didn't like Marilyn being involved. And he didn't like borrowing money from Carl. It felt wrong.

But he couldn't think of anything else to do at this point.

Marilyn hadn't cried in hours, so he assumed she was more confident than he was about this exchange. There was a logic to it. He appreciated that. Put the money in a hiding place so that the kidnappers can pick it up whenever they want—when they're confident they won't be seen. It made perfect sense if you were a kidnapper.

But from Duff's perspective, he was forced to put trust in people who were untrustworthy. He and Marilyn and Eddie were forced to have faith that these people were going to follow through on their end of the deal. Duff didn't like trusting criminals. Most of them would lie to their own moms to make a score. And if the money was for drugs, which seemed likely considering these guys were willing to accept such a small ransom, they'd be even more prone to screw up the arrangement.

Criminal drug addicts were the worst. They were less predictable than wild animals. At least wild animals had to follow their natural instincts. These meth-heads burned away their natural instincts. Their emotional reflexes were tainted. They were mush-brained.

Duff had seen the worst of the worst when he worked on the SFPD Tenderloin Task Force, and he was afraid he was dealing with the kinds of people whom he'd seen shacked up in residential hotels, living every day for the next score, sometimes crafting fantastical plans to get what they wanted. Desperate reprobates, always the most dangerous.

If both sides just followed the plan, everyone would be safe. Duff just didn't trust that these people were capable of even remembering the plan. But he was happy that Marilyn seemed to think all was well. He appreciated her optimism.

"Crossing paths with Carl was really lucky," she said and smiled as they pulled up in front of his house.

"He's a good dude," said Duff.

"The best," she said and opened her door.

"I don't think we all need to go in," said Duff. "I'm just going to grab the money, and we're off."

"I want to thank him," said Marilyn.

Eddie didn't say anything. He'd been quiet, said he felt sick.

"Okay, Eddie," said Duff. "You wait out here. We'll be out in a minute."

Eddie nodded, and Duff wondered what he was thinking about. He wondered if Eddie could see this coming to an end but then having to start all over with Kim, if that was even an option. Duff wondered when Eddie would have to tell her about Angie, if any of that even mattered anymore.

Duff somehow felt guilty about Angie's death even though he'd never met her while she was alive. Watching that zipper run up over her face was going to stick with him. He knew that. But he assumed Eddie had it much worse. Eddie must have been wondering how much his relationship with Angie had to do with her demise. There had to be a connection. If it was Al Young or the Romanians, Eddie's relationship with Angie had to be connected to her death. Why else would they have included him in the body disposal business?

When they got across the street and walked about halfway up the path, Duff noticed that the door was open. He stopped and grabbed Marilyn's hand.

"What?" she said.

"The door."

"It's open," she said.

"Yeah," said Duff. "That's usually not a good sign."

"What do you mean?" she said.

Duff put his arm around her shoulder and looked into her hopeful eyes. "Does Carl seem like the kind of guy who would leave the door open?"

"Maybe he left it open for us," she said.

Duff shook his head and looked back at the door. "Maybe he'd leave it unlocked," he said. "But open? Something's not right."

"What do we do?" she said, sliding her arm around Duff's waist.

"You're going back to the car," he said and turned her around so that she'd know he was serious.

Eddie had the window open and as they approached, he said, "What's going on?"

Duff felt Marilyn look up at him, but he kept his eyes on Eddie. "Probably nothing," said Duff. "But just to be safe, I'm leaving Marilyn with you." He opened the door and watched her climb inside silently.

After he'd made it back across the street and was just about where he and Marilyn had stopped on the path, he heard Eddie say, "You want me to come?"

Duff didn't flinch. He kept moving forward.

When he saw the drops of blood on the stone path, he kept an even stride and angled his body so that the door gave him some cover. He wanted to yell out for Carl, but he didn't want to alert whoever else might be in there.

The table near the doorway was tilted up against the wall, and the tackle box had slid down so that it was balanced between the wall and the table. The Persian runner was at an oblique angle, pointed toward the staircase instead of straight ahead. The house was quiet, and Duff made a quick trip to all the rooms on the first floor. Nothing else was disturbed.

He knew the stairs made him vulnerable, but he had to check the second floor. About halfway up the stairs, he heard wheezing. It wasn't the short, labored breaths of someone who was hyperventilating. It sounded almost like snoring.

Duff tip-toed down the hallway and followed the sound to Carl's bedroom. Maybe it *was* snoring. Duff peeked into the room and looked directly into Carl's eyes, which were wide open. He was definitely awake and sitting in a pool of blood that was leaking out of the head of one of the bald brothers, who was lying prostrate next to Carl. The bald guy had a hole above his eyebrow. His entire face was covered in blood, and his head was tilted toward Carl, so everything was leaking into a pool that was damming up next to Carl's bare leg. He was in his underwear and had a bunched up, blood-stained robe tangled behind him.

He was also using two hands to point a gun at Duff.

"I think I might have gotten the other punk as well," he said.

"Carl," said Duff. "I think you're right, but can you put that gun down."

"He just left," said Carl. "Do you think he'll come back for his brother?"

"If he does," said Duff, "Marilyn will call and warn us. She's out in the car. But I don't think he's coming back. He probably thinks you already called the cops."

"This one's only slightly dumber now than he was when he was alive," said Carl, who pointed the gun away from Duff and then placed it on top of the dead man.

Duff tried to avoid looking at the body. "Why did you shoot these guys, Carl?"

"Oh," he said. "They wanted to take my money and then kill me."

"How do you know?" said Duff, thinking maybe Carl was losing it, remembering back to his earlier performance as the senile old man but thinking now maybe it wasn't a performance.

"They told me that's what they were going to do," said Carl. "But the older asshole got away."

Duff nodded. "I guess we need to call the police now."

"I was pretty brave, Duff."

"I bet you were."

"I shot him backwards, over my shoulder," he said. "One shot."

Duff had no idea what to believe at this point, but he knew they needed to call the police. This was a crazy-looking crime scene, and now he was part of it. The money drop was looking unlikely at this point. He assumed the brother had gotten away with the money, and Duff was going to be stuck here talking to the police, probably for hours.

"Are you hurt?" asked Duff.

"I was so scared I felt like I was freezing for a second," he said. "But bravery's about being able to function at a high level while simultaneously shitting your pants."

"That's true," said Duff.

"And I shot this piece of human garbage from over my shoulder," he said and pointed down at the dead man. "I still don't hear so good."

"Carl," said Duff, raising his voice a bit. "Are you hurt?"

"I think they broke my hand or my wrist or both," he said. "And I might be concussed."

"I'll tell them to bring a medic."

"It's nice to know I did something brave before I die," he said and smiled.

Duff smiled back and nodded. "Good for you, Carl."

And then Carl's face lit up. "My pockets!" he said.

"Huh?"

"Help me check my pockets," he said and shifted his body to free up the robe that was twisted behind him.

"Do you want to stand up?" said Duff.

"I guess I should," he said.

Duff grabbed both his hands and pulled like you see basketball players do after someone takes a charge. And once he got Carl to his feet, Carl wrapped his robe back around himself and tried to tighten the belt the best he could, but he was clearly having trouble using his right hand. Duff moved forward to help him, but Carl waved him off. Then Carl reached into both pockets at the same time and pulled out two envelopes.

Duff shook his head at the old man and smiled. "Son of bitch," he said and immediately went back into planning mode. He figured he needed to get the money out to the car before the police got there so that Marilyn and Eddie could get it out to the drop site while Duff dealt with Carl and whatever first responders got there first.

Carl was waving both envelopes over his head like a cartoon lottery winner, wincing and grinning at the same time.

The bald guy was lying there with Carl's gun resting on his chest. The blood was clotting around his eyebrow and looked almost black in the darkened room.

## 46

Derek was in a parking spot on Ocean Avenue in front the optometrist's office, just up the street from the drugstore. He'd bought two rolls of paper towels in the drug store and stuffed a wad of them up near his shoulder to help with the bleeding. His jacket was ruined. When the old man had shot at him, the bullet clipped the doorframe, and a small chip of wood splintered into the hallway, tore through his sport coat, and wedged itself in the soft tissue between his collarbone and his shoulder blade.

He thought he'd been shot.

He managed to pull the chunk of wood out, but he was still bleeding like hell. He'd replaced the paper towels a couple of times already and was just now beginning to get control of the wound.

His brother was dead.

In the split second he'd peeked into that room, he saw enough to know. Alex's eyes were open, but he was lying next to the old man, and his head was tilted wrong. He looked like a doll, dropped on the floor for someone else to pick up.

Derek carried that image with him down the stairs when he ran out the front door. He wanted to go back and get Alex, but he knew the police would already be there. The whole thing was a shit show now. He wanted to know what stupid thing Alex had done to end up like this. His mind kept shifting between incendiary anger and paralyzing grief.

Sometimes the anger was directed at the old man, and Derek could feel it rise up in his chest and spread into his shoulders and arms and fists. But when Derek thought about his brother's stupidity, the grief would ooze into his neck and head. It would settle in his temples and throb steadily while the same image would materialize again and again as if it were playing on a loop.

For brief moments, he let himself consider the pending conversation with Cristian, but he pushed away those thoughts. He knew the man was too old to physically fight Derek on his own, but he also knew that Cristian would want him dragged around the club by his hair. Maybe that's why Derek had shaved his head in the first place. He knew there was going to be a time when he'd have to face Cristian, but he had other things to attend to first.

He was reading the real estate agent's business card he'd found in the box in Angie's closet. *Eddie Bilker*. Business address and phone number on the front and a handwritten address and phone number on the back. Derek took this to be the man's personal contact information. Since the moment he found the card, there was something that didn't feel right about it, and it had been eating at him the whole day. He didn't like that Angie had been talking to a realtor, and he didn't like that the guy had given her his personal contact information. What possible reason would this guy have for giving her his address? He couldn't help thinking that Angie and this real estate agent had something going. He just couldn't figure out if it was business or pleasure or both.

He flicked at the card with his finger and looked out through the window into the optometrist's office—a whole wall of glasses, all staring back at him. He knew he was missing something, his vision still not clear.

His brother was gone. His wife was gone. Cristian was sure to either banish him or kill him. So, he wanted to see clearly again. He wanted to know how all this came to be.

It was time to meet the realtor.

***

Derek knew the neighborhood fairly well. He liked the burrito place across the street. He decided to catch this guy, Eddie, in the office instead of going to his house, but it didn't look like it would happen. It was already past five, and there was only one light on in the building.

He pulled on the door, but it was locked, so he peered inside. There was an empty office on the left, but the one on the right with the lamp was occupied by a guy right off one of those suburban realtor bench billboards. His hair was just right—clean part. And his starched shirt had a conservative cut but enough flair to catch someone's attention—subtle pinstripes, but they were purple instead of blue.

Derek was holding the business card in one hand, and he knocked on the glass door with his other. The guy looked up from his work and shook his head. *We're closed*, he mouthed.

"I want to buy this house," said Derek and pointed at a random offering posted on the window.

The guy wasn't mouthing the words anymore. "Can you come back tomorrow?" he said.

"Can't do it," said Derek. "Getting on a plane in the morning."

This got the guy up out of his desk. He unlocked the door and let Derek in. "I'm Dan," he said and extended his elbow, trying to observe the new protocol but not wearing a mask.

"Derek," he said and offered his elbow. "Thanks for seeing me."

Dan moved his eyes from Derek's elbow to his shoulder. "You okay?" he said.

"Huh?"

"Your shoulder," said Dan.

"Oh, yeah," said Derek. "I was at a job site earlier." He pulled the bloody wedge of wood out of his pocket and presented it to Dan. "Rookie laborer could have killed me. I'm lucky it didn't hit me in the face."

"Jesus," said Dan. "I'll say."

"Where's this guy?" said Derek, holding up Eddie's card.

"Did he show you the listing?" said Dan.

Derek didn't want to get too involved if Eddie wasn't even there. "Someone recommended him to me," he said.

"He didn't come in today," said Dan. "But I can probably help you."

Derek looked at him, thinking Dan was ready to steal Eddie's commission. Then Derek looked over at the empty office. "Is this his desk?" he asked and walked over to look around. He didn't know what he would find, but he thought it was worth a look.

"Yeah," said Dan, following Derek over to Eddie's area. "But he's not coming back tonight."

"Can I leave him a note?" said Derek.

"You can just tell me," said Dan.

"You were ready to steal his client," said Derek. "This is a personal note."

Dan stared at him for a moment, maybe a little scared now, glancing at the bloody shoulder before saying, "Go ahead," then heading back to his desk.

Derek pulled the top page off a notepad and wrote *Angie recommended I come see you about some property. By the way, have you seen her?* He folded the paper over once and stapled it closed. The note wasn't important. It was just a pretense to scan Eddie's office. See if there was anything that might be interesting. It was just normal stuff. But there were two pictures on the desk. One was Eddie with a woman who must be his wife. The other looked like it was a shot taken with his true love: a new Porsche. Eddie was leaning up against the car and wearing a blue suit that matched the blue sports car. He had good posture.

Derek didn't like him, but he could see how Angie might. Time to stop by Eddie's house.

\*\*\*

The address on the back of the card led Derek to a foggy neighborhood just east of the zoo. It was difficult to see the addresses on the houses unless they were lit up. Most were not, so Derek cruised slowly around Country Club Drive, looking for 71. When he got to 83 and saw that the next house was 85, he knew that he'd passed it. But this street looped all the way around, so rather than making a three-point turn, he just kept going.

His gun was on his lap. He was still pissed that he hadn't brought it into the old man's house earlier that day or that he hadn't just choked him out in the front entrance as soon as they'd gotten there, considering they didn't even need him to open the safe. This same kind of thing had gotten him in trouble before—making a show out of something that could have easily been done quietly.

And now his brother was dead.

Derek couldn't help thinking that he'd let his emotions get the better of him. The old man was a phony. He'd been putting them on for months. And having sex with Angie the whole time. Derek was starting to feel it in his chest and arms again, and he was gripping the wheel like he was going to tear it right off the steering column.

He'd keep it simple with the realtor. Bullet to head. Eddie Bilker was part of this. Derek wasn't sure how, but he knew the realtor was involved in Angie's disappearance. Derek was convinced that Angie and this guy had somehow plotted to sidestep The Organization on a real estate deal—maybe the one that was never really going to happen with Carl's house.

He took a deep breath and relaxed his hands. He almost felt liberated for a moment. He felt that he had nothing to lose. He could either run or face Cristian. If he ran, Cristian would find him. A man, not unlike Derek, would be in charge of tracking Derek down. Nothing really mattered. He was a dead man walking. So, he wanted a few people to pay before he left this world.

As he made his way around the curve, he squinted at some addresses. He was getting close when he saw a set of brake lights blinking like morse code about fifty feet away. As he got closer, he could see that it was the blue Porsche.

He lifted the gun off his lap and rolled down his window. He couldn't figure out why the realtor was tapping on the brakes. Maybe he was listening to music outside his house. It didn't matter. Derek had made up his mind. Eddie Bilker was going to die in the Porsche.

With the fog and the tinted windows, Derek didn't have a clear view into the driver's seat, but he could visualize where the man's head would be. He slowed his own car to a stop, opened his window, aimed, and fired. When the window of the Porsche shattered, Derek still couldn't see very well, but he could hear a woman screaming. She was straddling the driver, who was, indeed, dead, but he didn't look like the realtor. In fact, both the driver and the straddler were black. The woman looked right at Derek and continued to scream.

He fired two shots at her and then one more at the driver. The screaming stopped, and Derek drove off even more confused than he'd been when he saw his brother lying on the floor in Carl's bedroom.

He felt like he was losing his mind.

## 47

Duff was glad to be out of Carl's house and on the way home.

He didn't know any of the cops who'd responded to the 911 call, but most of the cops had heard of Duff. The infamous gang bounty on him as well as his abrupt departure from the force was now a part of SFPD lore, even though Duff simply wanted to be known as the guy who ran Elmore's Boot. But just like his dad, Duff's experience in the SFPD was following him despite his best efforts.

By the time he walked into his house, Marilyn and Eddie were already there, looking disheveled and sitting next to each other on the couch. Apparently partners in crime now.

"How'd it go?" said Marilyn.

Duff sat down in the chair by the window and said, "How'd it go for you guys?"

Eddie was sitting forward with his elbows on knees. "The money's in the ground," he said and then shrugged as if to suggest *it's in God's hands now.*

Marilyn had her legs crossed at the knee and looked as if she were folding into herself, a human origami. Poor thing was sitting like someone who'd been strapped into a straitjacket. "Is Carl okay?" she asked.

"He'll be fine," said Duff. "Are *you* okay?"

"He must have been terrified?"

"It looks like he has a compound fracture of the wrist," said Duff. "But it doesn't seem to be bothering him. He's really proud of himself."

Eddie stood up and walked over to the fireplace. He leaned up against the mantle and said, "You didn't have time to tell us what exactly he did when those assholes showed up."

"I guess he killed one of the bald gypsies and wounded—or maybe even killed—the second one."

Marilyn released herself from the straight jacket and smiled. "How'd he do it?" she said.

"I don't think it happened the way Carl says," said Duff. "He made it sound like it was a trick shot, like you'd see in an old west show."

"A trick shot?" said Eddie, leaning forward away from the fireplace now.

"An old west show?" said Marilyn.

Duff had to think back to remember how Carl had described it. "He made one of the guys think he was helping them out, making it look like his death was a suicide and eliminate the brothers as suspects." Duff shook his head. It sounded so ridiculous. "He somehow had the guy put Carl's hand on the gun to leave his prints, and then Carl put the gun up to his own head." Duff smiled now, picturing it. "Then Carl somehow moved the gun enough to avoid hitting himself and shot the poor son of a bitch backward, over his shoulder. A trick shot, only without a mirror."

"And he hit the guy?" said Marilyn.

"In the head," said Duff. "One shot."

"Jesus," said Eddie. "And now he's proud of himself?"

"He should be," said Marilyn. "These dudes are nasty pricks."

"Sounds like self-preservation to me," said Eddie.

"Carl was complaining about his hearing," said Duff. "I guess the gun went off next to his ear, but he was smiling the whole time."

"Well, I think he was brave, Michael," said Marilyn.

"So does he," said Duff.

\*\*\*

The next move was to get over to Eddie's house. Duff didn't know when or where the kidnappers would release Kimberly, but he figured she would probably go home after. Where else would she go? He wondered if they were out there digging up the money right now.

Duff was just hoping these people didn't assault her. The trauma of being held for ransom was going to be difficult to overcome, but if they assaulted her, he didn't know if she'd ever be herself again. He was also worried about how she was going to react to the news that Eddie had been cheating on her. They would have to introduce that subject gradually after they could gauge her emotional state. Marilyn would, of course, insist on disclosing this information, and Duff had no problem with that. Eddie deserved whatever he got from this ridiculous escapade. Duff knew they might never find out who was responsible for the kidnapping, but he was confident that Eddie's lifestyle was the catalyst for the whole sordid mess.

When they crossed over Sunset Boulevard and turned onto Country Club Drive, Duff saw a skinny, middle aged black man running out of the neighborhood, back up toward the shopping center.

"Who's that?" said Duff and pointed at the guy who'd just scampered through the headlight beams.

"He's not from our street," said Eddie. "I know everyone."

As they made their way around the curve, Duff watched the black guy in his rearview mirror. The man was just a shadow now, blending into the shrubs and signs and parked cars until it was as if he never existed.

When Duff shifted his eyes back to the road in front of him, he saw a small group of people in the street up near Eddie's house. He wondered if Kim had already been released and made it home. Two men and a woman were standing next to Eddie's car. The woman was making frantic gestures.

"That's Susan," said Eddie.

"Who's that?" said Duff.

"She lives next door."

Duff pulled up near Eddie's parked car. Eddie opened the window and leaned his head out. "What's going on?" he asked.

Susan looked at him with her mouth open and ready to talk, but she didn't say anything for a moment.

"Susan," said Eddie. "It's me. What's going on?"

She just pointed at his car but didn't say anything. A large man wearing a hoodie, his hands in the front pouch, walked up to the window and addressed Eddie. "That's your car, right, Ed?"

"What's going on Tom?"

"I think you need to look for yourself," he said.

A second large man was standing in front of the car's front window, so Duff couldn't get a good look inside, but he saw the glimmer of broken glass on the asphalt. He put the truck in park and pulled up on the parking brake. Before he got out, he said, "Stay in the car, both of you."

He kept his engine running and the headlights on. He walked around the front of the truck until he was face to face with the guy shielding the driver's side window of the Porsche.

"You don't want to look in there," said the woman standing behind him. "I'm not even sure what I saw, but I knew to look away."

The guy in front of the window said, "We heard gunshots a while ago, so we called the cops and waited a few minutes before we came out. This is what we found."

He stepped away from the car and let Duff have a look. "Well, shit," said Duff and looked over his shoulder at Marilyn. "Stay in the car," he said again before staring into the interior of the Porsche, where he looked a second time at the half-dressed couple dead in the driver's seat.

The two of them were in the middle of something when someone shot them both where they sat. The woman was on the man's lap. She had no shirt on, and her face was obscured by her hair, which appeared to be a blonde wig that was half falling off her head, which was thrown back and resting in the space to the left of the steering wheel. Her mouth was open, and some of the wig was covering her teeth.

"I was gonna cover her up," said the first man, Tom. "But I didn't want to mess with the crime scene."

Duff nodded and leaned in a bit to see where all the blood was coming from. A lot of it was leaking out of the neck and cheek of the guy in the driver's seat. His face was pretty messed up, but once Duff's eyes adjusted to the light, he recognized Al.

His brain was trying to process it all. He hadn't been this close to four killings since his years on the gang task-force, where it was fairly common to see a gangland murder followed by any number of retaliatory killings in the same week. But as far as Duff could surmise, the only element tying these four bodies together was Eddie Bilker.

Duff walked back to the passenger side of the truck and leaned in. "Don't worry about that payout to Al Young," he said.

Eddie said, "What?" and leaned his head out to try and see past Duff.

"Al's gambling days are over," said Duff, looking back at Eddie's Porsche. "Someone killed the wrong idiot."

## 48

Kimberly Bilker was ready to go. The money should be in place, and she was excited to get home so that she could start planning how to *leave* home or kick Eddie out—one of the two. She hadn't decided yet. As soon as Eddie came clean about Angie, Kim was going to do a full examination of their assets and call Eddie out on his draining of their accounts. The smart move was probably to just sell the house and deduct the money he'd stolen from the proceeds. Knowing Eddie, he'd probably want to include his commission as part of the sale.

She figured the divorce would be quick. He wouldn't contest it. He was a cheater and a thief. Kim was fully aware of the fact that she, herself, was a murderer, but she'd done that by accident, and, at this point, Eddie had no idea she was involved. All the atrocities he committed against her were done on purpose. Cheaters were bad. Kim hated cheaters. But a cheater who steals from his own wife was a special kind of asshole.

At her old parish, there was a priest who'd gotten caught molesting altar boys. Before his trial, he embezzled from the parish and fled to Mexico. Kim was thinking about Eddie in the same way that she thought of that priest. You can't stay married to a man you think of in that way. Kim could never understand the women in books and movies who stayed with men who were abusive or unfaithful. The thought of it made her sick. She was a self-reliant woman. Why would she need to stay with a man who didn't treat her right?

Leo had also done some bad things in his life. Kim was sure of it. But he was also deeply loyal. She wanted to be around more people who were deeply loyal. She now considered it an underrated quality, a prerequisite for future friends and lovers. To her right now, loyalty felt like the most important trait a human being could possess, especially as she was getting ready to drive to the casting pools to go pick up the money that Eddie had scrounged together to pay off her kidnappers. She needed to be around people she could trust. Eddie coming up with this money was the first selfless thing he'd done for her in as long as she could remember.

"You can stay here, Kim," said Leo, tying his shoe and looking up at her. "No reason for both of us to be running around the park at night."

"Leo," she said. "I'm coming with you."

"You sure?" he said, working on the other shoe now.

"How do I know you won't run off with my money?"

"Are you ser—?" He caught himself and looked up from his shoe. Kim was surprised he'd bitten. She was smiling now and winked.

"Got me," he said. "For that, you can do the digging."

\*\*\*

Leo parked on Lincoln Boulevard so that the two of them could walk the quarter mile into the park. There was a park curfew, and Leo didn't want to draw any attention. He brought a trowel, which he was carrying in his back pocket, and he had a flashlight, which he wasn't going to use until they needed it. Kim had told Eddie not to bury the money too deep, so he thought the little shovel would be enough, and they'd only have to use the flashlight for a few minutes.

As they walked the dirt path above the Polo Fields, Leo was in the process of trying to figure out his relationship with Kim. He sure liked her, but the context in which their relationship was being built probably didn't provide an ideal litmus test for love.

She knew some of what he'd done in his life, and he now knew the worst that she'd done. Mutually assured destruction wasn't a good place to start a relationship.

He didn't care, of course. He was all in now. He wanted to see how this would end up. Even if things didn't work out, someone could write a song about them.

"Aren't we almost there?" she whispered, holding on to the back of his jacket as he navigated the narrow dirt path down the side of the hill toward the casting pools.

"They're right in there," he said and pointed between two tall pine trees at the quiet cement pools. The fog had lifted, and the moon was reflecting off the water. Leo was looking at the spot where he'd instructed Eddie to make the drop. It was at least fifty yards away, but the moonlight made it possible for Leo to see the stack of pinecones where he thought they'd be.

"Do you see it," he said, as they crunched over gravel, and the path opened up to the concrete deck of the first pool.

Kim stepped around him so that they were walking side-by-side now. "I think so," she said.

They were taking small, soft steps when Leo realized they were holding hands. He felt like he was on a date. "Now do you see it?" he said.

"Yes," she said, released his hand, and did a short sprint to the pile of pinecones.

Leo checked the corresponding number stenciled by the side of the pool. 105. This was it. He watched Kim moving the pinecones, and then he took out the flashlight and shone it on the spot. "Here you go," he said and pulled the trowel out of his back pocket.

"You're really going to make *me* do it?" she said.

"Absolutely," he said. There was just enough light for him to see her smiling.

She grabbed the trowel and after about five scoops, she was pulling the bag out of the sandy soil. "For some reason," she said, "I'm surprised it's here."

Leo wasn't. He knew Michael Duffy would get it together and make sure the drop was done correctly. But Leo also wanted to get the hell out of there just in case Duff was hidden somewhere planning an ambush. It wouldn't be a great idea on his part, but he'd been a bit of a cowboy back when he was a cop, and Leo wanted to avoid some kind of showdown out here in the dark.

Leo turned off the flashlight and said, "We should get out of here."

"We should," she said, grinning and holding the bag up in front of her. "I'm looking forward to slipping into a warm bed."

"Well, that might not be for a while," said Leo. "Depending on how your husband wants to handle this, you might be up late answering questions, making sure you have your story straight."

"I wasn't talking about my bed, silly."

Leo felt his weight shift to his heels as he watched her approach him and then drop the bag in the dirt. She pressed herself against him and looked up at him under the trees, the reflection of the moon on the water providing enough light for him to look into her eyes. Then he pulled her into him, and he kissed her, knowing how absolutely stupid this whole thing was getting.

## 49

When Derek woke up, his shoulder was throbbing. He drank so much when he got home last night that he fell asleep sitting up on the couch with his feet on the floor. But at some point, he'd tipped over in his sleep, and now the white couch had a bell-shaped blood stain where Derek's shoulder had been. He was sitting up again now and didn't remember putting on two band aids before he sat down last night, but he must have. By now, they'd both soaked through, fell off the wound, and were crisscrossed on the couch next to him. Apparently, the upholstery had done a good job of stopping the bleeding, but the couch was a goner. He didn't mind. He never really liked the couch, and he didn't really care about anything anymore anyway.

He decided to go see Cristian. He wasn't going to be a runner for the rest of his life. He was going to tell Cristian everything. Well, almost everything. He wasn't going to talk about the black people. Cristian didn't need to know about the misunderstanding down by the zoo. But Derek would explain that the old man had been gaming Angie, and he killed Alex.

Cristian would tell Derek that Carl's money was already budgeted, and that Derek was now responsible for reimbursing him that money. Derek didn't really know how he was going to reply after that. He figured he would just read the room. By that point in the conversation, Derek was confident he would know whether or not Cristian was going to have him killed. Then Derek would have to decide the best way to die with honor.

He cleaned up, dressed the wound, put on a clean suit, and headed down to the club.

Derek had never been in Cristian's office before, but that's where the two men led him. They seemed to be waiting for him when he arrived. He'd seen them both before, but he didn't know their names. They were members of the inner-sanctum and didn't really associate with Derek and the other foot soldiers.

Cristian was sitting behind the desk. He had a magazine open in front of him, and he was shaking a box of Tic Tacs. After he popped several in his mouth, he held the box up toward Derek, who was standing between the two chairs in front of the desk. Derek shook his head. "No thank you," he said, waiting for Cristian to offer him a seat. He did not.

"So, times up," said Cristian, taking off his glasses and placing them on the magazine.

"Sir?" said Derek, but he knew.

"Your wife," said Cristian. "You haven't found her."

"No," said Derek. He'd been trying to look Cristian in the eyes, but he let his gaze drop to the desk. Even from upside down, Derek could tell that the magazine was written in a foreign language. His eyes moved just a fraction to the right, and he saw the jar. He'd heard stories about the jar, but he'd never seen it. Here it was.

"Do you believe she's dead?" asked Cristian.

Derek was still looking at the thumb floating in the jar, but he raised his eyes to Cristian. "I don't know," he said. "My brother and I tried to follow some leads, but ..." He heard himself trail off and his eyes moved back to the thumb, which seemed perfectly preserved in the clear liquid.

"Your brother should be here," said Cristian.

"He's dead, sir."

Cristian stood up and walked over to the portable bar tucked into the corner of the room beneath the built-in bookshelf. He poured himself a glass of a brown liquor out of a crystal decanter and then returned to his chair. "I'm sorry for your loss," he said and took a long swallow.

Cristian didn't ask how Alex died. He just sat there, staring at Derek.

"Carl shot him," said Derek.

"Ah," said Cristian. "Killed by an old man." He put the glass down near the thumb jar. "What do you think it's like to be killed by an old man?"

Derek felt light-headed for a moment. He wondered how much blood he'd lost yesterday. He wondered if those two goons were standing right outside the door. He wondered how Cristian planned to do it. Finally, he wondered how it had come to this. "I imagine it's a terrible feeling," said Derek. "Getting killed by a shriveled-up, old, impotent bastard is a shameful way to die."

Cristian reached for his glass again and took a small sip before saying, "Why do you think Carl is impotent?" His smile was crooked. "I believe he was having sex with your wife. Yes?"

"I wasn't talking about Carl," said Derek.

Cristian stared. The smile was gone. He looked very old, the corners of his mouth heavy and his wrinkled hands folded on the magazine.

Derek, who had been standing this whole time, stepped closer to the narrow desk and said, "I don't have any desire to get old." Then he reached across and grabbed Cristian's drink. He smelled it first and then took a sip. Derek didn't like scotch, but this one was good, smokey and smooth. He placed the glass back on the desk and said, "Getting old is just like being a baby again."

Cristian eyed his drink. He didn't seem to be interested in the conversation anymore. Derek wondered if there was some button somewhere that Cristian would press to summon the men who would be killing him in the next few minutes. "Like a baby?" said Cristian.

"Yeah," said Derek. "You end up having people feed you and wipe your ass for you. I don't have any interest in that."

Cristian nodded but said nothing.

"What's it like?" said Derek, enjoying this now, curious what Cristian's next move would be. Derek knew he should be shitting his pants at this point. This was likely the last conversation he would ever have. But the one swallow of scotch seemed to remind him of the feeling of being intoxicated. He felt good. Loose.

"You don't want to talk about it?" Derek said, taunting Cristian now. "That's all right. You should probably be having your nap soon anyway." Derek was feeling excellent, liberated by his impending doom. "Dying in my prime won't be a bad way to go."

"You call this your prime?" said Cristian, laughing now, mouth still closed but with staccato breathing pumping out of his nose.

"I guess," said Derek, and he reached down for the drink again but ended up going in a different direction. He snapped up the thumb jar, leaned over the desk, and smashed the jar on the side of Cristian's head before Cristian could even raise his arm in defense.

It wasn't loud. A muted pop. Like someone clapping inside a casket. He'd caught Cristian just above his ear, but Derek somehow knocked the old man's teeth out. He watched them arc out of Cristian's mouth and spray on the Persian rug next to the desk. Derek was transfixed by the teeth, simultaneously surprised and delighted at the sight of them. After a moment, however, he realized that he wasn't looking at teeth. The white bits were Tic Tacs.

Derek actually laughed before he looked back at Cristian, who was still conscious but had blood running from the wound near his ear. It was oozing down his neck and under the collar of his white shirt. "I thought those were your teeth," said Derek, still laughing to himself while he walked behind Cristian, who could produce only a breathy groan.

The whole room smelled like pickles, and Derek smelled his hand before wiping it clean on the back of Cristian's jacket.

Cristian tried to turn around to see what Derek was doing, but he seemed to be having a hard time after the blow to the head. Derek wrapped his arm around Cristian's neck and applied pressure. He'd never done this before, but he knew wrestlers used the hold. Derek clutched his own wrist so that he'd be able to use both arms to pull back on Cristian's throat. As he continued to squeeze, Cristian put his hands up to Derek's forearm and tried to loosen the hold, but he was too old and too weak. Cristian's mouth was still closed and the last of the air was escaping from his nose.

When no one had come in after Derek smashed the jar off the old man's skull, Derek assumed the door was thick enough to muffle most of the sound inside. It was probably designed that way.

"Don't fight it, sir," said Derek. "It's all for the best."

When Cristian's hands dropped to his sides, and Derek could feel the life running out of him, Derek looked down over the man's shoulder and was shocked to see Cristian's pecker peeking out of his fly. Derek blinked once and recognized what it really was: the thumb. He looked at it and laughed out loud—the second optical illusion in the last twenty seconds. Alex would have found this hilarious. Derek reached for his phone to take a picture but stopped himself. He didn't have anyone to send it to. He looked down at his boss one last time.

He could see that Cristian was dead, so Derek straightened him in the chair and adjusted the old man's head so that it was tilted slightly toward the ceiling, his neck resting against the chair back. The thumb was balanced vertically on his zipper. Derek picked it up like he was handling a lit cherry bomb. He didn't want to hold it for very long. It was milky white and lighter than Derek imagined. He used one hand to separate Cristian's lips. Then, with the other hand, he placed the thumb in Cristian's mouth.

Derek's steps crunched on the broken glass when he approached the door. He rubbed the bottoms of his shoes on the edge of the rug. Then he took a deep breath and opened the door. The two henchmen were standing on either side. Derek closed the door behind him and nodded at them as he walked down the hallway toward the bar. He remembered how Alex used to run from stray dogs when he was a kid, and the dogs always chased him.

Derek slow-walked it down the hallway, listening for heavy footsteps behind him.

## 50

Duff had been up most of the night. The cops cross-referenced the two murder scenes in two neighborhoods that hadn't seen any murders in decades. And when Duff's name popped up on both reports, there were a lot of questions that had to be answered.

Duff shouldn't have been involved in either mess. He could have easily left Carl's before the cops arrived, and he could have driven right past the Al Young debacle. But he didn't. He hung around both scenes, and now he was a person of interest in both cases, even though Carl had been bragging to the cops about the over-the-shoulder trick shot. The implausibility of the story seemed to have stirred misgivings among the officers on the scene. Several had looked sideways at Duff, as if he might have had something to do with Alex's condition, sprawled on the floor of Carl's bedroom, little bits of his brain mixing with the blood and leaking onto the floor.

But the only crime Duff had committed in the entire shit-show was helping Eddie bury the body. And Duff knew that as soon as Kim was released and home, he was prepared to explain everything to law enforcement. Any crimes he might have committed or been accessory to were committed in an attempt to save another life, but he was having trouble figuring out how to explain it correctly. His mind kept drifting back to the scene in the Porsche, and none of it made any sense.

He, Marilyn, and Eddie were sitting in Eddie's front room now after the long night. They were waiting to hear from Kimberly. Duff was having trouble keeping his eyes open, but he didn't want Marilyn to think he was uninterested in the current situation, so he was playing mind games to stay awake. He wouldn't look at any one thing for more than a couple of seconds. He was trying different kinds of breathing. He stood up every couple of minutes and walked to the window. He wanted to slap himself in the face or put his head in some ice water. Ultimately, he succumbed to the fatigue, and nodded off on the couch.

His dream featured an extremely competitive game of cornhole with Al Young. Duff felt a lot of pressure to win, but Al was good, and the referee seemed to be giving Al an advantage. Duff didn't question the fact that Al was alive again or that there was a referee in a cornhole game, but he did feel like he recognized the ref from somewhere.

They were in Carl's front yard, the lawn manicured, bees flying around the flower beds. The two bald brothers were sitting on a porch swing with Carl between them, his tackle box resting on his lap.

Al threw the next beanbag directly into the hole. It didn't even touch the board. "Nothing but hole," he yelled. "Air mail, youngblood!"

"That's a point, Michael," said the ref, but his voice sounded like Kimberly's. And then Duff recognized the ref. It was the dude they saw running out of the neighborhood last night. When Duff looked up above the porch swing, Angie was staring out the front window, a red scarf around her neck. Duff felt himself take a short breath.

"Michael," said Marilyn, pulling him back into Eddie's living room.

"What?" he said as his brain thrashed to finish the puzzle left on Carl's front lawn.

"You're snoring," she said.

"Sorry," he said. "The cops had me at the station until four in the morning. I can't keep my eyes open."

"It's okay," she said. "I just want you awake when Kim gets here. You always seem to be able to calm her down."

"I think I'm fine now," he said. "How long was I out?"

"About a minute," she said.

"Well, I just got my second wind," he said and muscled up a tired smile.

"How are you going to handle the topic of Angie's body?" she asked.

"You mean with Kim?"

"No," she said. "I mean with you and Eddie and the police."

"I think what we did falls under *duty to rescue*?" he said, thinking back to his criminal law classes in the academy.

"What's that?" she said.

"I don't think this is a perfect fit," he said. "But there's a law where you're supposed to at least attempt to rescue someone if the situation arises."

"Um," she said, a slanted smile on her face, "Angie was already dead, Michael, and you guys buried her. How would that be considered a rescue of any kind?"

"Not Angie," said Duff. "Kim."

Eddie was looking out the front window. "She's not here yet," he said, sounding far away.

Marilyn shook her head at Eddie and then looked back at Duff. "You're saying that you were rescuing Kim when you buried Angie?"

"In a way," he said.

Marilyn nodded but didn't look convinced.

"I'll just say this," he said, feeling more awake now. "If we didn't bury Angie like we were told, and the kidnappers ended up killing Kim, I think we might have been violating the duty to rescue law."

"Do you think they killed her?" she asked.

"Angie?" he said.

"No," said Marilyn. "My sister."

"I don't know why they would," said Duff. "Unless she's seen their faces or tried to escape." Duff's mind went back to the last time he'd heard her on the FaceTime call. She sounded surprisingly confident, so either these people were doing a good job of duping her, or they had no intention of taking her life. "What did she look like on that last call?"

Marilyn tilted her head back and closed her eyes. She remained this way for a half a minute before her eyes snapped open. "Kim thought these guys were going to let her go."

"Why do you say that?" he said.

"Because she's my sister, and I know her better than anyone."

"Good," he said. "Then we should be seeing her soon."

"She wasn't scared, Michael."

"How do you know?"

"Again," she said, sounding a bit frustrated now. "I know my sister."

"Got it," he said. "Do you mind telling me how this lack of fear manifested itself on the FaceTime call?"

Marilyn could do a thing with her mouth that always let Duff know it was time to shut up, that he was somehow crossing a line. He could tell that she was biting the inside of her bottom lip. Most of the time he knew what he'd been doing to annoy her, but not always.

"Even if she thought they were going to let her go after the money drop," said Marilyn, "she still should have been scared, Michael. She was being held captive. That would scare anyone. That would scare *you*."

"You're damn right it would."

"So why isn't she scared, Michael?"

Duff didn't know. "Stockholm syndrome?"

"After three days?"

"You tell me," he said.

Marilyn looked over at Eddie. She didn't say anything. The sun was shining through the window now, so Eddie was a slumping silhouette, his head turned north toward the entrance to the neighborhood. Duff wondered what Marilyn was thinking. He wondered if she thought Eddie was somehow involved. Duff was mad at himself for not seeing whatever it was that Marilyn was seeing. Eddie was a complete moron, but he was also one of the wounded, albeit one who was culpable of his own set of crimes.

It reminded Duff of a band some kids from his high school had formed as seniors: The Guilty Victims. It had a ring to it.

## 51

Kim put on the clothes that she'd worn for the FaceTime calls and was sitting on Leo's couch, awaiting further instructions. "So, where's the best spot to leave me?" she asked, ready to get on with the business of the day.

"I'm leaving you at the beach," he said as he finished the last of his toast and then wiped the corners of his mouth with his thumb and forefinger. "It needs to be somewhere with no security cameras."

Kim nodded.

"They're gonna go after the people who did this to you, so they'll pull all the security footage from the area where you get dropped. I think the far end of Sloat Beach might work."

"And I can actually just walk home or walk to Marilyn's house."

"Exactly," he said, now rubbing the back of his neck. "I think maybe go all the way to your house. They would probably all be there."

"Or I could stop at Java Beach and call home?"

"That could work," he said. "Is that what you think you'd do if this really happened to you?"

"I think so," she said. "It's far enough away from my house that I think it might look weird if I walked right past it."

"Agree."

"Should I act crazy?"

"At Java Beach?"

"Yeah."

"Some tears would look good."

"I can do that," she said. "I'll start about a block away and then keep it going when I'm asking to use the phone."

"Try to look at least a little distraught the whole way up the beach," he said. "The cops might try to talk to witnesses, and you never know where there might be cameras."

"Makes sense," she said. "But how are you going to drop me off without being seen?"

"We'll go way down to the end of the parking lot, and you won't get out until the coast is clear."

"Literally," she said.

"Huh?"

"We'll literally be on the coast waiting for it to be clear," she said, smiling, ready to put on a show, get this over with, and start her new life.

Leo smiled too, but she could tell he was nervous. He was trying to look cool, and his voice was clear and steady. He sounded like all the anesthesiologists she'd worked with, but Leo was avoiding eye contact and was in constant motion. She knew he'd done his share of nasty business, but the last few days had to be the worst, and he wasn't doing this one for her dad. This was for her. And it wasn't for money or loyalty. Kim really felt that he was doing it for love. She was smart enough not to try to analyze her own emotions while she was in the middle of a crisis, but she knew she cared for this man. In many ways, he was the total opposite of Eddie, who cared about appearances more than anything else. Looking back now, she had no idea how she'd ended up with Eddie. He was likeable enough, but even if this current disaster hadn't occurred, she couldn't imagine staying with him for the rest of her life.

She wasn't sure she could fall head-over-heels for the ghost either.

"And when they start asking questions, just be consistent," he said.

"They wore masks the whole time," she said.

"And they made you wear a blindfold when you were out of the room."

"Yeah," she said. "And they didn't really talk to me except when they told me what to say on the FaceTime calls."

"What did their voices sound like?"

"Nothing distinct. No accents. Two or three men. I couldn't tell."

"That's good."

"The cops'll probably connect this somehow to Angie's people, huh?"

"There's no logical connection unless they find out she was sleeping with Eddie, which they might."

"And what would that narrative look like?"

Leo's eyes moved to the ceiling. "Gypsy wife cheats on her husband. Husband performs an honor killing of the wife and then tortures the lover by kidnapping that man's wife and asking for a ransom."

"That actually feels like a logical chain of events."

"I think that's all we can hope for at this point."

Kim felt relieved that Leo had put together a story of what could have happened. She knew she could convince herself that it went down that way, as long as she could keep repeating it in her mind over and over. She did not kill that woman on purpose. She knew it in her heart. So why should she live the rest of her life feeling guilty for something she did by accident? No, she would do everything she could to scrub away any remnants from her own brain. Whatever it took. She would erase from her mind the image of Angie lying on the floor in her garage.

In fact, she'd already started the process to a certain extent. Everything about her brief personal encounter with Angie had blurred edges and muted colors. The experience was becoming a faded polaroid in her mind, and she would keep working on it until it became overexposed, the shapes mashed together into a flash white glob with no meaning to anyone.

The problem was that no matter how hard she tried, she couldn't erase the slow-motion memory of Angie and Eddie walking out onto that deck at Mission Rock, Eddie enjoying the attention of being in the company of this beautiful woman. For some reason, this memory was going to be harder to eradicate. The colors were vibrant, the movements clean. All the details had defined lines. If she closed her eyes, she could be there, on the top deck, looking down at the two of them. She could even hear their footsteps on the splintered planks and smell the salt in the air.

The memory was stubborn, but she had immediate worries as well. "Are you certain Duff will want to bring the cops into this?" she asked, sitting at the edge of the couch, hoping that might signal to Leo that she wanted to get going.

"You know him better than me," he said. "But I think you should insist on it regardless. If anything ever happens, and that body turns up, Eddie and Duff could get dragged into an awful mess."

"Yes," she said. She didn't want Duff or Marilyn to get into any trouble. She would insist that they call the police and report the crime against her and the coerced burial of the murdered woman. She wondered about the grave site. She wondered if the body was still inside Eddie's travel bag. She wondered what it would be like when the family was notified and questioned. Those people would surely be suspects. For a split second, Kim believed that the family *did* have something to do with it before her mind corrected itself.

"You okay?"

"I'm just running through different scenarios," she said. "The less I know about my captors, the better."

Leo reached down to her, and she took his hand. He pulled her up off the couch and held her close to him. "Once I drop you off," he said, "I have to stay away for a while. Do not call me under any circumstance. If they start to suspect any funny business, they'll get a warrant to tap your new phone once you get one."

This scared her a bit, but she nodded into his chest.

"No matter what happens," he said. "You stick to your story. It's okay to be confused. It's okay to forget things. You've been through a lot."

"I have," she said and meant it.

"Go ahead and let them know that you've lost track of days, shit like that."

"I actually have," she said and smiled. "It feels like it was a year ago when I asked you to spy on Eddie."

"I don't spy," he said. "I do surveillance."

"That's right," she said. "Spies are bad guys."

## 52

Derek looked down at Angie's things strewn across the bed. Photographs, coins, the old driver's license, an Italian pin. Lots of worthless shit. But the phone bill and the sheet of paper with the passwords was important to him now.

He'd done some research and learned there was an app that could locate an iPhone even after the battery had died. The last entry in Angie's password list worked to get him into her account, and it only took a few minutes to find an address—some place way down at the end of Geary Boulevard, near the Cliff House. If he'd found the phone bill on the first day she'd gone missing, he would've driven down to the place and yanked her out of there. Then he would've brought her back to Cristian so that she could explain herself to him. She could tell them all what she'd been planning, why she'd run off the way she did. Cristian probably would have had her killed at the club. He would've forced Derek to watch. In fact, he might have made Derek do the deed.

For a moment, Derek felt strangely heroic, as if by taking three days to find her, he'd actually saved her life.

He could feel the sweat that had dried and left a thin film over his body. He considered changing his clothes. The bleeding had started up again and ruined another suit. He looked at himself in the long mirror in the hallway and laughed. The blood stain had turned the color of clay and covered most of his shoulder and the top half of his lapel. He looked like a gangster movie villain now. His eyes were bloodshot. He had a cut on the bridge of his nose. He had no idea how it got there. He was a mess, but he thought he looked good. Mean. Ready to go.

Alex was dead. Cristian was dead. Those two black people in Eddie's car were dead. And it looked like Angie was shacked up with someone out in the fog belt now. But he wanted to talk to her. He didn't want to try to reconcile anything—he knew it was too late for that—but he thought she'd be proud of him for standing up to Cristian. He wanted her to know that. He wanted her to like him again.

\*\*\*

The house was a dump. Everything in this neighborhood seemed to be rusted. Stop signs, parking meters, cars, fences, and gates. Everything metal seemed to be corroding away, including the knocker on the front door.

Derek rapped it three times and watched paint flakes from the door float to the worn-out mat under his feet. He waited a few moments and then looked at his phone to make sure this was the right address. The number he'd put in his notes matched the tilted one barely hanging on to the stucco next to the mailbox.

He tried to peek in through the front window, but the curtains were pulled tight. He peered into the mail slot, but the garage looked dark and empty. He stepped back and surveyed the property. It was fenced all the way around, so he'd have to climb the fence or knock it down if he wanted to try to get in through the backyard.

When he walked to the front of the house again, he noticed that the roots of the big palm tree had caused the concrete in the driveway to buckle, which prevented the garage door from closing all the way. Derek looked around to see if anyone was watching. He wasn't overly concerned, but he didn't want to deal with a neighborhood watch group either, so he looked up and down the street before he reached under the garage door and yanked it once, hard.

The door groaned and then gave. He pulled it up just far enough to crawl underneath. If the suit wasn't already ruined, he wouldn't have been crawling around in it. He still felt odd letting the knees of his slacks touch the dirty concrete, but the feeling didn't last very long, and he managed to slide under the heavy door.

He pulled it closed behind him and then toured the nearly empty house. The garage still had some stuff in there, but once he got into the house, it was clear that no one was living there. He thought he might find a blow-up mattress in one of the bedrooms with some of Angie's stuff, but all the rooms were empty.

He reviewed the terms and services of the phone app, which would help Derek find the phone wherever it was as long as the battery was charged. If the phone had gone dead, the app would lead him to the last location where the phone had power. Derek assumed that's where he was now. But he couldn't figure out what Angie would have been doing here. And he also found it odd that she'd left this place but never recharged her phone. It didn't make sense.

He was standing in the kitchen, leaning up against the counter when his mind went back to the front door. There'd been something hanging on the doorknob, and Derek had ignored it when he was looking for a way to get in, but now it was bothering him, so he opened the front door to inspect the outside knob, and hanging from it was a lockbox. He reached down and shook it. He could hear the key rattling around. Then he was down on his knee once again, looking at the backside of the lockbox, where a laminated business card had been attached. Derek used his thumb to wipe the grit off the plastic. He squinted at the card and then blinked it into focus. *Eddie Bilker.*

Derek stood up a little dizzied. He felt the possibilities buzz around his head like gnats, haphazardly whizzing in all directions, confusing him, and then startling him into clarity before confusing him again. Obviously, Eddie was selling this house, but Derek wondered if the man was also using it to meet with Angie. She'd obviously been in the house. At some point, her phone lost power here. Derek was confident now that the plan was for Eddie to help her sell Carl's house, but he didn't know how Angie planned to do it without getting caught. And none of this was going to happen anyway because Carl never intended to leave her the house in the first place. Angie had been bamboozled by the old man.

Derek walked back inside feeling nauseous, wondering if the loss of blood was finally affecting his body chemistry. He took a deep breath to see if he could shake off the queasiness and then walked right through the house to the back door and out into the yard. There was a little brick patio, and he sat down on the ground, still trying to make sense of it all.

He wondered if Angie was running now because she was scared of Cristian. That would make sense. But Derek didn't know how many trusted contacts she had in The Organization. He wondered if she knew that she didn't have to run anymore. Did someone inside contact her to give her the heads up about Cristian?

He stared out at the weed-covered yard, thinking about what was next for him. He wanted to take another run at Eddie, but the shooting in the Porsche had to have tipped the sneaky bastard off that someone was after him. Eddie would be on high alert now, and he probably had that other guy looking after him. Maybe they were all in it together—Eddie, Carl, the dude with the cop vibe, Angie. Could Angie be working with these people?

He started to cramp up a bit, so he stretched his legs out in front of him. He kept his back straight, so he was in the shape of an L now, his heels sinking slightly into the soft soil in front of him.

He looked at the dirt. It didn't look right to him. The entire backyard was covered in weeds, except for the thin rectangle of softer soil directly in front of where he was sitting. The house was covered in dust, and the yard hadn't been touched in what looked like several years. Except for this rectangle.

Derek felt a tingle in the back of his neck, but he didn't move yet. He wanted to think this through. The fresh earth in front of him didn't seem wide enough to be a grave, but that didn't stop him from considering it. He stood up and walked around the area, mentally calculating the dimensions. He'd once read a book about Montana and the moonshine they served in an old, modified boxcar out by a river. The name of the booze was 3-7-77. Those were supposedly the dimensions of a proper grave, a fitting name for the vile liquor they served at Black Jack's bar. And Derek was pacing off steps now, but this rectangle seemed to be about 2x5, nowhere near the standard 3x7. But still. Those dimensions included a coffin.

He looked around the yard and saw a plastic, five-gallon bucket resting on its side in the weeds over by the fence. He felt like an idiot, like his mind was screwed up now and making him think strange thoughts, but now he had the itch and needed to scratch it.

He walked over to the bucket, bent over, and looked inside. A light layer of dirt dusted the bottom of the bucket. He grabbed the handle, walked back to the rectangle, and started removing bucket after bucket of soft soil and creating a small hill behind him. He knew he should be tired, but he had more energy now than he had in days. He felt like he was born to do this work. He was on his knees and leaning into the hole, waiting for his back to give, but it didn't happen. And once it got deep enough, he stepped into the hole and dug out the dirt on both sides of his feet.

He worked himself into a rhythm in which he was taking deep breaths before every scoop and then letting out the air when he dumped the dirt behind him. There were no roots, and he was working mostly with wet sand, like the stuff you'd use to build a castle—easy to work with until he got deep down into the hole. Then he had to lift the dirt above his head to get it out, and his arms started to ache.

At this point, he had no doubt about what he'd find. It would take time to figure out how it happened and why, but he was certain Angie would be down there.

He struggled to push the bag out of the hole. It was heavy, and he had no strength left in his arms. But he had it lying on the patio and decided to start with the side pocket of the big bag. He was putting off the inevitable. Angie's purse was in there. He dumped the items on the bricks and saw the phone bounce a few times before it settled next to a lipstick and a set of earbuds.

Then he rolled the bag over and stared at the zipper.

## 53

When Marilyn took the call, she immediately started crying. Duff walked over and stood next to her so that he could try to hear what was going on. He could tell it was a woman's voice, but he didn't know if it was Kimberly's or not.

Duff bent over so that his ear was closer to the phone. Eddie stood by the window. He looked like he was paralyzed by the possibilities intrinsic to this call. Everyone wanted this to be over, but Duff knew that Eddie was probably already broken by the events of the past three days, and who knew what these people had done to Kim and how it would affect her moving forward. Duff continued to look at Eddie but concentrated on trying to hear the words coming from the phone. He actually thought he heard the word *Jabba*, like Jabba the Hutt. He wasn't a big *Star Wars* guy, but he was confident that he'd heard a reference to that fat blob who'd taken the Princess hostage.

Marilyn finally ended the call and held the phone up to her chest. "Kim's okay," she said, the tears coming one after another, like they were on a timer.

"Where is she?" said Duff.

"Java Beach," she said. "She called from Java Beach."

"Okay," said Duff, taking Marilyn's hand. "Let's go get her."

Then he looked back over at Eddie, who was leaning against the window. Eddie's eyes looked the way they would get after his third Guinness—wet and dim at the same time, like a shark's eyes, no emotion but with a kind of dogged purpose. "C'mon," said Duff. "Are you okay? We gotta go."

Eddie didn't say anything. He walked past Duff and Marilyn to the front door. Duff wondered if Eddie was excited and happy to see his wife, or if he was worried about the judgement that would take place when he had to explain the details of his relationship with Angie. There was no way around it. Marilyn knew about the relationship, so Kimberly was going to find out whether Eddie had the balls to come clean or not.

"Hey, Eddie," said Duff. "Let's take my truck. Remember, they impounded the Porsche."

Eddie had his hand on the doorknob. He stopped and looked back at Duff, maintaining the glazed look that had taken over his face ever since Marilyn first provided the good news of Kimberly's safety. "Not enough room," he said, standing in the hallway with his hands folded in front of him.

Duff considered telling Eddie that he would have to ride in the back of the pickup. Instead, he said, "Eddie, you drive the truck and take Marilyn. I'll wait here."

Marilyn said, "No, Michael. You're coming with us. Eddie can ride in the back."

Duff smiled. "It's a two-minute drive, hon. I'll just wait here, and we'll figure everything out when you guys get back."

Marilyn stared at Duff for a long moment—too long, considering her sister was waiting for her down at the coffee shop. "Gimme the keys," she said.

Duff handed them over and then followed Marilyn and Eddie out the door. He planned to sit on the front stoop until they got back.

***

After some tearful hugs in front of the Java Beach regulars, Kimberly got into Duff's truck. She sat between Marilyn and Eddie, and no one said anything for the first couple of blocks. With her right hand, Marilyn kept wiping the tears from her cheeks while she steered the truck with her left. Kim didn't even look over at Eddie, but he did pat Kim's knee every time Marilyn sniffled.

"Are you hungry?" he said finally.

It was hard for Kim to hold back. She wanted to tell him to go screw himself. She wanted to tell him that if he didn't cheat on her, none of this would have happened. She wanted to tell him that he was a worthless thief, a terrible husband, a selfish piece of shit. She thought it was important for him to know that she was aware that he was trash, that he never cared about anyone but himself, and that he was incapable of participating in an authentic adult relationship. It was difficult for her to resist the temptation to let him know that he wasn't wired to share anything with anyone. She wanted to punch him in the balls.

Instead, she shook her head and tried to push out some more tears.

"We'll get you home and into a shower," said Marilyn. "Then we can sit down, and you can tell us whatever you want. Whatever you need to say. You don't have to get everything out all at once. You can do this gradually while you get reacclimated."

Kim felt herself patting Marilyn's knee now. She knew she'd eventually confess everything to her, but—as Marilyn said—she needed to do this gradually. Kim didn't like the fact that, at some point, Duff was going to know all the details. Without trying, he had a way of making people feel guilty. Which was odd, because the man would go out of his way to try to make people feel comfortable about their decisions. He was the least judgmental person that Kim knew. But the way he lived his own life seemed to have an effect on the way people viewed their own choices. She was still thinking about Duff, actually picturing his face, as they turned onto Country Club Drive.

She wondered how long it would take to sell the house and get her share of the money she'd dumped into it over the past few years. She wondered about the divorce and the best way to start the process. She wondered how Eddie planned to tell her about what he'd been through over the past few days—what she'd put him through. She wondered if he realized what an awful human being he'd turned out to be.

As soon as they turned the corner, she could see someone standing on the front lawn. It was a man in an athletic stance, like he was getting ready to start a marathon, but he was facing the house and had one arm extended in front of him. It took only another second or two before she realized he was pointing a gun at the stairs. With all the cars parked along the street, she couldn't see the bottom of the stairs until they were about two houses away.

Michael Duffy was sitting on the third step. He was leaning forward with his elbows on his knees. He looked like a lifeguard during adult swim at the community swimming pool. The angle of his head told Kim that he was looking at the gunman, but he didn't seem to be worried.

Simultaneously, Eddie was saying "Oh no," while Marilyn was saying, "Michael!" The duet gave Kim chills.

Marilyn sped up for about twenty feet and then slammed on the breaks. The truck squealed to a stop at an oblique angle, partially facing the driveway. Kimberly felt her body jerk against the seatbelt before she fell back again. She felt pressure building in her head and realized that she'd been holding her breath since she saw the man with the gun.

## 54

Duff wished he had his gun. He'd reached for it in the morning, but it wasn't in its spot under his nightstand. He couldn't remember bringing it to work, but he must have at some point. There was no other place it could be. He hadn't touched it in so long that he couldn't remember why he'd brought it to The Boot. But that didn't matter now. The only thing that mattered was the gun the bald brother was pointing at him.

"Where's Eddie Bilker?" he asked after he parked his car, blocking part of the driveway.

Duff didn't know Derek's intentions, but he knew the guy was upset. His brother had been shot and killed by Carl the day before, so he couldn't be in a good mood. "Sorry to hear about your brother," Duff offered, not moving from his spot on the stairs.

"You heard the old man shot him?" he said.

"I did," said Duff. "It sounds like it might have been self-defense."

Derek nodded but didn't say anything right away. "The old man was scamming my wife," said Derek.

"Yeah?" said Duff. "Sounds like a lot of people were scamming each other." Duff thought about the maneuver he would have used if he had his gun. He used to practice stuff like that when the gang-bangers put the bounty on him. He was quick. He was never as accurate as he wanted to be, but Derek was standing only about twelve feet away. Duff felt he would have been able to put him down pretty easily.

"Scamming," said Derek. "I guess that's how all this started." He tapped his gun against his chest.

"Too bad about the suit," said Duff. "Looks like it was a good one."

"It was," said Derek and smiled. "Wood chip."

Duff had no idea what that meant, but it was time to find out what he wanted. "Why're you looking for Eddie?" he said. "And, oh yeah, there's no need for the gun."

"I need the gun for Eddie," he said. "He killed my wife."

Duff thought about that. Duff still had no idea how this went down, but he was pretty certain that Eddie didn't have anything to do with it.

There were moments over the course of the past few days when he considered the possibility, but he always went back to the shock and horror on Eddie's face when Duff had pulled the zipper on that big piece of luggage. The guy just didn't have the acting chops to pull that off. Carl could. Even Kimberly could. She'd been an actress in high school. But Eddie wasn't sophisticated enough to do it. He didn't have enough empathy to know how to fake real emotions.

Duff shook his head. "You got the wrong guy," he said. "Eddie doesn't have the stomach for it."

"Yeah?" said Derek. "But you don't know everything that I know."

Duff took a moment to think this over. Duff might not have known everything Derek knew, but the opposite was also true. Derek had no way of knowing what Duff knew. He gave Derek a half-grin but continued to work through the possibilities. He got stuck on Al Young. Al could have done it, but there was no way to get a confession at this point. And it still seemed like a stretch. How was killing Eddie's girlfriend going to accelerate payoff from a bet? It didn't make much sense. But thinking about Al Young activated another idea. Who killed Al Young, later found dead in Eddie's car? Duff couldn't connect the dots about why Al was in Eddie's car, but if Derek was out looking to kill Eddie, Duff could see a mistake being made.

"Why'd you kill Al?" asked Duff.

"Was he the black dude in Eddie's car?"

"He was," said Duff.

"That was an accident," said Derek.

"I've made some mistakes in my day," said Duff, "but that one …" He shook his head and let the words trail off.

"I was in a bad place," he said and put the gun in his other hand.

For a moment, Duff considered charging him. Most people can't shoot with their off-hands, but Duff hesitated, and now Derek was aiming at him again. Duff didn't think Derek had any intention of shooting him, but he was worried that he'd fire at Eddie when they pulled up and hit Marilyn by accident.

"Why'd you kill the lady?" he asked.

"It was dark," he said. "And she was screaming. Going crazy." He put the gun back in his right hand. "And as I said, I was in a bad place."

"Well, can you do me a favor?" said Duff.

"You're not really in any position to ask for favors, my friend."

"Yeah," said Duff. "But this is an easy one."

"Just for fun," said Derek. "Let's hear it."

"Eddie's going to be arriving pretty soon. My girl will be driving the truck, and her sister's going to be sitting in the cab as well. I'm just asking that you let the two women get out of the truck before you start firing."

"You're like a knight," said Derek, smiling. "What's the word for you?"

"Are you talking about chivalry?" said Duff. "I'm not trying to be a knight or anything. I just want to make sure you don't miss Eddie and hit one of the women or knock glass in their eyes or anything like that. They're not really involved in any of this."

"No," said Derek. "Not chivalry. Gallant. That's what you are, friend. You're gallant. Is that the right word?"

"If that means I don't want my girlfriend and her sister to get shot, then yes, I'm gallant."

"You are," he said. "I should have been more gallant, I think. Maybe my wife would still be alive."

Duff knew this was his opportunity if he was ever going to convince Derek that Eddie didn't kill Angie. "Just so you know," he said, "Eddie had nothing to do with your wife's disappearance. I know that for a fact."

"I didn't think you'd be the type of guy to play games," he said. "Do you know where I found Angie?"

Duff swallowed hard. He was not anticipating that Derek had found the body, but if he had, then he might know Eddie's connection to the house. This wasn't good. He didn't know what to do, so he went with, "I imagine some place connected to your organization?"

Derek smiled and shook his head. "You've heard of The Organization?"

## 55

Marilyn was surprised that she'd lost control of the truck, but she had it stopped now, so she threw it into park and stomped down hard on the emergency brake. She rushed to get out of the truck, but she looked over the bald guy's shoulder and saw Michael. He was looking relaxed and signaling with his hand for her to stay put. Then, when he saw that she wasn't going to get out, he signaled again, this time to roll down the passenger-side window, closest to him and the bald man.

She did, and then looked past Kim and Eddie as the guy with the gun approached the truck.

He was pointing the gun in their direction but not aiming. He periodically looked back at Michael, presumably to make sure he stayed in his spot on the stairs. As Derek walked toward the truck, Eddie was whispering frantically, "Get outta here, Marilyn. Let's go."

But Marilyn wasn't going anywhere with Michael sitting over there and a crazy gypsy waving a gun around. "Shut up, Eddie," she said and turned toward her sister. "This guy's a conman, Kim. In the beginning, we thought he was the one who took you."

At this point, Derek bent at the waist so that he could see into the truck and said, "Hi, everyone." Then he tilted his head and looked across the cab at Marilyn. "You must be Marilyn," he said and smiled.

Marilyn smiled back and nodded.

"You guys make a great couple," he said and looked over his shoulder at Michael.

"Thank you," said Marilyn, trying to figure this guy out. He looked like he'd been through hell, like the survivor of a shipwreck or multi-car pile-up. But he was talking like they were sitting around a mixed table at a wedding reception, trying to get over the awkward introductions. Marilyn had her hand on the door handle, but she didn't have a plan. She just kept thinking if she stayed calm that he'd stay calm.

"I'd like you to turn off the ignition," he said. "I have just a few things I need to take care of, and I'll be following some of Mr. Duffy's suggestions to make sure some of you are safe."

***

Eddie found himself holding Kim's hand. He was pissed at Marilyn. All she had to do was drive right past Derek. They all saw the gun. Eddie didn't understand why someone would stop a car in front of a person holding a firearm.

Eddie was sitting by the open window listening to Derek give Marilyn instructions. Derek had a mean cut on the bridge of his nose that made him look like he was scowling even when he was smiling.

"You girls are going to stay here in the truck," he said. "But hand me the keys, please. I don't want you to miss the show."

Marilyn handed Kim the keys, and she moved to pass them over to Derek, but Eddie stopped her with his forearm.

"Hey Derek," said Eddie. "We're just gonna get outta here. You don't seem like you're in a good place right now, and—"

"Eddie Bilker!" he said, still smiling and reaching across Eddie for the keys. "I've been looking for you, buddy." He was leaning fully into the car now and tapping on the roof with the barrel of the gun. For a moment, Eddie thought about trying to open the door as quickly as he could to smash Derek in the midsection and hopefully get the gun from him. But when he shifted his eyes to the door handle, he could see that it was locked, and he knew Derek would notice if he reached for it.

"I haven't been hiding," he said and tried a smile.

"Not hiding," said Derek. "But maybe having other people drive your car? Things like that?"

Eddie knew he should've put this all together as soon as he saw Derek standing there with the gun, but Eddie felt like his mind wasn't firing on all cylinders at the moment. A part of what was happening seemed to be almost dreamlike, as if his brain was trying to spark into action but wasn't firing fast enough to provide a full picture of the scene unfolding in front him. He wondered if Al Young had felt the same way the night before when Derek pulled up on him sitting in Eddie's Porsche, looking over and seeing Derek pointing the gun at him. Eddie wondered if this glazing over of the mind was some kind of internal defense mechanism.

"I don't know why that guy was in my car," said Eddie, surprised that his voice sounded as calm as it did.

"It doesn't matter, Eddie. Just step out of the car, please."

Eddie hesitated and looked back at Kim. For a moment he considered saying *I love you*, but he didn't want Marilyn to scold him for being a phony, so he just sat frozen for a moment. He felt his mind shutting down. This would not be a dignified way to die. He knew Derek intended to shoot him, and it appeared that he wanted people to witness the murder in broad daylight. In some twisted way, Eddie sympathized with the man. Eddie figured that Derek blamed him for Angie's disappearance. It had to look that way to Derek if he'd found something that connected him to Angie.

Eddie's first instinct was to say that he was only sleeping with Angie but never did anything to hurt her, though that kind of statement could produce the same outcome as saying nothing at all. And then it hit him—a second epiphany in the last ten seconds. Maybe Derek had already killed the man responsible for Angie's death.

"Hey, Derek," he said and put both hands on the dashboard, trying to look even less threatening than he actually was. "Y'know the guy you shot in my car?"

"You need to step out of the car, Eddie."

"I think you actually got the right guy," he said.

"I have the right guy right now," said Derek

"The guy in my car was taking it because I owe him money," said Eddie.

"Step out of the car," said Derek.

"I think he might have killed Angie because of my debt."

"Why would he do that?" said Derek. "What does Angie have to do with you?"

"He might have found out that Angie and me ...." Eddie let the words trail off. He'd talked himself into a circle and was right back where he started.

Derek sneered at him now. "Time to get out of the car, buddy."

Eddie nodded. He didn't look back at the sisters. Derek stepped away from the door to give him room. The air was cool. He felt like he was stepping into a tomb, but he also knew that Duff was over there on those stairs, probably thinking of some way to step in and save the day. That's what the man was known for.

So, Eddie unlocked the door and opened it slowly. He looked at Derek and put his hands up in a half-hearted surrender. He took a deep breath and felt a pounding in his ears. The bones in his legs and feet felt hollow, like plastic straws that might buckle if he stepped too hard.

At the very edge of his peripheral vision, he saw Duff move.

## 56

As soon as Derek saw Eddie's eyes shift in the direction of Duffy, Derek spun and fired. He missed wildly and put a hole in the garage door, but he got Mr. Duffy's attention, and the whole neighborhood for that matter. It was quiet, and the sound of the gunshot seemed to reverberate up and over the houses that lined the little street. It was if the gun had gone off in a tunnel.

Duffy got the point. He sat back down and raised his hand in surrender. "Just stretching the legs, Derek," he called over and offered a lazy salute.

Derek nodded at Duffy but said nothing. Then he focused his attention back on Eddie. He put the truck keys in the pocket of his jacket and pointed the gun at Eddie. "You see the Lexus?" he said and pointed to his car, parked behind the truck.

"Yeah," said Eddie, looking like he was dazed, like a guy coming out of surgery.

"Can you please go get my luggage out of the back seat?"

Eddie looked over at Duffy.

"Don't look at him," said Derek. "Just do what I ask. Get my luggage out of the back seat of the car and place it here on the front lawn."

Eddie was hunched over now, shuffling over to the Lexus like an old man. Once he had the back door open, he reached all the way inside. He looked like he was struggling to find the handle.

Derek took the opportunity to check on Duffy, who was now sitting with his legs stretched out in front of him. His ankles were crossed and so were his arms. He looked like a little kid who'd been benched in the basketball game and was pouting now because he wasn't playing.

Derek glanced over at the truck. The beautiful sister was looking right into his eyes. Derek stared back for a moment and then shifted over to the other woman. She had her head down. For a moment, he thought she might be crying, but then he realized she was probably texting. He knew he should have taken all their phones, but it didn't matter. If the cops got him, at least he wouldn't get killed by someone from The Organization. If The Organization got him, at least he wouldn't have to spend the rest of his life in prison. He really didn't have a preference at this point. He just wanted Eddie to have a worse ending than him, and he liked the power he felt now being in charge of Eddie's fate.

He couldn't see all the mechanisms in the Rube Goldberg mousetrap that led him to his current position, but he knew there were many. He suddenly felt sad that he was never going to find out how it came to this and what tiny machinations were involved in leading him to this lawn in this neighborhood with these people. He knew he worked in a dangerous field, but he also knew there had to be some bit of happenstance that, if removed, would have resulted in a different conclusion. If there was just one bit of machinery that malfunctioned, things might have been different for him, different for Angie, different for this poor son-of-a-bitch who was about to get a bullet in the brain for whatever part he played in this mess. He didn't feel sorry for Eddie, but it hit him that Eddie could be standing there, thinking the same thoughts, wondering what ball bearing or spring or lever could have malfunctioned to allow them both a different fate, but the gears were already turning, and there was no way to change things now.

The luggage was caught on something, and Eddie was struggling. He climbed partly into the car to free the luggage strap from the seatbelt. He finally pulled it out gingerly and used the wheels to roll it, first on the sidewalk and then on the grass, where he carefully placed it near Derek's feet.

Eddie didn't make eye contact. He kept his head down and stood with his hands at his sides. This guy was one of the least threatening people Derek had ever met. Derek was more concerned about Duffy, about twenty feet away on the steps, sitting tight for now, waiting to see Derek's next move.

Derek swiveled his head to get a 360 look at the surroundings. There were people in windows now, looking down at him, judging him without knowing what he'd been through. He was tempted to fire into one of the windows just to get the rest of them to go back to Netflix or sour dough recipes or whatever bullshit they were doing before his life became their entertainment.

"Stand over here," he said to Eddie and pointed to a spot on the lawn that would allow Derek to watch Eddie and Duffy at the same time without having to keep turning back and forth. The police would surely be there soon, but he had a few things he wanted Eddie to do before he closed the curtain on the whole thing.

"Would it be too much to ask you to apologize to my wife for what you did?" he said and pointed at the long bag.

Eddie looked like he was starting to feel the adrenalin now. He was a little shaky when he said, "I can do that." Then he looked at Derek and said, "Do I say it to her or you?"

"Say it to Angie," he said.

So, Eddie looked down at the bag, and Derek was tempted to tell him to unzip it and look at her, but Derek couldn't bear to see her again. The experience of digging her up and opening the bag had done something to him. Once he'd unearthed the bag, he knew what he was going to see. The duct tape on her throat was the only surprise. But his knowing didn't prevent what happened when he closed his eyes. His mind went back to the last time he'd seen her in the club, but it wasn't just that he could see the scene. He was in it. And he could feel the fabric of her dress, hear her glib voice, smell the fresh varnish in the room, and taste the bile in the back of his throat. It was as if shame were a liquid injected into his veins.

Eddie didn't waste any time. He acted like he was trying to reduce his remaining, agonizing minutes on the planet. "I'm sorry for burying you instead of calling the police," he said.

"That's an odd apology?" said Derek.

"I was set-up, Derek," he said. "Someone put her in this bag and then put her in the trunk of my car."

Derek smiled. He thought Eddie would come up with something better. "So why not call the police?" he asked. "What possible reason would you have for doing this on your own … or with Mr. Duffy … however this went down?"

"They had my wife," said Eddie. "They were going to kill her if I didn't do what they said."

Derek pointed the gun at Eddie's head. "That's not an apology," he said again, trying to figure out what Eddie was talking about, who *they* were. "You're telling me that you buried the body of the woman you were cheating on your wife with in order to save your wife?" Derek looked over at the truck to try to gauge whether or not the wife knew, but she was looking out the back window of the truck. He couldn't even tell if she'd heard him.

"For what it's worth, he's telling the truth," said Duffy. "I wouldn't have helped him if I thought he'd killed someone."

This man sounded truthful to Derek.

He looked up and watched the wind push white cotton candy clouds across the blue sky. Then he closed his eyes for a moment, but the images of Angie flooded his senses again. When he opened his eyes, he looked around at the neighborhood—the identical houses lined up on either side of the street, the manicured lawns, the faces in the windows, a grey-hooded jogger on the opposite side of the street.

Then he looked down at himself—the bloodstained suit, his muddy shoes, the gun. The people in the windows must have seen him as a trespasser. He was the vomit in their new Volvos. Dog crap on their walkways. Dirty graffiti on their garage doors. The loud motorcycle at two in the morning.

It was time to leave.

He wanted to know more. He wanted Duffy to tell him who had been holding Eddie's wife. He wanted Eddie's wife to tell him if she knew about Eddie and Angie. He wanted to talk to the goons who'd found Cristian's body after Derek had left. But Derek was just now seeing himself as a man on a rampage—an active shooter. The trespasser in the neighborhood. And he was done now. He'd done enough. And he'd never find the answers this way.

It was time to leave.

## 57

When Derek closed his eyes, Duff considered taking a run at him again. It would take Duff four or five steps to get to him, but he could make it in a couple of seconds. He had his hands on the stairs, ready to push off and jump into action, but Derek opened his eyes again and looked around at his surroundings.

Duff could hear sirens now. One of the neighbors must have called. He guessed there'd be at least three cruisers, and they were just a couple blocks away. This was all going to be over in a few minutes one way or another. The people in the windows were taking in the show.

The jogger must not have seen what was happening on Eddie's lawn because he just kept coming, bobbing along slowly, soundless. Almost like he was floating above the sidewalk before he stepped off the curb and ran down the middle of the street. He wore a grey hood and a Covid mask. He had an odd stride, swinging one arm back and forth like a speed-walker but with his other arm stiff against the front pocket of the hoodie. He was wearing old-school grey sweats to match the hoodie. And he had a pair of canvas sneakers, like some weekend runner from the 1970's.

Duff watched Derek glance at the jogger once but then turn his attention back to the people in the windows. "I'm sorry," he shouted, raising both hands above his head, like a television villain, surrendering to the police after a long standoff. Duff remained in the ready position in case Derek turned his back to him one more time. "I'm sorry," Derek shouted again at the neighbors' houses, then looked at Duff. "Sorry," he said.

Then Duff watched the jogger make a quick turn in front of the truck. At first, Duff thought the man had stumbled. But a moment later, the jogger appeared more athletic as he pivoted toward Derek and pulled a gun out of the front pouch of his hoodie. Derek didn't seem to notice him, but Eddie must have seen him because he dropped to the ground next to Angie and covered his head with his arms.

The jogger fired three times. The first shot got Derek's attention. His hands were still up, and his reflex was to fire a shot into the clouds. The second shot from the jogger brought Derek to his knees, and the gun fell from his hand. The third struck his head, very close to the same spot where the bullet had hit Alex the day before. Derek dropped sideways onto the grass, but his knees remained bent so that he fell into the position of a man in a tortured sleep.

The jogger adjusted his hood, turned around, and started running back toward the entrance to the neighborhood. The sirens were getting louder. Eddie was still lying face-down on the grass. Angie was now flanked by Eddie and Derek. Both sisters had gotten out of the truck. And Duff watched as the jogger and the police cars crossed paths near the curve at the end of the block.

Duff thought about having to explain to the police how it came to be that he was connected to another homicide. He almost laughed. It was probably time for Eddie to come completely clean about everything. But Eddie Bilker's version wouldn't explain the jogger or the body in the luggage or the dead sheriff in Eddie's car. Derek might have been able to fit these final pieces of the puzzle into the broader mosaic, but not now. It would all be speculation at this point.

Duff was staring at Eddie on the lawn when he felt Marilyn holding him around the waist. He smelled her hair and pulled her in tighter. "Did you get a look at him?" he asked.

"He was wearing a mask," she said.

"I saw him," said Kim, who was leaning up against the truck, stoically examining the scene on her front lawn.

"Was it one of the guys who kidnapped you?" said Marilyn.

"No," she said. "It was a ghost."

# About the Author

*The Wrong Idiot* is Tim Reardon's fourth novel. His previous novels, *Shadow Lessons, Part of the Game,* and *Infinite Worth,* are all set in his hometown of San Francisco.

**ALL THINGS THAT MATTER PRESS**


FOR MORE INFORMATION ON TITLES AVAILABLE FROM
ALL THINGS THAT MATTER PRESS, GO TO
http://allthingsthatmatterpress.com
or contact us at
allthingsthatmatterpress@gmail.com

Made in the USA
Middletown, DE
23 August 2023

37255068R00157